SORRY CAN'T SAVE YOU

A MYSTERY NOVEL

WILLOW ROSE

MYSTERY/THRILLER/HORROR NOVELS

- Sorry Can't Save You
- In One Fell Swoop
- Umbrella Man
- Blackbird Fly
- To Hell in a Handbasket
- Edwina

HARRY HUNTER MYSTERY SERIES

- All The Good Girls
- Run Girl Run
- No Other Way
- Never Walk Alone

MARY MILLS MYSTERY SERIES

- What Hurts the Most
- You Can Run
- You Can't Hide
- Careful Little Eyes

EVA RAE THOMAS MYSTERY SERIES

- Don't Lie to me
- What you did
- Never Ever
- Say You Love me
- Let Me Go

- It's Not Over
- Not Dead yet

EMMA FROST SERIES

- Itsy Bitsy Spider
- Miss Dolly had a Dolly
- Run, Run as Fast as You Can
- Cross Your Heart and Hope to Die
- Peek-a-Boo I See You
- Tweedledum and Tweedledee
- Easy as One, Two, Three
- There's No Place like Home
- Slenderman
- Where the Wild Roses Grow
- Waltzing Mathilda
- Drip Drop Dead
- Black Frost

JACK RYDER SERIES

- Hit the Road Jack
- Slip out the Back Jack
- The House that Jack Built
- Black Jack
- Girl Next Door
- Her Final Word
- Don't Tell

REBEKKA FRANCK SERIES

- One, Two...He is Coming for You
- Three, Four...Better Lock Your Door
- Five, Six...Grab your Crucifix

- Seven, Eight…Gonna Stay up Late
- Nine, Ten…Never Sleep Again
- Eleven, Twelve…Dig and Delve
- Thirteen, Fourteen…Little Boy Unseen
- Better Not Cry
- Ten Little Girls
- It Ends Here

HORROR SHORT-STORIES

- Mommy Dearest
- The Bird
- Better watch out
- Eenie, Meenie
- Rock-a-Bye Baby
- Nibble, Nibble, Crunch
- Humpty Dumpty
- Chain Letter

PARANORMAL SUSPENSE/ROMANCE NOVELS

- In Cold Blood
- The Surge
- Girl Divided

THE VAMPIRES OF SHADOW HILLS SERIES

- Flesh and Blood
- Blood and Fire
- Fire and Beauty
- Beauty and Beasts
- Beasts and Magic
- Magic and Witchcraft
- Witchcraft and War

- WAR AND ORDER
- ORDER AND CHAOS
- CHAOS AND COURAGE

THE AFTERLIFE SERIES

- BEYOND
- SERENITY
- ENDURANCE
- COURAGEOUS

THE WOLFBOY CHRONICLES

- A GYPSY SONG
- I AM WOLF

DAUGHTERS OF THE JAGUAR

- SAVAGE
- BROKEN

If I lie, I lose it all. If I stand or if I fall, I've got to lay it all on the line.

Adrenaline Mob

Part I

Dispatch: 9-1-1 what's your emergency?

Caller: She's dead.

Dispatch: Excuse me? Who is?

Caller: The woman.

Dispatch: What woman, sir?

Caller: (breathing heavily) She's dead.

Dispatch: I need you to calm down and try to talk to me. What's your name?

Caller: It doesn't matter. Just send someone; she's dead.

Dispatch: Who is dead? Is it someone you know?

Caller: Just send someone, please.

Dispatch: What's the address?

Caller: 13 Mountain Creek, Bryson City, North Carolina.

Dispatch: Okay, got it. And, sir, I need you to stay with me for a little while. Sir?

Caller: Just send someone, please.

Dispatch: I'm working on it. But tell me, what happened?

Caller: She was killed.

Dispatch: (pauses) Did you kill her, sir?

Caller: Yes.

Dispatch: And you're sure she's dead?

Caller: (Breathes heavily) She will be.

Dispatch: (pauses, breathes jaggedly) What do you mean, *she will be*? Is she still alive? Sir? Sir? Sir?

Chapter 1

THE WOMAN in the hospital bed is barely moving. She is lying eerily still, looking like she's staring into the ceiling, reminding him mostly of a porcelain doll. Only her chest heaving up and down in a rhythmic motion reveals that she is, in fact, alive—that and the beeping monitor next to her, counting her every heartbeat. Her eyes are half-closed, and the big bruise on her cheek hasn't healed yet. It's still purple and swollen. Her arm and shoulder are bandaged, and blood has seeped through the gauze in patches. Her shoulder-length hair is spread out on the white pillow, looking like a red halo surrounding her.

"Has she said anything so far?"

FBI Special Agent Jonathan Caine looks at the small woman standing next to him by the window in the ICU. She belongs to the local law enforcement in the mountain town where they have sent him.

Bryson City, North Carolina.

In the heart of the Great Smokey Mountains—it's known for its wildflowers, streams, and the gateway to the Appalachian Trail.

Jonathan had never even heard of this town before his boss called him with this assignment. He's still exhausted from the drive there, and his back is killing him, but there is no time to rest. They need this woman's testimony in the books, while it is still fresh in her memory. Before coming to the hospital, Jonathan drove by the scene up by the cabin where they found the body, and it wasn't pretty. The woman behind the glass is the only one who can tell him exactly what happened. She's the lone survivor.

"Not yet," the local law enforcement officer, who goes by the name Victoria Grande says. Jonathan can't stop smiling when she talks because of the irony of her name compared with the actual size of her body. "We've been waiting for you."

"And you say she was found inside the cabin when you arrived?" he asks. "That's what I was told."

Victoria Grande nods. He wonders if she has children or if she's married, then looks at her finger and spots a ring. It looks new. It's still shiny, and she keeps touching it like she isn't used to wearing it yet. It doesn't surprise him that she's married, even though she is young. Victoria Grande is pretty, and a girl like her should be married. He just hopes he's a nice guy. He hopes she found a guy that prioritizes her. He hopes he's nothing like himself, who messed up his chance at happiness and marriage by letting work get in the way. No woman deserves a man like that.

"She was sitting in the chair in the living room, her face beat up, blood running from the gunshot wound in her shoulder. She was barely conscious when they brought her to the hospital."

He nods. That's what the report said. It's been three days since she was found in the cabin up there. She is originally from Florida. She was vacationing in the mountains when the incident happened. That's all he knows about her.

Grande hands him a wallet, or rather a small purse, one of those many women have today, carrying both their credit cards and a phone. He opens it and takes out the driver's license. The phone isn't there, naturally, since it will be with the techs, who will be doing to it what they do best. Jonathan barely recognizes the woman from the other side of the glass when he looks at the photo on the card. The red hair tells him it is her, but the beat-up face on the woman in the bed doesn't look much like the woman in the photo.

At least not anymore.

SHE SITS up when they enter. Her eyes are barely open. The right one seems not to be able to open properly, as the lid refuses to lift, and decides to dangle in front of her eye instead. Her upper lip is swollen and cracked, and it looks like it hurts as she opens her mouth. She's about to say something, but pain holds her back.

"Laurie Davis?" Jonathan says, and she tries to nod, but groans in pain, then leans back on her pillow.

It rubs him the wrong way, seeing a woman like this. In his time on the force, he has seen his share of beaten-up women, and it never becomes something you just get used to seeing. It stirs him up every time in a way he can't always control. Whether it is because his own mother was subjected to his father's rage, he doesn't know. But he suspects it is. He has seen first-hand what a terrorizing father can do, how much damage he can provide, not just to the woman he beats, but also to the children.

"Yes," Laurie answers. "And you are?"

He reaches out his hand, and they shake, her using her left hand since the right is in a sling, so she won't rip out the newly stitched gunshot wound in her shoulder.

"FBI Special Agent Jonathan Caine and this is Detective Victoria Grande. I think the last part of her name refers to her big heart, not the size of her body," he says and winks at her.

That makes Laurie chuckle. Not a happy chuckle, but it is more than would be expected in a situation like this. Jonathan is known for making people feel relaxed in his company, and when they are comfortable, they talk. The words seem simply to flow easier.

"Nice to meet you both," she says.

"Wish it could have been under different circumstances, huh?" he says and grabs a chair. Victoria Grande does the same. They sit next to her bedside.

Laurie closes her eyes with a deep breath. "I guess there's no use postponing it anymore, huh?"

Jonathan shakes his head. "We need you to tell us what happened up there. And do take your time. We want all the details; we want the entire story. Also, what went before this. If anything seems too small and insignificant, tell it anyway. We can always *eat the meat and spit out the bones, afterward,* as my dear mother used to say. We have all the time in the world. I'm not retiring till later this year."

He says the last part with a small laugh and hopes the two women don't detect the fear in his voice—because it is there. There is nothing Jonathan fears more right now than being retired—old and with nothing else to do. He recently turned fifty-six but feels like he's still in his forties. He can live with the age. It doesn't bother him. In most jobs, he would still be considered young, just not in the eyes of the bureau. The thought of being out of a job is what scares him. What is he supposed to do all day? Just stay at home with absolutely nothing to do? No one needing him? To Jonathan, that is the most terrifying thing in the world, and he has seen his share of atrocities in his line of work. But there's no way around it. Agency policy declares he must retire at fifty-seven if he's had more than twenty years in service. He can scream and fight it all he wants to, but it is coming. Now, he just needs to figure out what to do with the rest of his life.

He doesn't even like to fish.

Laurie leans back on her pillow, then uses the remote to raise her headrest to make herself comfortable. She looks at Jonathan with her left eye, then takes a deep breath through her nose, opens her cracked lips, and says:

"All right, then. I guess it all started with Cheerios."

"Cheerios?" he says and looks up from his pad, where he was getting ready to write his notes. He is also recording everything through the app on his phone, but he likes to write down key points as well. It helps him to get a better overview.

She nods.

"Yes, Cheerios."

Chapter 2

THE THING IS, I didn't buy the darn Cheerios, and that's what we were fighting about on our way back home in the car—the kids and me. That's my son, Damian, and my daughter, Isabella. Now, when I say fighting, I mean my youngest, Damian, who is six years old, is having a raging fit. He is screaming at the top of his lungs inside the car, and there is nothing that can calm him. Damian loves his Cheerios, and more than that, he needs things to be the way they used to be. He doesn't do well with changes, and there have been a lot of those recently. Too many for such a young heart to carry. I should have known that was what it was all about, but I was so frustrated, so worn out, I didn't have the strength to deal with his fit. So, I yelled back. I yelled at him and told him to eat something else for once—that it won't harm him.

"But there is nothing I like," he screams back at me. "It all tastes bad."

"Just do it for me, okay? Just this once?" I say.

"No."

I look at my son in the rearview mirror. He crosses his

arms in front of his chest and pouts. His sister, who is fourteen, rolls her eyes at him and looks out the window just as I drive up the street. We live on base—Ambridge Air Force base near Dundee Beach, Florida. My husband is a pilot in the Air Force. My kids go to the local school outside of base and come home by bus when I don't pick them up on my way back from Publix. I prefer to shop at Publix outside of the base since I can get more organic groceries that way, and I try to keep my family healthy. It's funny how you try to control the little things when everything else is out of control, right? I mean, it's absurd; here I am, not knowing if my husband will have killed himself, and all I worry about is whether my children are eating organic or not. As if it even matters. They don't really know that it is better, do they? All the experts, I mean. Do they even have proof that organic is better for you? I didn't eat organic food when growing up, nor was I gluten-free or dairy-free or any of that stuff, and I'm still alive, right? But I guess it makes me feel in control when I make sure the kids stay healthy. It's probably why I also tend to go to the gym constantly when Ryan is overseas. I do cross-fit, and it makes me feel stronger, so I tend to do that a lot when he is away for a longer time. This was his fifth deployment, and he had just returned about a month earlier. I say returned, but the thing is, I wasn't sure he ever returned from this trip. I know a part of him didn't; that's for sure. He came back changed. It's hard to explain…he was just not the same man. Anyhow, I'm getting off track here. Where was I…? Oh, yes. I turn onto our street on the base, where we live. It's all government housing, our street, a row of two-story gray houses squeezed onto a small strip of land between the river and the ocean. The houses are all the same; I'm talking completely identical, and more than once, I've parked in front of the wrong house, thinking it was ours, ha-ha, but that was mostly in the beginning, in the first years we lived there. Now, after eight years, I'm somewhat of an expert at telling the houses apart.

What I am not an expert in is dealing with my husband's PTSD. Do you know how many of them come back with PTSD? No, neither do I, but it's a lot more than you'd think. And after four trips over there, I was pretty certain it wouldn't happen to him, that he knew what he was dealing with by now, so it wouldn't happen. Not to my Ryan. But it did. And we realized it too late. It's not like there's a sign to look for, like a rash or a fever, or that he's even aware of it himself; it just sort of happens, you know? The little things he can't deal with all of a sudden.

"Is that Dad?" my daughter says as I drive up toward the house. Both my children shriek when they see him. He is sitting outside on the doorstep, looking dashingly hand-some as always. My heart skips a beat as I lay my eyes on him.

"It is; it's Daddy," Damian yells, while the groceries in the back clank and scramble as I turn the minivan into the driveway and stop.

"It is him!"

Damian jumps out the minute the car stands still and runs to his father. Isabella follows him, but she is more cautious.

"Hi there, peaches," he says to her as she approaches him, Damian already hanging around his neck.

"Hi."

He pulls her into a hug. I fight my tears as they well up in my eyes. I am overwhelmed with so many emotions right now; it's unbearable. I can't contain it. He sends me a feeble smile like he knows he has screwed up.

"Where have you been, Daddy? Where have you

been?" Damian says. "I got a new bunny. Do you want to see it, Daddy? Do you?"

"Really? You got a new one, buddy? That's amazing," Ryan says and looks up at me, his eyes questioning. We had agreed no more pets, but that was before he left. Things are different now. Rules and agreements are being broken in the name of survival.

Damian rushes inside to get the new bunny.

"If Mom keeps giving him bunnies every time you're not home, we're gonna need to go live on a farm," Isabella says.

"Yeah, well, he needed a distraction," I say as Isabella goes inside, ignoring my excuses. She has heard them numerous times before and still doesn't believe them. She knows I gave him that bunny to make him stop whining and moping, so I could catch a break.

I grab the groceries and slam the back of the van shut, then walk up toward Ryan. He grabs one of the bags from me and carries it inside when Damian comes running with his new pet, the black angora rabbit called Tigger. It's named after Damian's favorite character in Winnie the Pooh, and since they could both jump, it was the right name for it, he argued. He already has two other bunnies, Ollie and Wanda, and the last thing we need is one more mouth to feed, but it seemed like a good thing at the time. It was the only thing that cheered the boy up when he realized his dad had left again after only one month home, and we didn't know when he was coming back.

"HOW HAVE YOU BEEN?"

Ryan helps me put the groceries away. I have a jug of milk in my hand and have it halfway into the fridge when he asks the question. I pause, then close my eyes for just a second before placing the jug on the shelf and closing the door to the fridge a little harder than I intend to.

Ryan looks up from a paper bag, a pack of Annie's Organic Mac and Cheese Deluxe in his hand.

"How have I been?" I ask with a light scoff. "How have I been? Well, let's see. Ever since you ran out on us and decided to stay away for the past week, I've pretty much been trying to keep everything together. I feed the kids; I help with their homework, I arrange playdates, I go to parent-teacher conferences, and I nod and smile and tell them everything is fine. I tell my parents, using my calmest possible voice, that you'll be back, not to worry, and then I cry secretly in the bathroom, praying the children won't hear it. I build Legos with Damian, hoping he won't ask for you; I do math with Isabella, praying I know what I'm doing. I answer their questions, and I take their fits of rage as they turn their anger and blame on me. I tuck them in at night; I get them up in the morning, I wash their clothes while they're in school and make sure they're folded and that none of my tears hit their dinner as I serve it. I can't stop eating, and I think I've gained about ten pounds just this past week because I worry; I worry like crazy about you and when we'll see you again. And once we do, how long will you stay this time? You leave without a word, and we don't know when or if we'll ever see you again. I don't know where you are, where you're sleeping at night. You don't even freaking call them and say goodnight. At least you did that when you were deployed, Ryan. At least you'd call us. The kids need you, you know? They finally got their dad back, and now you're gone again without a word, without even a goodbye or an explanation. What do you want me to tell them? They're trying so hard to be brave, and then…then I forget one thing like those freaking Cheerios, and suddenly everything breaks down. I try to convince them—along with myself—that their dad hasn't left for good. That you'll be back one of these days, maybe tomorrow, while the hope dwindles inside me. And I feel so abandoned. You might as well have died in that war over there. Maybe the pain would have been less invasive. That's how I've been. How's your day going so far?"

The minute I say all this, I regret it. I can tell by the look in his eyes that he is embarrassed. I blush with guilt. I have made him feel worse. That wasn't my intention. I guess I just needed to get it off my chest.

"I'm sorry," he says. He is rubbing his eyes and hair excessively, and I can tell he isn't feeling well. The last thing I need right now is to scare him off, to make him run away again now that he is finally home.

No. I'm sorry, Ryan. I know you can't help it. You're not well. It's just so…I will behave. You're the one who's in pain here. You're the one suffering.

Those are the words I want to say. But I can't seem to get them across my lips. Instead, I wipe the sweat off my brow and keep unpacking, putting cereal boxes away, annoyed that I'd forgotten those stupid Honey Nut Cheerios. The thing is, I had done it on purpose. I meant not to buy them—to cut down on the boy's sugar intake. It's all he ever eats, sometimes straight from the box. It can't be healthy. The kids are supposed to be eating healthier; the therapist told me, especially my daughter. Sugar isn't good for her anxiety, which often torments her during tests in school. But who am I kidding? I'm not going to be Super-Mom of the year anyway. I just want to get past this week, heck even this day would be nice.

I finally get the courage to ask:

"Will you stay the night?"

He twitches and nervously touches the edge of his shirt.

"I should…I need to…"

My heart beats violently in my chest as he says the words. He can't be serious. He can't be talking about leaving already. I want to tell him please don't go.

Stay, and we'll make popcorn, we'll watch a movie, anything you'd like, doesn't have to be just for the kids. I'll cook. I'll make the lamb you love so much; you remember that? I can make that for you, every day if only you'll stay with us. We can have a glass of wine; we can sit in the living room, holding hands, not saying anything if you don't want to.

His eyes avoid mine, and he turns away. I feel the desperation rise inside of me. Did I do this to him? Is this my fault? Am I pushing him away?

"I…can't. Not tonight…"

I have barely opened my mouth to try and talk him out of leaving before he runs off. The screen door slams shut, hard, and Damian comes out to me. He has just been in his room to put the bunny away.

Only gone for one second.

The boy stares at the door, then up at me. "Where is Dad? Where did he go? Did he leave again?"

I lean on the counter as I feel like the entire ground has been removed beneath me—the carpet literally pulled away.

What have I done?

"Did Dad leave again?" Isabella asks a second later when she comes into the kitchen too. Then she looks up at me, her eyes fuming.

"What did you say to him?"

Chapter 3

I DON'T KNOW what to do, where to go. I try to go to the bathroom to let the tears flow, but my son soon knocks on the door because he has to go—now—and I leave. I walk into the pantry, then sink to the white tiles, crying between cans of diced tomatoes and baked beans, water bottles, and pasta. I cry, feeling like an idiot. Why did I have to go off on him like that? Why couldn't I have been more kind to him, make him feel more welcome in his own home? Why did I have to say all those awful things? The fact is, he can't help it. It's just too hard for him to get back to an everyday life with everyday problems and little—to him insignificant—things that need to be done.

It started after just a few days at home. I woke up because he was awake, walking around in circles in the bedroom. Sometimes, he was crying; other times, he was just restless and couldn't lie in bed with me. One night, he wasn't there when I woke up. He had left in the middle of the night and came home reeking of alcohol. That started a new pattern where he'd go drinking at night with his war buddies, the other soldiers from his flying squadron. Night after night, he'd be gone. Then the anger came. We still have punched holes in the doors around the house to remind me, and the kitchen chair he kicked was never the same even after he tried to fix it. No one sat in it after that.

Then, one day, a week earlier, he backs me into a corner and starts yelling at me, screaming into my face in front of the children. I get hysterical, and I am screaming, threatening to call for the Security Forces, the SP's. He then grabs me around the neck and holds my throat tight like he wants to strangle me, his eyes piercing me. Everything is chaos. The kids are screaming at him to stop, and once he realizes what he has done, he lets go, then stares at me for a few seconds before he grabs a bag, fills it with a few things, and leaves. I beg him to stay and tell him it's alright; I'm not mad at him. I want him to get better, and maybe we can get some help…that I know it isn't him, but a disease that makes him do those things.

But it is too late.

"I don't trust myself around you," he says, then leaves.

I can't believe he gave up on us that easily. I just want my husband back.

"CAN I go to play with Joe?"

I lift my head and see Damian standing in the entry to the pantry. He doesn't even wonder why I'm sitting on the floor, crying. He has seen it too much; he's gotten accustomed to seeing me like this. The thought makes my stomach churn. Why am I such a wimp? Why can't I just be strong for the kids?

I grab a bag of Oreos, then eat one and hand one to

Damian. He takes it, and I nod. "Go ahead. I'll pick you up a little later."

Joe is the kid who lives across the street from us, and Damian's best friend. Those two hang out every afternoon, biking in the street or skateboarding. That's what I like about living on base. You can let your kid run around the neighborhood without having to worry about anything bad happening to them. Joe, Jr.'s mother, Sandra, was in Ryan's squadron in Afghanistan at Fagrad Air Base on their latest deployment. I often think about asking her what happened to my husband…if she knows. But I feel like I'd be prying, asking her to share details she can't or doesn't want to.

What happens in Afghanistan apparently stays over there. That seems to be the mantra between them since I never hear them talk about anything, even when we have barbecues or hang out otherwise. They never talk about what they did or mention things they experienced. Not even the good stuff.

Damian smiles, then asks for a second Oreo, and I give it to him, then eat a couple more myself, thinking I deserve it, going through what I am.

Then, my phone rings.

IT'S my mom who calls. And my dad. My mom always has the phone on speaker, so my dad can be in on the conversation, which I am actually very happy about. I find it a lot easier to talk to my dad than my mom. He's less judgmental and doesn't always tell me what I'm doing wrong and what I ought to do.

My dad used to be a pastor at a church up in the panhandle of Florida, where I was born and raised in a small town called Crestview. I grew up as a pastor's kid in a very safe environment. We never had much money, but we never lacked anything either, and my parents were always around, which I liked a lot. They always believed in being close to their children, and since my dad retired, they too moved to the Atlantic Coast and live now in Dundee Beach, where they have bought an apartment close to the beach. They follow my life closely, especially now that Ryan and I are having trouble. They want to be there for me, which I appreciate, I truly do, but I just so wish I had better news for them.

"Has Ryan come home?" my mom asks, just like she asks every time they call. I can hear the anxiousness in her voice. It's vibrating in that way she can't hide from me, even though she almost chirps the words out like she is asking me about the weather or something else less uncomfortable.

"As a matter of fact, he has," I say with a deep sigh.

"Really?" she says, and I know she is looking at my dad, smiling and relieved. I also know he is nodding reassuringly, like he is saying, *told you he'd come home*. It's been rough on my dad since he loves Ryan like a son. Growing up, there was only my sister and me, and she's not married. He and Ryan used to bond and talk for hours. He has more than once asked me if he should have a talk with him and try to convince him to come back home, which I have, of course, told him not to. It would only embarrass Ryan, and he doesn't need that right now.

"But then he left again," I say with an exhale. I can just see their disappointed eyes as they hear the words. "He… it's just too difficult right now."

They're silent for a few seconds. I can hear my mother's heavy breathing and know they're still there.

"It's okay, sweetie," my dad finally says. "He'll be back. He'll come around. He just needs time, is all."

"Yes, he needs…time," my mom repeats. I know she doesn't mean it. She thinks he's a wimp for running away from his family and that he needs to act more like a man and take care of us. My mom is old-fashioned like that, and she doesn't understand. She's also the one who told me just to stop thinking sad thoughts when I went through a period of post-partum depression after having Damian. She doesn't understand why depressed people don't just stop, why they don't just not think about the things that make them sad. So hearing her say this, I know she's at least trying to be understanding.

I close my eyes and rub them tiredly. "Listen… Mom…Dad…"

"I'm sure it'll get better," my dad says. "Put your faith in God. Put Ryan in God's hands. He'll help you both get through this."

"I will, and I am," I say.

"We'll pray for him," my dad says, and I smile warmly. I want him to come over and hug me in his bear-arms so badly. I miss him terribly. I just can't really deal with their sad and concerned expressions right now, so I've been avoiding them. Also, my house is an utter mess, and I don't want my mom to see that. I can't take her worried looks and the disapproving shaking of the head.

"Let's have lunch soon," I say, hoping they'll want to meet somewhere else, so I won't have to clean. I don't want the kids to be there either. I'll just end up having to excuse them constantly.

He's going through some stuff right now… She's in a bad mood; you know how it is with teenagers… He doesn't normally act like this… Maybe she's coming down with something.

"Sounds good, sweetie," my mom says. "You know I like that lobster place. Maybe we should go there? Maybe Tuesday next week?"

I nod, knowing I won't have the energy and will probably cancel. Still, I play along for now.

"Let's do that."

I have barely hung up and gathered myself before I hear my son scream.

Chapter 4

I DROP the phone and run outside, heart in my throat, worry nagging in the pit of my stomach. Has he hurt himself on his bike? Did he fall from that magnolia tree in Joe's yard again, even though I told him to stay out of it? I sure hope nothing is broken. I can't spend the rest of the day at the ER again. I simply can't do it.

"M-O-O-M!"

"Damian?"

He is running toward me. He doesn't seem hurt; I am relieved to see. There are no visible bruises, no blood, and no limping or grasping of the arm.

"What's going on, Damian?"

The boy stops. I feel confused and scared, yet strangely calm now that I can see he is physically alright.

"Damian, what happened?"

He stares at me.

"Where's Joe, Jr.? Did he do something?"

Damian shakes his head. He looks determinedly at me, then pulls at my hand.

"Come."

I sigh. "Damian, if nothing is wrong, then can't I please go back to the house? I have so much laundry I need…"

"No," he says. "Come."

I stare into his eyes. Something in them makes me decide to follow him. Plus, I can't take another argument right now. He's dragging me inside Sandra's house. I hope she won't be angry with me for walking in like this without knocking.

"Hello?" I say. "Sandra?"

Damian pulls me toward the stairs. "Come."

"Damian, Joe, Jr.'s mother needs to know I'm here. I can't just…"

"Come!"

I walk up the stairs, feeling more and more worried as I take each step. Something seems to be strangely off here. Where is Sandra? Why isn't she answering when I call her name? Isn't she here? Has she left her kid home alone? No, that wouldn't be like her; she wouldn't do that.

Maybe she's in the backyard? Or could she be asleep?

"Damian, maybe we should…"

"Come, Mom. Come," he insists.

I follow him into the master bedroom, protesting, telling him we can't just walk into people's bedrooms. It's not right. Yet, we do it anyway.

He stops in front of a closed door. I know it leads to the master bathroom since the house is exactly the same as ours. Damian grabs the handle and turns it. I pause, thinking this is odd. Why is he taking me to Sandra's bathroom?

"What's in there?" I ask.

He doesn't answer but opens the door. Inside, I see Joe, Jr. He's standing, bare feet on the floor, staring at the bathtub. The water is overflowing, and he's getting soaked on his feet and the bottom of his pants. But that's not the worst part. It is what he's looking at that makes my blood run cold. Inside of the tub lies a person. Inside of the tub, half-sunken into the water lies his mother.

"I DON'T THINK the boy even realized she was dead," I tell Investigator Rick Thibodeau from the Special Investigations Office, who arrives along with the ambulance after I called for help. After realizing what had happened, I grabbed both boys, and I took them to our house, where they are now playing on the floor with their toy cars. I am struggling to keep it together, but I do it anyway. My hands are shaking, but I hide them behind my back. I speak slowly to sound normal. I don't want to frighten the kids.

"I'm not even sure he understands it now," I add. My breath is ragged, and the words kind of jumble out of me. I'm not even sure it makes any sense, but by the look on the investigator's face, I think it does. "He was just staring at her in the bathroom like he expected her to get up at any moment."

"But you were certain she was dead?" he asks.

I nod. I keep seeing Sandra in front of my eyes, images of her in that water, her skin blue, almost purple, her eyes staring dead into the air in front of her. When I touched her, she felt so cold; it made me shiver. I tremble again just from thinking about it. I keep seeing her face, over and over again, and her arms.

Those deep cuts on her wrists.

"There was blood in the water and on the floor. There was no pulse when I felt her throat. She was ice-cold when I touched her. I'd say she's been dead for quite some time, probably even before Joe, Jr. came home on the bus. He might not even have noticed anything until he needed to go to the bathroom."

I say these words without even knowing if I'm right. Where did all this come from? Am I just guessing?

The investigator nods and takes notes on his pad.

"So, it was suicide; I take it?" I ask cautiously. I saw the cuts; I feel confident in what I have seen. Yet somehow, I still want to be reassured.

He nods again. "Looks like it."

"I guess you get that a lot?"

He sighs and sends me a warm smile. It doesn't feel comforting; on the contrary, it gets a little creepy. Maybe it's just the situation. Everything about it makes me feel sick to my stomach.

Those dead eyes.

I shake my head. I can't keep thinking about them, or about the rest of her in that water, that blood-filled water. I have to focus on where I am right now, talking to the police.

"It happens," he says. "It can be tough coming back, you know?"

I swallow, thinking about Ryan. The words linger in my head for a long time, and I don't really hear what he says next. *It happens. It can be rough getting back.* This is my greatest fear. This is exactly what I worry about every waking hour of my day—that the love of my life will give up. That he'll decide it's not worth the fight anymore. If only he'd let me help him…if only he'd talk to me and tell me what was going on. If only he'd seek help.

I nod, looking at the kids playing behind me. Joe, Jr. seems oddly oblivious to the fact that his life has just been changed forever.

"I know."

"All right, Mrs. Davis," he says, closing his notepad. "Can the boy stay here till we get ahold of his father?"

I nod. "Of course."

Suddenly, my heart bleeds for Joe. This is going to kill him. Sandra and Joe are divorced, and Joe lives off base now. He had an affair while she was deployed, and they split up right after she came home. But they were good at sharing the kid, and the divorce seemed decent. It wasn't brutal, as far as I know.

How do you tell your child that his mother is dead? How would I ever tell my children if Ryan wasn't here anymore?

I sit down as the Special Investigations Officer leaves us, but I don't stay seated for long. My hands are trembling, and I am a mess. I get back up, then walk to the cabinet, grab Ryan's scotch, and pour myself one. I drink it all in one gulp, trying to subdue all my emotions and force away all my fears while the boys continue their play.

I stifle my tears while secretly praying this won't happen to my children. I don't know how any of us would be able to live on after a thing like this. Yet, I still prepare myself mentally for it, for the fact that this could be Ryan.

Maybe not today, but one day.

Chapter 5

TWO DAYS LATER, we have a barbecue at the Colonel's house. I sit with the wives and one husband in the patio chairs, as usual. I glance toward the soldiers from Ryan's unit who are standing by the grill, all in civil clothing, which is rare to see, each with their beer in hand. I am hoping Ryan will show up, at least to hang out with his war buddies, but I don't know if he will. He hasn't called or contacted me since he was in our kitchen a couple of days ago.

I find it absurd for them to have a barbecue only two days after one of their own killed herself. Sandra isn't even buried yet, and still, they insist on making burgers and eating hotdogs. They don't mention her at all, at least the spouses don't. I don't know what the others are talking about. I wonder if it is because they're terrified like me. Maybe they're scared to talk about suicide and PTSD—because talking about it brings forth the fear, makes it real somehow. I wonder what Joe is doing tonight. And Joe, Jr.? Is he all right? Have any of them even stopped by to check on them? Make sure they're okay?

I kind of want to bring it up in the conversation because I'm scared of Ryan hurting himself, but I don't dare to. They're talking about school right now and the new principal that no one likes. It seems like a safe topic. No one can get upset, or maybe everyone is upset about it, but they're allowed to be. The guy is an idiot who has made the rules for absences even tighter. If you're late by even just a minute, you'll get detention. A lot of moms are complaining about that. I'm not. My kids ride the bus. They're always there on time. Besides, I can't worry about something like that. To be honest, I wish that was all I had to be concerned about. But it's not. I doubt it is for the other spouses, either.

The food is done, and the kids are getting burgers and hotdogs first. Spouses next. We eat, and I compliment the salad that Lisa McCandless, who we usually call Lotty, has created. She is the wife of the squadron commander, Colonel Chip McCandless, and they're the hosts today. It is a really good salad and has cranberries in it, along with some type of seed that tastes good. And kale, of course, but I am not that fond of kale. Not like everyone else these days.

Still, no Ryan.

Is he even coming? I know he has been invited. The guys love him, and I know they see each other, even though he is on leave due to his injury. They probably mostly meet up at the bar outside of the base. But I am certain he knows we're all here.

So, why isn't he here? Is he just staying away because he knows I'll be here?

Vera sits next to me, eating a hotdog with extra ketchup. She hasn't taken any of the salad. She's no one's wife, but her sister was in the unit as well, deployed with the rest of them. She came home in a casket before everyone else. According to what the Air Force has informed Vera, her sister, Clarice, was killed after leaving her duty station. Initially, her family was informed that Clarice was killed in action from "hostile enemy fire." The Air Force later revised its statement, saying that she had died in a "non-combat-related incident." The family believed it was a case of "friendly fire," but then the Air Force later ruled her death a suicide. What was clear was that she was found dead of a single gunshot wound to the head, near a chapel, inside the secure airbase. Vera, who is also enlisted and lives on base, is a close friend of mine. But since she received the news of her sister, she hasn't been the same. She has grown this spite, this resentment toward the Air Force that I never saw in her earlier. She only stays because she has a contract, she tells me. I'm not opposed to her resentment, as I feel it growing in myself as well. I'm not happy to admit it since the Air Force has been our entire lives so far, ever since I married Ryan. But I don't like what being deployed does to our loved ones. I don't say it out loud, of course. Not like Vera, who airs her resentment publicly any chance she gets.

"So, when are you going to let Ryan come back home?" Lotty suddenly says. The question catches me completely off-guard, and I stare at her in confusion. I look for an answer, something clever to say, but there's nothing ready.

"I...I...he's the one who left," I say. "I didn't throw him out."

"He's been sleeping on our couch the past couple of days," Lotty tells the other women around the table, to justify her question. Like she at least deserves to know what she's dealing with here, how long he's going to stay. I am happy to hear he's at least been sleeping somewhere safe. I fear he spends the nights in bars or maybe even sleeping on the street downtown. I know he goes off base a lot since I have this app that I use to spy on him. It gives me his location, not a completely accurate one, but enough for me to know a little about where he goes. I downloaded it last year on all of our phones to be able to track my teenage daughter. I could never have guessed I'd need it for this. But watching him on the app has made me more paranoid, and I realize it is doing me no good. Yet, some nights, I can't seem to stop. I worry whether Ryan is hooking up with someone…if he's hanging out with women. I don't think that is what he is doing, but the worry lingers in the back of my mind; of course, it does.

Lotty tilts her head as she looks at me. "Really? Isn't it the same? Don't you think he just left because he didn't feel welcome?"

"Excuse me?"

"I mean…well, now, don't get me wrong, but maybe you should think about creating a more…uhm… welcoming environment."

I don't know what to say, literally. Okay, maybe I have a lot of things I'd like to say, involving lots of bad curse words, but I hold it back. I have never been good at comebacks, and more than often, I regret the ones I do sling out. It's better to keep my mouth shut. I have learned that the hard way.

Vera comes to my rescue.

"Are you serious right now? How can you even say something like that? You don't know what Laurie and Ryan are going through."

I send her a grateful look. Vera is the only one I have confided in. I've told her everything about how Ryan felt different, how he changed when he came back, about the nightly bar visits, and the fists planted in doors and walls at the house. I even told her about the day when he grabbed my throat. But I have a feeling that Lotty knows these things too. I went to her husband, who is Ryan's superior, right after, and told him everything. I even asked him for help. I asked him if he could talk to Ryan. Tell him to get help.

He told me to *deal with it myself*. This was above his paygrade. "Everyone else deals with these things within the four walls of their home. Why can't you? Why do you have to tell everyone your private affairs?"

So, I went to a mental health professional on base and told him everything too, thinking he'd know what to do.

He gave me a Valium and told me to go home.

That's when I realized that the Air Force doesn't want to deal with wives.

"I'm just saying that I believe it is our duty as wives to make sure our husbands feel welcome once they get back from deployment," Lotty continues.

As she speaks, I can't—for the life of me—understand why she is still talking. How is she even from this century? She can't be serious about what she's saying. No one stops her, and she just yaps along about how important the wife is to her husband's good return and how her Chip has never had any issues coming back. The more she talks, the more she makes it sound like it is my fault that my husband has ended up the way he has. I don't want it to, but it still gets to me.

Because that's also what I fear.

"I just think that if you try a little harder, then I'm sure Ryan will be able to come home. That's all."

That's all, huh? It's that easy? Why didn't I think of this earlier? Thank you for enlightening me. From now on, my life will be a lot easier.

As she folds her hands, finishing her sentence, I rise to my feet, grab my kids, and tell them we're leaving. Damian complains because he's playing with Lotty's son, while Isabella is relieved to go home finally. The men are playing football now, and Chip is in the grass fighting with Ted.

"You're leaving?" Lotty says. Her voice is shrill, and it makes the hair rise on my arm. I hate her right now; I hate her so much I want to punch her. Instead, I walk away. I don't even say goodbye. I just send Vera a look, so she understands. I know she does.

"Don't be like this, Laurie," Lotty yells after me. "We're only trying to help."

Chapter 6

I CAN'T SLEEP. I keep thinking about Sandra and those deep cuts in her wrists. I keep thinking about Joe, Jr. and his dad, and how no one even mentioned them at the barbecue or even talked about Sandra. Was it because it was simply too unpleasant to even think about? Because it hit a little too close to home for so many of us? I keep wondering if the same thing would happen if Ryan had killed himself. Then, I wonder where he was. Why he didn't show up. I don't know why I expected him to. Because they were his buddies, his friends? Why did I assume it was easier for him to be with them and not me? Because I feared Lotty was right? That I scared him off? Made him feel unwelcome in his own home?

I get out of bed, sick of staring into the darkness. I know I'm not getting any sleep anyway, so I grab the laptop and turn on Netflix. I want to watch an episode of *The Crown*. I am halfway through the last season. I hope it will get my mind off things and maybe make me sleepy. I am about to open Netflix when I decide to go on Facebook instead. Just a quick check to see if anything is new.

Then I do what I promised myself I wouldn't. I go to Ryan's page and see if he posted anything. He hasn't. He never does. The last picture is of him and me as he said goodbye to me at Orlando airport, kissing me. That was more than a year ago. The picture makes me feel sad. I remember that day so vividly. It was the last time he was himself.

I touch the screen gently while smiling softly. I wonder if he'll ever be that guy again—the one who was completely devoted to me and our family. The one who'd post pictures of me from the gym, then tell the world he was *a lucky SOB*—the guy who made a picture of him and the kids his profile picture—because they were his every-thing. We were everything to him.

Where did he go?

Will he ever be back?

I sigh and lean back, thinking about the last time I saw him a few days ago. Did he seem better? I wonder about the leave they gave him for being wounded in combat...if that is a blessing or a bad thing for him. He isn't right; he isn't himself. But the fact that he doesn't have to get up for work every day, does that maybe make it worse? I know he goes to physical therapy at the medical center, and he shows up for that a couple of times a week. He has also started running again; I've seen him on the tracks by the landing strips, driving by one day, so I know he is keeping himself in shape. But what does he do all day? I was happy to hear he is sleeping at Chip's place. Those two are close friends and have been through a lot together. Ryan was the one driving the squadron commander on a ground mission when the truck hit a powerful mine that blew off its rear end and flipped it over. Ryan was the first one out, and he helped Chip escape while under heavy fire. He earned the Purple

Heart after sustaining a back injury and a possible concussion in the explosion.

He wouldn't talk about the incident when he got back, and after a while, I stopped asking. I don't know if that is what is bothering him still, or if it is just the fact that getting back to everyday life rather than life-or-death situations is getting to him. Is it the trauma from the explosion? He won't tell me, and he gets so angry if I ask. At least two of the holes in the doors in our house are from me asking about it.

I scroll down and stare at an old picture of us, taken on our Valentine's trip to St. Augustine two years ago. We are holding two cups of water in the air, from the fountain of youth.

How were we so happy back then?

I know it's silly, but I can't help thinking that maybe there's more to the way he acts than a trauma. I fear he's seeing someone else. The thought knocks the air out of me. I feel like I'm losing him; he's sliding away from between my hands, and I don't know how to hold onto him.

I stare at the Facebook page, then do the last thing I ever thought I would. I log off my own Facebook profile, then log onto his. I know all his passwords. He thinks I don't, but I do. He's not that hard to figure out. He only shifts between three passwords: my birthday, Damian's birthday, and Isabella's birthday. It's all he has ever used. I start with mine, then move onto the children's. It works with Damian's birthday. I am logged in and now have access to his profile.

IT'S the first thing I see. It pops up in a separate window, and my heart rate quickens immediately. I see now that he has been on Facebook, probably using his phone. And he has been messaging someone. A girl. Not just some girl.

Sandra.

I barely breathe as I scroll up and begin to read the messages. Apparently, they had been talking for a few days before she died. He's the one who wrote to her first.

Ryan: We need to talk.

Sandra: I don't want to talk to you, Ryan.

Ryan: We have to.

Sandra: No, we don't. We're home now. It's time we forget what happened. Things are different now that we're back.

Ryan: I need to see you. I'll be over tomorrow at noon.

Sandra: All right. Just for coffee. Nothing else.

I STARE at the words on the screen, then read them again and again. There's a couple of days between some of them, but the last one was written the day before she was found dead. This realization makes my throat feel tight. I struggle to breathe. I suddenly remember something from the day I walked into her house, guided by Damian. There was something on the breakfast counter. Two cups had been left out. The kitchen was completely clean otherwise, Sandra never left anything out. Her kitchen was always annoyingly clean. Those two cups, and this message…does that mean…was Ryan visiting right before she killed herself? The thought makes me dizzy. The wording of the messages makes my stomach churn.

Just for coffee? What did that mean? Did she fear he expected something else? Did they have an affair? Had they slept together while deployed, and now that they were home, he wanted to continue while she didn't?

Now that I think about it, I was worried that Ryan had been with someone else while being away. I noticed right away that Ryan was different in bed. He felt different, more aggressive. I told myself it was the PTSD. I had explained it with intimacy problems, which are typical for people with PTSD. I even read about it online. He didn't want to look me in the eyes. He was like an animal, demanding and raw.

The thought makes me feel sick. I can't help but wonder if he has been lying to me all this time.

And why did Sandra end up killing herself right after he visited?

Chapter 7

IT'S DRIVING ME CRAZY. The next day, I send the kids off with the school bus. I am washing clothes, cleaning the bunnies' cage, and walking Rosie, our Golden Retriever. I drive to Publix outside of the base, and, of course, I'm taken aside for a random inspection at the gate, so it takes forever. I buy three boxes of Cheerios, just to be sure Damian is happy while thinking about Ryan. So many thoughts rush through my mind all day. I can't believe he would cheat on me and then come home and make me feel like it's my fault. It all makes sense now. It explains his distance and why it was so hard for him to be with us again. He's plagued by guilt. But does that mean he's leaving us? Why did he come to our house after he went to Sandra's? He was at our doorstep when we came home, and I wonder why he did stop by?

Did he sense Sandra wasn't happy? Was that why he stayed away from the barbecue? Because he felt guilty? Because he feared he was to blame?

I avoid that other thought that keeps nagging at me

because it doesn't make me feel good. Besides, Sandra had cut her wrists. She wasn't killed.

Yet, I can't stop worrying. He was there. Did he say something that made her want to end it all? I don't want to. I really don't, but the thoughts keep popping up in my mind. I keep thinking about his aggressive behavior and feel his hands on my throat from the day he left—the day he almost strangled me.

No, Ryan would never do that. He'd never hurt anyone.

Except he isn't my Ryan anymore. This guy is different.

I CAN'T CONVINCE MYSELF, and the worry gets to be too much for me, my paranoia taking over, so I call a friend. I call Frank, who is a military forensic investigator on the base.

"Laurie. Long time no see. How's it going?"

I give him a long chat about how things are great, busy as usual, and how the kids are growing. I tell him we should get together soon; maybe he can come over for a cookout? But I don't really mean it. I mean, I like him, I always have. He's a nice guy and all, but I am just not in a place where I feel like having people over. Finally, he asks how Ryan is doing, and I become suddenly honest. I don't like lying to people or even pretending.

"He's not so well, I am afraid," I say. "It's tough to get back and well…he's suffering this time. He's been staying with friends for some time."

"I'm so sorry to hear that," Frank says, but I am not sure he means it. Frank has always liked me, in that way that makes it necessary for me to keep him at a distance. We can still be friends, at least I hope so, just not close ones. As I think about this, I realize that if my husband really has been unfaithful to me, then I don't have to worry about this anymore. I can have male friends and admirers if I want to.

The thought doesn't make me happy. On the contrary —it makes me feel sad. I don't want to get a divorce. I don't want to be on the market again. I was never good at being single. Ryan saved me from my loneliness when he came along, tall and dashing. I was still in college, getting my journalism degree, and he had just signed with the military. We didn't see each other much, but the little we did was so thrilling that I soon started to dream of a life with him—even though I knew I'd be one of the military wives—one of those who'd have to send their loved ones off to war, not knowing if they'd come back. I thought I could deal with it…that I could take it. I have always been strong, and I loved him so much; I knew if anyone could survive this, it'd be us. We would be the ones to get through it.

"So, what do you want from me?" Frank asks. "I know you didn't just call to have a chat. That'd be a first, at least."

"I need your help with something. It's important."

He goes silent. "Okay?"

I tell him what I've found. I read him the messages from Ryan's Facebook account and tell him I am concerned. He chuckles on the other end.

"I can understand your concern about him cheating on you, but I'd hardly be worried about him killing her."

"But what if it was an accident? What if he lost it the way he did with me? He got angry with her because she didn't want him, didn't want to sleep with him again? He might not have meant to kill her, but then he did?"

"And then made it look like suicide afterward? That's a little calculated, don't you think?"

"He's changed, Frank. I feel like I don't know him anymore. Just tell me, okay? What did the autopsy say?"

"All right. Give me a sec."

I hear him tapping on a computer. I am so happy to know a guy like him, who'd do anything for me. I know he is risking his job. I'll have to make it up to him someday.

"Here it is. It looks like it was ruled a suicide—nothing out of the ordinary. She cut her wrists with razor blades, then bled out in the water. Time of death is dated to between noon and two o'clock."

I swallow. Ryan had said he'd stop by at noon for coffee. At two o'clock, he was sitting on my doorstep. How long had he been there?

Stop it! You're being paranoid!

"There is nothing strange about this death," Frank says. "I think you can let go of this thought."

I breathe relieved. He's right. They had an affair. Ryan came over, then left, and she killed herself afterward. Maybe he didn't want her anymore. He wanted to take care of his family. Maybe he told her that? No matter what, it doesn't have to be suspicious. Tragic, yes, devastating too since it's the end of my marriage, but it's not murder. There could have been a ton of reasons why she killed herself. It didn't even have to be about Ryan. It could have been something she experienced while over there. Things she couldn't talk about—like Ryan refuses to talk about that mine and the rescue of Chip. Only Sandra herself knew what she was carrying, what kinds of terrible experiences she had to relive in her nightmares. They all had them. I knew that much.

"Thank you," I say.

"I hope it makes you feel better."

"It does. It really does."

I hang up, then realize it's a lie—because there's

another thought that has struck me. One I can only think and not say out loud.

What if they did something awful over there? Something they were covering up?

Why did he *need to talk to her*? Why did she say *it's time we forget what happened*?

What if that doesn't refer to sleeping together?

I look out the window at the house across the street where she used to live. The house is empty now; no one lives there anymore. I can still see those cuts in my mind… and those dead eyes and feel her cold skin against my fingers as I frantically searched for a pulse.

That's when I realize that I have to ask him. I have to know what they discussed.

———————————————

Chapter 8

———————————————

I TEXT Ryan and then call him. He doesn't answer either. He never does. It annoys me. Damian returns from school, and I make him a bowl of Cheerios, then help him with his homework. Except I am not really there. I am constantly thinking about Ryan and Sandra. I think of them sleeping together. I picture them sneaking off at the camp, finding a remote place where they know no one goes, then having sex. I picture them in different positions—him on top, her on top. Then I decide I'm an idiot, close my eyes, and return to Damian's math problems. As I stare at the numbers on the piece of paper, I see them kiss; I see them smile at one another secretly when no one is watching. I cast the thought away, but then realize if they aren't having an affair, then it could be something much worse. And I don't want it to be that. Maybe I do. Maybe I want them to have killed someone over there by accident and then tried to cover it up—maybe some local woman at the village, who they thought was carrying a bomb, when it was, in fact, just groceries. Maybe that's what they're running from; maybe that's what's tormenting them. I've seen movies about stuff like this. It happens. They meant well, but they were under pressure; they thought it was them or her. But they were mistaken, and maybe they realized it too late. Yes, that could be it. It could be as simple as that. Awful, yes, but no sex involved.

I check my texts every five minutes or so, then realize it's time to pick up Isabella from her friend's house. She lives off base, and this is the only way my daughter can get home.

I am driving across the small town while Damian is in the back seat, playing on his iPad. I see a homeless man sitting on a bench with his head bent like he's either crying or sleeping. I wonder if it is Ryan. I worry it is him. I think I see him many places all day—from the window at the coffee shop downtown…when driving to the hairdresser… when driving to school to pick up the kids if I pick them up and they don't go by bus. I think I see him when I walk down to the beach to do my powerwalk, and I see a group of homeless people hanging out by the pier drinking, or see one of them sleeping leaned up against a pillar. I worry about him all the time. Is he eating properly? Why can't he be with us? Has he hurt someone? What did he do over there? Will he kill himself like Sandra did?

WE EAT dinner in town at a small Puerto Rican place with the best shrimp tacos in the world. Isabella gets the nachos while Damian gets a Caribbean burger. We sit outside, since it is hot out, even for January. I look at the stars above us while we eat, then wonder what Ryan is eating. I check my phone, but he still hasn't answered my texts or called me back. I think about opening the app and seeing where he is but stop myself. I don't want to go there. It's a dark place and leads to nothing but me imagining the craziest of things. I don't want to be that lunatic wife.

It's dark when we return to base. Damian is tired, and I have to carry him inside even though he is getting way too heavy for me. Isabella isn't saying much as usual. She's been very quiet since she saw her dad attack me. I can't blame her. I often still feel those fingers around my neck, and sometimes I wake up at night and can't breathe, dreaming I am being strangled. That feeling of not being able to breathe—it's awful.

"Did you do your homework?" I ask her as we walk up toward the house.

"I did it with CC," she says, sounding annoyed. I know she hates it when I ask, but I need to know. Her grades have been going down lately, sliding slowly, and I fear she's giving up. You can't slide much before you fail in school these days. It was different when I was a kid. We could easily get by with a lot less. Today, the kids need to perform constantly—test after test, almost every day. I fear for her. She gets anxiety, and I fear it'll break her.

"Okay," I say. "Just checking. No reason to be upset."

"But that's the thing, Mom. You're not just checking. You don't trust me. You don't think I know I need to do my homework or study for tests, but I do. And I am always prepared for school. You never recognize this. You act like I am two years old."

I chuckle, holding Damian close to me, carrying him toward the door, reminding myself to enjoy these years before he turns into a teenager too.

"Well, to be fair, you were only two years old just the other day, and you'll have to forgive me, but it takes a while to get used to you being so big all of a sudden. It feels like just a few days ago that you needed me for everything."

Isabella growls, but she can't help smiling too. She likes

talking about when she was younger, back when Mom and Dad were happy and still together in the same house. I know she must feel insecure about the future.

I know I do.

"What's that light?" she asks as we approach the house. She points toward our house in front of us. "In there?"

I look and see that there's a light turned on in the guest room downstairs, the one we never use.

"That's odd," I say. "I don't remember going in there recently, do you? I don't think I have been in that room for weeks."

Isabella shakes her head. "I never go in there. It's just a lot of boxes and old stuff anyway."

"Then how come the light is on?"

I stare at the window, feeling frightened. Is someone in our house? I open the door using my key, then put Damian on the couch, where he continues to sleep. I walk to the closet and grab one of Damian's baseball bats. With it lifted, praying it's not a burglar, I walk to the guest room and push the door open. Inside, I see him. Ryan. He's sleeping, lying on the bed on his side, curled up into a ball.

"It's Dad," Isabella says behind me.

I lower the bat as my fear goes away.

I signal for her to be quiet, and we look at him together. He doesn't look homeless. His hair is clean and recently cut. He smells good too. He doesn't smell like alcohol at all. He is taking care of himself. I wonder if he knows about Sandra…if he has heard. I am sure his friends have told him. He is sleeping heavily and doesn't even notice we're there. I'm guessing he needs his sleep. I sigh, turn out the lights, and we leave him in there, closing the door quietly.

At least I know where he'll be tonight.

Chapter 9

I DREAM about Ryan again that night. Nothing unusual in that. I dream about him most nights, just like I think about him most days. What is unusual is that he is crying. He sits in a corner and cries, his body shaking. As I try to comfort him, he starts to scream. I jump back, my heart beating so fast it's almost painful, and I fear it'll never relax again. I wake up with a start and realize I am completely soaked in sweat. Tears are streaming down my cheeks, and I fight to breathe and calm myself.

That's when I realize I am not alone in the room.

Someone is sitting in the chair by the door next to my bedside, in total darkness, staring at me. Frantically, I turn on the bedside light and look at him.

It's Ryan.

"Geez, you scared me," I say and clasp my chest. "How long have you been sitting there?"

He doesn't answer. He stares at me, his red-rimmed eyes almost glowing. He looks upset. Angry.

"Are you okay, Ryan?" I ask.

Then, I see the tears. They're running down his cheeks.

His face is strained, and he can no longer keep himself composed. His body is shaking. I don't think twice about it. I jump out of bed and go to him. I hug him and hold him tight while he cries.

"Is it because of Sandra?" I ask as I feel him calming down slightly in my arms. "Are you crying because of her?"

He nods, then sniffles loudly. "I don't think I'm doing so well."

"Oh, sweetie," I say and hug him again. His tears and snot wet my shoulder. His body is shaking, and he smells like alcohol. On the bedside table stands an almost empty glass. There's a little bit of scotch left on the bottom. The bottle next to it is completely empty. He's been drinking while watching me sleep.

"What's going on, Ryan?" I ask, squatting in front of him. "Can't you tell me what is happening with you?"

He shakes his head, still crying. I stare at his lips, missing them terribly. I have the oddest urge to dive in, to let go of all my issues, all my worries, and just do it. After all, I don't know with certainty that he has cheated on me. Their meeting could have been about something else, something completely different. It might not even be anything terrible. Maybe he just missed her because they were friends? I know I am lying to myself, but I don't care. I need this distraction right now. I need this.

I kiss the lips. I lean forward and kiss him. He kisses me back. We stay like this for a few seconds until he pulls away. I don't understand, so I look at him, puzzled. His shoulders are shaking. I raise my hand and put it on his neck. He doesn't push it away. I pull him closer, and we kiss again.

"I'm sorry," I whisper. "If I haven't made your coming home easier. I want to, but you have to help me. You have got to talk to me. Tell me what's going on."

He pulls back forcefully. I realize I have gone too far; I have pushed him again. He doesn't like that. He straightens up, then pushes my hand away from him. Then he laughs. It's a bitter laugh. The terrifying sense of panic is rising inside of me, devouring me. I don't feel like I can count on him. He seems out of it—like the time he tried to strangle me. Remembering this, I pull back.

"Ryan?"

I can see the veins underneath his skin. He gets up and grabs the empty bottle next to him. I want to go to the front door, but he is blocking my way. I have to get past him first, and I don't want to, not now that he's holding that bottle in the air, his other hand in a clenched fist.

"Please, Ryan," I say on the verge of tears. I raise my hands to protect myself. "I'm sorry."

The bottle hits the wall behind me and shatters. Glass rains onto the carpet, and I sink to my knees, terrified. Seeing this, Ryan stops. He reaches down toward me, grabs me by the shoulders, and helps me get up.

"I'm scared," he says. "Don't you understand? I am so terribly scared."

"Of what?" I ask, crying. "What is it you're so scared of?"

"I've been to war! Don't you get it? I have seen rocket-propelled grenades that just missed me by inches. I have been shot at, blown up, and I have seen children die. I was almost killed myself."

His shoulders slump as he says it. I feel my heart grow soft. My fear dissipates. He's not dangerous. He's a broken man. He's hurt.

I rise to my feet and take him in my arms. He leans on my shoulder and cries again. Then we kiss some more. I feel his body close to mine. He kisses me now, demandingly, grabs my hair and pulls it; then he pushes me down on the bed. He is on top of me, taking off my clothes, and we make love right there on top of the bed. He is rougher than he used to be with me, and it scares me a little, but I also enjoy being close again.

———

"I STILL CAN'T BELIEVE she's dead."

Ryan shakes his head. He's sitting on the edge of the bed when he starts to talk. It's unexpected, and I sit up, worried that I might ruin the moment if I say anything.

He turns to look at me. His cheeks have color in them, probably from the sex.

"Sandra," he adds. "I can't believe she'd kill herself."

I swallow. It takes me a few seconds to finally find the courage to ask.

"When was the last time you spoke to her?"

He scoffs. "I don't even remember. Right after we got back, I think."

He puts on a sock, then pulls it up. A ton of alarm buttons go off inside my mind. Ryan just lied to me.

Ryan never lied to me before.

He sighs and looks at me kindly. He reaches over, places a finger under my chin, then lifts it and kisses me.

"I think maybe it's time I come back home, huh?"

I stare at him, not knowing what to say. He sees it, then exhales.

"Listen, I know what happened was bad. That's why I left that day. I didn't trust myself around you or the kids. But I'm better now."

I look toward the broken glass on the carpet. I still have the picture frame he broke the last time in the top drawer of the dresser by the front door, the one with the palm trees. It's the picture of him and me together from before we had children and went to Italy on our honeymoon. On the day he tried to strangle me, he threw it on the floor, then stomped on it, breaking the glass. Frightened, I put it in the drawer where it has been ever since. I haven't wanted to take it out. I don't want to be reminded of that day.

"You don't trust me," he says. His eyes are on me, scrutinizing me. He shakes his head a little like I am some child who has misbehaved. "Do you?"

I don't know what to say to him. I want him to come home, yes. But do I dare to have him here? Do I believe he's truly better? He just lied to me. Things change when people start to lie.

"I want to," I say, stifling my tears. "I want to believe you're okay…but I don't."

He nods and moves closer to me. He pulls me into a kiss. A tear escapes my eye, and he wipes it away with his thumb.

"Then I'll just have to prove myself to you, won't I?"

Chapter 10

I WAKE UP, and the bed is empty. Ryan is gone. I exhale and feel his pillow, remembering how we had fallen asleep in each other's arms, just like when we were younger and had just met—back when everything was easy and exciting. He had whispered in my ear how much he had missed me and that he needed me more than ever and for me please to be patient with him. He was coming around. He just needed me to wait for him.

And I had enjoyed every second of it. It was all I had wanted since he got back—to feel his closeness, his breath on my skin, his heart beating close to mine.

We made love three times during the night. It was like he was insatiable…like he couldn't get enough of me. Every time I thought we were about to doze off, he had wanted more. And I didn't stop him; I didn't want to. I enjoyed him wanting me this badly, feeling his deep desire for me, and the more we were together, the gentler he became. It was like we found each other this night, slowly got to know one another once again. We found the pace. Or re-found it. It was quite intense.

But now, he is gone. His side of the bed is empty, and I am filled once again with grief. I hate not knowing where he is, not knowing if he'll stay or be going. I hate that he won't tell me what drives him to go. It is, after all, Saturday, and we could have spent the day together.

I had hoped we would.

With a deep sigh, I sit up, then check my phone. No messages. I stare at the screen, wondering if it's something I said or did. Maybe it's what I didn't say or do? Am I not comforting enough? Am I not understanding enough?

Am I not enough?

That's when I hear the voices—laughing voices, and happily yelling voices. They're coming from the kitchen downstairs. I get dressed, fast, then rush down. By the breakfast counter, I spot Damian. He's eating something, and it isn't Cheerios. He sees me, and his face lights up.

"Mom! Dad made pancakes!"

I walk closer and see Ryan behind the stove. He is wearing his old jeans and a white T-shirt while flipping the pancakes and placing them in a stack next to him.

"It was supposed to be a surprise," he says, grinning. "But Damian couldn't wait."

Isabella has heard the ruckus and comes into the kitchen, then sees Ryan. "Dad?" she says, her voice raised. "What are you doing here?"

Ryan reaches out his arms. You can see his muscles flex underneath the T-shirt. He has been working out a lot and looks very fit. "Isn't it obvious? Making pancakes, of course. Come, dig in before your brother eats all of them."

Isabella sits down, and Ryan serves her a plate, then pours syrup on top of her pancakes and drizzles them with chocolate. Just the way she loves it. He then winks at me, grabs a cup and pours coffee in it, then hands it to me, leans over, and kisses me.

"Thank you," I whisper and hold it between my hands. I feel like I am blushing like a schoolgirl—like when we first met.

"No, thank *you*," he whispers back. "For last night."

I chuckle and sip my coffee while he prepares a plate for me and serves it on the counter. I stare at him, thinking, if I didn't know better, I'd think it was a dream. Has he really returned to being himself? The way he's goofing around with the kids, the pancakes—it's almost like he's back to his old self.

I should be happy. I should be thrilled. This is what I have waited for…what I have dreamt about.

Then how come I feel more terrified than ever? How come the hairs in my neck rise every time I see his smile?

WE EAT BREAKFAST TOGETHER, just like in the good old days before Ryan's last deployment. The kids get into a fight about something silly, and Ryan and I exchange looks —just like we used to. It all feels so familiar and pleasant… if only there hadn't been that stupid lie last night.

I can tell the kids are excited to have their dad here, especially Damian, who gets almost ecstatic. I hear Ryan promise to play ball with him later in the yard before the boy runs to his room to take care of the bunnies. He's in charge of making sure they're fed and have water while I clean out the cage. Our dog, Rosie, lays at Ryan's feet and refuses to leave him. She has always been very fond of Ryan and might be the one enjoying his return the most.

When he's done eating, Ryan leans back in his chair and stretches. "It feels good to be home."

I sip my coffee. I don't know how he does it, but Ryan's coffee always tastes better than any other coffee out there. I close my eyes and sigh, taking in the moment, trying to push that feeling of dread away. I don't want to feel this way. I want to be happy. I deserve to be happy.

As I open my eyes, I accidentally glance out the window across the street at Sandra's house. Immediately, she's on my mind again, and I remember the messages they sent one another. I can't stop thinking about them, even though I don't want to. I really don't want to. I risk ruining this moment.

Yet, I can't help it. I have to know.

I sip my coffee, looking at Ryan over the rim of the cup. He is staring at me, head slightly titled, his tongue playing with the inside of his cheek. He saw me looking at Sandra's house. I wonder if he knows what I'm thinking about. It feels like it.

"It's kind of odd, don't you think?" I say.

He squeezes his eyes almost shut. "What is?"

"That there weren't any signs beforehand. I mean, I saw her almost every day, and I couldn't feel that she was even depressed."

Ryan frowns, places his right elbow on the table, and cups his mouth. "I guess you can't always tell when people are depressed. A lot of times, they put on a show and pretend to be happy. The suicide comes when they can't pretend anymore."

I nod. He's right. That's what they always say. It often comes as a surprise to the people who are close to them. It frightens me greatly. "But she didn't even leave a suicide note. Don't they say that people usually leave a note for those they leave behind?"

Everything inside me is screaming to let it go, to stop talking about it, but I can't. Ryan fiddles with his cup. He doesn't look at me when he answers.

"I don't think there's like a rule for that. Clarice didn't leave one either before she shot herself at the base."

He suddenly lifts his glance and looks directly at me. It feels like he's looking straight through me. His hand is gripping the table.

"Why are you asking about this?"

"I don't know. I was just wondering," I say, my face reddening. I sense I have overstepped a line here and made him uncomfortable.

"You can't do this," he continues. "You don't have any right to ask these questions, do you hear me? You weren't there. You don't know what it's like to come home. You don't have any idea what we're all going through, what I'm going through. Geez, Laurie. I really thought you were smarter than that."

I shake my head, feeling ashamed. He's right. I haven't been to war. I don't know what it's like to be a depressed soldier with PTSD. I don't know the weight of what they're carrying around. But I am married to one, and I would like to know just a little more about what signs to look for, what to be aware of, so I can act before he might kill himself. I don't find it that strange to ask these questions. But I have angered him. I can tell. This is his territory, and I am not allowed to enter.

I don't say another word. I don't want to ruin his mood, but I do keep thinking about it for the rest of the weekend—especially about Clarice, Vera's sister, the girl who killed herself while they were deployed. When Ryan mentioned her, I suddenly remembered something that Vera had told me at the funeral.

I ignored it then, but not anymore.

Chapter 11

I CALL Vera and ask her to meet me for lunch the following Monday. It's her day off, and she can be a civilian for once, not wearing her uniform. We go to a café outside the base in downtown Dundee Beach. I have a salad and then a piece of chocolate cake for dessert. I also have a large latte and a strawberry smoothie. Vera has a ham and cheese sandwich with pesto sauce on sourdough bread. We sit outside since it's seventy-three degrees out, and the air feels really nice. It took me a while to figure out, but January is probably the time of year you sit outside the most in Florida. From April to October, it's too hot to be anywhere that isn't the beach. Right when we moved there, I met people who'd say to me how wonderful it was when the temperatures dropped in January and February when the wind blows from the north, and I thought they were silly because why would anyone like that? But now, I get it. Once the temperatures drop, it becomes really nice, and even on the few days when it is in the fifties in the mornings, you learn to enjoy that because it's so rare that you just can't help but want to be outside and feel it nip at your skin. Usually, by afternoon, it's back in the sixties, so you gotta enjoy it while it lasts. To me, temperature around the low seventies is just perfect—cool enough to wear jeans, and that is a treat when you live where I do. We usually say that by the time you find your winter clothes in the back of the closet, Florida winter has already come and gone.

But I haven't asked Vera to meet me in order to enjoy the weather. I am not there because I enjoy her company either, even though I really do. Vera is fun and always pleasant to be around. And even though she is enlisted, and has been deployed herself, she doesn't have that thing where you can't talk bad about the Air Force that most of the people on base have—at least the ones who are around me.

"It's like a cult," she'll often say. Then she'll laugh, but you can tell she means it. "Or it's like that song, you know…uh…you can check in any time…but you can't leave, or something like that. You know which one I'm talking about?"

Vera dreams of becoming an author one day when she's done with the airforce and will often refer to famous characters in books or talk about stories that I have no idea about because I rarely read. Not that I don't want to—I just don't have that kind of time with the kids and all that. Especially not with Ryan gone so much. I, for one, think she's gonna make an excellent author one day. She has that quirky mind, you know? Slightly crazy, and you're never quite sure if she's telling the truth or pulling your leg. She likes to exaggerate a lot, and everything is a potential plot. Everyone she sees or meets reminds her of some character from a book. She'll often go: "Doesn't that guy over there look just the way you'd think Rand from *Gone Girl* would look? He does to me."

Usually, I'll just nod and play along, even if I have no

idea who she is talking about. Again, I don't read as much as she does.

"So, what's up?" Vera asks as we're halfway through our meal. She knows me well and knows something is going on with me. "I hear Ryan is back."

I nod, my mouth full. I chew, then wash it down with my smoothie. "Yes. He came back Friday night and has stayed home all weekend."

"I bet you're happy about that?" Vera asks, her eyes scrutinizing me. "Or are you?"

Vera is probably the sharpest mind around here. I can't hide anything from her. She sees right through me.

"I ought to be, right?" I say.

"It's what you've wanted for a long time," Vera says, then shrugs. "But maybe it's not what you wanted it to be? Just like when he came home? I, for one, am worried about you. Remember how it ended last time."

I feel my neck and can almost sense his fingers around it, tightening their grip. Fear rushes through me, and I shiver lightly.

"But that's not why you wanted to see me, is it?" Vera continues, finishing her sandwich. "Something is troubling you."

I TELL her I'd rather talk to her somewhere a little more private. The café is a popular hangout for people from the base, especially around lunch, and there are more than a couple of others in uniform sitting near us. I don't feel safe talking about this here. So, we pay and take a stroll through downtown till we reach the beach. We take off our shoes and walk across the warm sand, then plunge our toes into the blue water. It feels good, a little chilly, but good. I finally relax a little. I don't feel like I've been able to relax at all, all weekend. I have been careful, constantly worrying that I might upset Ryan and ruin everything. I have been tiptoeing around him, trying so hard to keep him happy. I want him there; I want him to stay with us badly, mostly for the children's sake, but also for my own. And I certainly don't want to anger him. All weekend, I have been so careful about what I said, and even though I desperately wanted to, I haven't asked him more about Sandra and their meeting. I haven't told him I know.

Not yet.

"So, tell me what's going on?" Vera asks as we begin to walk. The sand and water feel wonderful between my toes, almost like therapy. I look up at her, biting my lip.

"It's your sister."

Vera frowns. The sun hits her face as she turns to look at me.

"Clarice?"

"Yes. I can't stop thinking about her ever since Sandra died. I talked to Ryan about it and about how she didn't leave a note, either, and that was when it struck me."

"What did?"

I stop and look at her. I place a hand on her arm, then look around us. I know there's no one there, no one is listening in, but I feel like I need to check.

"I remember you told me something at the funeral. Back then, I didn't think anything of it, I just thought you were grieving, grasping for answers. But then, the other day, it struck me. You said she called from Afghanistan a couple of days before she died."

Vera nods. She knows what I'm getting at.

"She did."

"Didn't she say something about being scared for her life?"

Vera looks at me, her nostrils flaring slightly. I hope I haven't upset her by asking. I know she doesn't like to talk much about it.

"Well, it wasn't as dramatic as that, but she did say she had concerns about something she had witnessed over there."

"But it was more than that, wasn't it?" I ask.

Vera sighs. She looks at her feet quickly, and I know it hurts to talk about it. She was close to her sister. They joined the Air Force together. I have a feeling Vera did it mostly to keep an eye on her younger sister.

"She also said that if anything happened to her, then we should investigate it."

"Yes, that's it. That's what I remembered," I say.

Vera sighs. "But Laurie, it's not something we…"

"But we need to investigate it," I say. "At least in her honor. It was her last request."

"We tried," she says with a deep exhale. "Do you have any idea how hard it is to get any information out of the Air Force?"

"You tried?"

"Well, my parents did. They've tried everything. But all they ran into were closed doors."

Chapter 12

SOMEHOW, I convince Vera to take me to see her parents. I don't know how I did it because she is very reluctant about it, and as we drive there together, two days later, she keeps glancing at me nervously.

Her parents live in Orlando, in one of those cookie-cutter neighborhoods, which kind of reminds me of the housing on base, only more expensive with a small water fountain at the entrance. But just like on base, all the houses look alike, a little too much for my taste. I know that, once I leave base, I'll want a unique house, preferably in a Spanish style. There's one I keep looking at every time I drive to Publix. It's located across the street from the beach and has beautiful arches around the windows and a cute red tile roof. I often dream that I live there and grow old there when I think about the future. I don't know if Ryan and I will ever be able to afford one like that once he retires from the Air Force, but a girl has a right to dream, doesn't she?

"Please, be gentle with them," Vera says as she stops the car in front of their house. The lawn outside is well taken care of, the flowers blooming. An orange tree in the middle of the lawn has fruit that is ready to be harvested. We have one similar at our house that we harvest from every January, then squeeze into juice. One orange can give enough for a big glass full, that's how juicy they are.

"They're still very fragile, and talking about Clarice is tough," she adds.

I nod. "Of course. I'm not here to upset them."

"It's not that they don't want to talk about her, they do, but it's just, well, my dad tends to get a little worked up about it, and he has a heart condition, you know? He takes pills for his high blood pressure. My mom tries to keep him calm."

I smile and think about my own parents. My dad has high blood-pressure but is otherwise healthy. Yet my mom does tend to worry about him anyway. It's like she doesn't have anything else to do, now that her kids are grown, and she can't worry about us constantly. I often think it's like she got into a habit of just worrying, and now she can't stop; she misses it if she tries. I also often wonder if I will be the same. Right now, I am always worried about Ryan, and of course, my kids, but for different reasons than my mom worries about. Completely different.

"I get it," I say with a reassuring smile. "I'll try not to agitate him."

VERA'S MOTHER serves us coffee in the living room, while her dad shows us pictures of Vera and Clarice from when they were younger.

"Those two were inseparable," he says and points at a picture of them together. Vera is no more than four or five years old, her sister even younger. "They loved one another so much and always wanted to sleep together, often in the same bed. We tried to give them separate bedrooms, but they always ended up in the same bed the next morning. They were so close in age; they even had the same interests."

"How far apart are they?"

"Only a year and a half. They've always acted like twins, doing everything together. Even sometimes dressing up to look alike so people couldn't tell them apart. Vera doesn't even remember that there was a time without her sister," he says. "But they could also fight. No one could fight like those two, oh, dear Lord."

"No one loves and hates each other out of a good heart like sisters," I say, thinking about my own childhood. There are three years between my sister and me, so I can relate. My sister and I are very different, though, and look nothing alike. I'm a redhead, whereas she has the most gorgeous long brown hair and blue eyes. She's also much taller than me, which has always annoyed me.

"We always told them that they had to remember that, once we were gone, they'd always have one another," Vera's mom, Hattie says. "That's how special it is to have a sister…and…" she trails off and doesn't say any more. Her eyes drift off, and she looks down into her lap at her hands, rubbing them lightly on her pants.

Seeing this brings a lump to my throat. I stare down at the table and my hands wrapped tightly around a mug.

"Anyone want a cookie with their coffee?" Hattie says, her face lighting up suddenly. She rises to her feet before we can answer, then disappears. Vera's dad, Samuel, or Sammy, as he told me to call him when he met us at the door, takes over. He closes the photo album, then says:

"Anyway, you didn't come here to hear all our silly

stories. You wanted to know about the last call we had from her?"

I nod, swallowing the lump. I feel awful for coming, and I wonder if it is even necessary. Am I just ripping open old wounds for nothing? Because I'm curious? I don't even know what my deal is, what I expect to get out of this meeting. I can't tell them how I think it is connected to what happened to Sandra. It's just a feeling, nothing else. Why am I ripping open their grief over a feeling?

"Well, Clarice called two days before we received the message that she had…that she wasn't…" Sammy trails off, then exhales. He doesn't seem to know I'm even there anymore. It's like he's talking to himself. "She sounded so different; I immediately knew that something was wrong. She was never happy over there. She didn't like being there. She had told us this earlier, in other calls. It was nothing like she expected it to be, not at all."

"It was her first deployment, right?" I ask.

He nods, still looking past me like I'm not really there. "I don't know why she was so eager to go over there. It was all she ever wanted. Remember that, Vera?"

Vera nods. She is not looking at him; she stares into her cup. "It was all she ever talked about. That was why she enlisted."

"She was an interpreter, right?" I ask.

Sammy nods heavily. His shoulders sag. "She studied Arabic and, naturally, that is very useful over there. She really believed she could make a difference, that she could be useful."

"So, why didn't she like it there?" I ask, praying I'm not going too far. But I do feel like they want to tell me this. They want to talk about their daughter. "You said she was disappointed at life at the camp. What was different? How was it different than what she expected it to be?"

Sammy shakes his head. He looks defeated. It's no surprise to me that he is a broken man; I can't imagine losing a daughter, but there's something else. There is spite in his voice and defiance in his brown eyes that tell me he hasn't gotten the closure he needs. There's a wistfulness to his voice that I don't think he's aware of. It's like he's missing these important pieces, and he's trying so hard to finish the puzzle without them, but it just won't fit.

"She wouldn't say exactly what it was, but she did tell us on her last call that she had seen stuff in her role as interpreter that she found troublesome."

"Like what?"

"I don't know much. Methods that were very different from what she was used to from her training."

I raise my eyebrows. "Torture?"

"Your guess is as good as mine," he says, "but that's the only thing that makes any sense."

"She did tell me about witnessing prisoners being burned with cigarettes at another time," Vera says. "Or stripped down and then taunted about their manhood. I got the feeling she only told me a little about what she had seen. She told me she wanted to talk to her supervisor about it because she didn't want to be a part of it. It was unethical, she said."

"Did she ever talk to her superior about it?" I ask.

Vera shrugs. "We don't know. There was a notebook that she wrote these things in, but it was never found."

"Really?" I ask. "And then she told you that if anything happened to her, she wanted you to investigate?"

Sammy nods. He doesn't look at me when he says the next part. He looks down at his fingers. He reminds me of my youngest when he is in trouble.

"Yes. I think she said it mostly as a joke. She said it

with a laugh at the end, you know? Like she didn't really mean it. That's what it sounded like to me."

The way he talks about it makes it sound like he doesn't really believe it was a joke. He has only convinced himself to think it was. I wonder why. Is it to make it easier to accept that she committed suicide? Because he doesn't know what to do about it if it wasn't? Because the Air Force has told him to think that way? Because his wife wants him to think that way, so he won't get worked up with his high blood pressure?

Because it's easier?

I lean back in my chair, pensively. It doesn't sound like a joke to me. Nothing about this seems like a joke. But what do I know, right? I wasn't there. I didn't know her very well and didn't know if she'd joke about something like this. Would anyone joke about something like this?

"But that's not the worst part," Hattie says as she comes back from the kitchen. She has been standing there for a little while like she was deciding whether to come sit with us or go back. She places the cookies on the table in front of us, then sits down, looking at her husband.

"Tell her, Sammy. There's no use in keeping it a secret. Tell her what you discovered."

Chapter 13

"WE WERE TOLD IT WAS A SUICIDE," Sammy says, folding his hands in front of him on the table while he speaks. "And immediately, we both knew it couldn't be true. We just knew."

"Not our daughter," Hattie says. "Not Clarice. Not my baby. She wouldn't do that to herself."

"None of us would believe it, so I took it upon myself to start digging a little," Sammy says, grabbing his wife's hand in his. They exchange a brief look before he returns to his story. "The first thing that rubbed me the wrong way was how she supposedly killed herself. We were told she shot herself in the mouth with a military-issued service weapon. Now, I am a military vet myself, and I knew that Clarice's service weapon was a forty-inch M-16. My daughter is only five feet tall and weighs maybe ninety pounds. She was a tiny little thing. She would have had great difficulty maneuvering an M-16 into her mouth and firing it. "

"But that isn't all," his wife says.

"No," Sammy says. "We were also told that she was

upset because a boyfriend had broken up with her via an email. That was their explanation. They said that she received the email, then slung her M-16 over her shoulder and went to the military store to buy a six-pack of soda and a pack of Hershey's chocolate. They said, at this point, she was with an unnamed male friend and that she returned to her barracks with him, but then she left alone. She then went to a tent belonging to a military contractor, where they say she found a can of aerosol and set the tent on fire, then put the M-16 to her mouth and fired. The Air Force's investigation showed that she killed herself. The Armed Service Committee in the Senate then signed off on her death, and the case was closed."

I stare at the both of them, my pulse quickening. "But…" I say, then look briefly at Vera. "Wasn't Clarice gay? I thought you told me that once."

Vera nods. "Yes, that's the problem. Only her closest friends knew this about her. She wasn't exactly open about it to the Air Force, but some of them knew."

"So, the boyfriend is made up," I say. "Someone made up that part?"

Sammy nods. "Yes. Someone who didn't know her well enough not to make such a mistake. And that makes one think. How much of the rest is made up as well?"

"We received her in a casket draped with the American flag, and they refused to let us see her," Hattie says. Her voice cracks as she talks, but she doesn't seem to notice. "They said it was for our own good. But my son…"

"Frank," I say and think about the chat I had with Vera's brother just a few days earlier when I called him about Sandra's autopsy report. He's a lot younger than Vera and Clarice, like ten years apart from them. I knew him before I met Vera, back when I worked as a journalist before we had Isabella. I used him as an expert for a series of articles I did on forensic work when they found a mass grave in the backyard of an old orphanage in Florida. He helped me get several articles to come to life. Since then, he has been my go-to guy when it came to forensic stuff I needed to have explained.

"You know how he works at the Medical Examiner's facility on base," Sammy says. He is leaning forward now, getting engaged in our conversation. I can tell he's getting agitated while talking. He's moving his hands more aggressively, and his nostrils are flaring. He is breathing in small huffs. "So, you also know that he has access that no one else does. We told him to look at her files, and he found out that they had actually performed an autopsy when she died, but it was just not made public. In it, he could see that Clarice had a busted lip, several broken teeth, and she had a lot of scratch marks on her neck. She also had a broken nose. He also noticed that the bullet wound in Clarice's head was too small to be from an M-16 and that it was on the left side of her face, even though Clarice was right-handed. Frank confronted the investigators about it, and they explained that the bruises and scratches were from before the suicide, days earlier, and she could have gotten them from a fall and that they believed it was definitely an exit wound from an M-16. Frank then went to two ballistic experts, and they said the wound was more consistent with a bullet wound from a nine mm pistol."

"Plus," Hattie said. "There was no trace of residue on her fingers and hands. She would have had that, had she handled the weapon herself. All this evidence was right in front of them, and yet they still concluded it was a suicide."

"We have tried to ask them to reopen the case, but they won't. The official response from them is still that the case is closed. They keep insisting she killed herself, that she was depressed and had shown signs of depression for a long time before the incident, that they had discussed putting her on suicide watch. But that just wasn't my sister," Vera says. "I spoke to her two days before it happened, and she wasn't depressed. She was looking forward to coming home for Christmas. I've started an online petition asking the Air Force to reopen the case. I have written to members of Congress, government and legal officials, and even they are met with the same reply when they try to help. The case is closed. There's nothing more we can do."

"We're not giving up, though," Sammy says. His cheeks are blushing, his fists clenched. "We just need to keep pushing until we wear them down."

***

I STAY with Vera's parents way too long. We talk about Clarice, and they tell me so much about her, what she was like as a child, how she always wanted to grow up and join the Air Force, and I can tell they enjoy being able to talk about her. I'm guessing not many people ask about her anymore, out of fear. People get like that when you lose someone, afraid to mention their name or talk about them. It's like they think you'd rather forget they were ever here, but that's not how it works. I know this because I lost a brother once, many years ago. He was only three years old when he developed an aggressive type of cancer that killed him within the next six months. It almost killed my mother, and it broke all of us to pieces. And we never talked about him once he was gone, which was the biggest grief for me. My mom would hush me if I mentioned him, or she'd tell me to go to my room. She didn't want to remember him, and I never understood that. I needed to talk about him and to remember. I was later told by someone that all people grieve differently, but I'm not sure my mother grieved at all. I think she shut it all out and refused to deal with it. In that way, I guess she never did.

I stay with them for so long that I realize I am late when I finally get up and grab my phone. I only have forty-five minutes until the kids return on the school bus, and the drive back is at least an hour. Luckily, both kids know where to find the spare key and can easily stay at the house alone on base. They're just not very used to it.

"It was very nice of you to tell me her story," I say as I hug them goodbye. Hattie holds me tight for a little longer, then smiles, her eyes turning moist.

"Thank you for listening. It's been a while since anyone wanted to."

I nod and smile gently, feeling awful for these poor grieving parents. To not only have to deal with burying your daughter but also having the doubt, the lack of closure because you don't know what really happened. It's gotta be tough.

"Thank you," Sammy says and hugs me with his strong arms. He's a small man, but still very fit, and it feels like he could easily crush me using his bare hands. He lets go of me but keeps holding my hands between his, then looks me deep in the eyes.

"You're a journalist, right?"

"I used to be once many years ago."

"Do with this what you want. You have our permission."

I look into his eyes and can tell he's not just allowing me; he's begging me. I suddenly get a strong urge to write a piece on this story. I feel like I owe it to them somehow. I also get the feeling that I have put my hand into the hornet's nest, and I have no idea what I have gotten myself into.

Chapter 14

RYAN IS home when I get back. He left in the morning to go to physical therapy, he told me. I don't know if it is true or not. I don't know if anything he tells me is true anymore. That's what one lie does to you.

"Where were you?" he asks, walking into the kitchen where I am taking out the meat for tonight's dinner. It's too late, and it probably won't thaw in time. "Where were you all day?"

He is smiling while he says it, but I have the sense that he's not happy. The smile comes off as stiff, and his narrowing eyes tell me he is pretending.

"I was with Vera," I say, putting the meat on the counter. I fill a pot of water to put it in, so it'll thaw faster. "It was her day off."

"You've been with her a lot lately, haven't you? Didn't you just have lunch the other day? What can you two possibly have to talk about so often? I didn't think she was your type?"

I pause. "And what is that supposed to mean?"

"I don't know. It's just that…Vera is the unmarried

type, the wild one, the one no man dares even to date because she's a little…crazy, you know?"

I shake my head with a small scoff. "No, I don't know that. Vera is nice, and she makes me laugh."

"Her sister was like that too. She was mentally unstable. I think that's why she killed herself. Not that I know much about it, but that's what I heard."

"How can you say that?" I ask, feeling sick to my stomach after what I heard earlier today.

He shrugs and grins. "I don't mean any disrespect or anything, but she wasn't all there, you know? Something was always off about her, in my opinion. I don't want you to hang out around her sister. Can't you find someone else to have lunches with?"

"You don't want me to hang out with her?" I ask, puzzled by this. Ryan has never tried to tell me who to hang out with and who not to. Is he trying to control me? "I'm not sure that's your call to make. I like her."

"Yes, you said that. She makes you laugh. I just don't think she's good for you. Besides, so do I. I make you laugh," he says. "Why not spend more time with me instead of Vera? We can go see a comedy show if you want to laugh more."

I put the pot down, my back still turned to him. I don't like that he is trying to restrict who I can see. Why is he suddenly trying to do that now?

I sense he is moving closer. He kisses my neck, and I shiver lightly. His hands move quickly onto my breasts, and he is moaning softly.

"I can be way more fun than she'll ever be," he says and nibbles my earlobe. "Don't you think?"

I chuckle. Not because I find it amusing, but because I don't know what to say. I don't push him away. I'm trying to save my marriage here, but that is actually what I feel like doing right now. Yet, I don't. I chuckle instead—a nervous and awkward chuckle.

"That wasn't meant to be funny," he says and lets his hand slide into my pants. He is touching me, and I let him, closing my eyes. I don't even hear the small steps behind us until the voice says.

"What are you guys doing?"

Ryan pulls away with a gasp. At first, I think he's laughing, but I realize too late that he isn't. He is shocked and turns around fast, then lifts his hand in the air, fist clenched, ready to swing it, to hit Damian, when I yell at him.

"Ryan!"

Realizing what he is about to do, he pauses with his hand still in mid-air. The boy stares up at him, eyes wide, a gasp caught in his throat.

Ryan freezes completely. The hand comes down slowly, and now he crumples. He turns away from Damian, and I grab the boy in my arms, then carry him away. Damian is not quite sure what is going on, but he starts to cry.

I caress his hair gently, then his cheek. "It's okay, sweetie. You didn't do anything wrong. You just can't sneak up on your dad, remember? We talked about this. He scares easily after what he has been through. He can't forget all those terrible things like bombs and people shooting at him. He's just afraid."

I glance toward Ryan, who is leaning against the counter, catching his breath. I know he's beating himself up. This isn't the first time it has happened.

"I am sorry, Daddy," Damian cries. "I am so, so sorry."

"Shh," I say and hug him, trying to calm my beating heart, kissing his forehead. "It's okay. You didn't mean to. Luckily, nothing happened."

I say the words, watching Ryan regain his composure. I can't help thinking, *not this time, at least.*

I MAKE SPAGHETTI AND MEATBALLS, and we eat, even though the atmosphere is a little tense around the table. I can't figure out if Ryan is angry or embarrassed. It might be a bit of both. Maybe he thinks Damian should know better by now than to sneak up on him; perhaps he doesn't know how to tell him how sorry he is for almost punching him. Isabella says she isn't hungry and leaves the table quickly after eating a few bites, claiming she needs to do her homework. I know she's just using that as an excuse since she told me earlier that she doesn't have any home-work, but I can't blame her for wanting to leave. She's very sensitive to tension and has a hard time dealing with it.

I wish for a second I could just up and leave like that. I'm still angry about Ryan trying to tell me not to talk to Vera anymore. I am not gonna do it, of course, but it still bothers me that he'd say those things—especially what he said about Clarice. I can't believe he could be so insensitive.

Ryan stabs his fork into a meatball a little aggressively, then shoves it into his mouth and chews with his mouth half-open. He shakes his head with a scoff.

"What?" I ask.

"I was just thinking about something funny," he says, then drinks his iced tea. He puts the glass down hard on the table, and the silverware clanks. "It's a military thing. You wouldn't understand. You should have been there."

"But maybe Sandra would have understood?" I say, not quite realizing I have said it out loud until it's too late. It just bursts right out of me.

Ryan stops chewing. He stares at me, the fork still in his hand. The silence is long and fills the room. Damian doesn't notice, at least I don't think so. He eats without even looking at us.

"What the heck?" Ryan asks. "Why are you talking about Sandra all of a sudden?"

I look down at my food, then shrug. "It's nothing. Just forget it."

"It's not nothing, Laurie. I know you. Why are you talking about Sandra?"

"It's just…well, did you have an affair with her?" I blurt it out. I don't care anymore. I need to know. I deserve to know. If we're trying to save our marriage, I have to know the truth. Can I trust him?

Ryan's grin freezes. The look in his eye changes. His gaze hardens, and his eyes get a gloomy look to them. I regret saying it; I want to take it back, but it's too late. Ryan turns to look at our son, then speaks with a firm voice. It's deeper than usual like it only gets when he is really angry, or very serious.

"Damian. Go to your room."

"But…I'm not done?" the boy argues.

"Now," his dad says, and the boy obeys.

I feel my pulse quickening. Why did I have to say that? Why now? Was it because I was mad about the things he said in the kitchen earlier? Was I trying to get back at him?

I can apologize, I think. If I tell him how sorry I am, maybe he'll let it go?

Ryan turns to face me, and I know it's too late. No apology will take back what I said. Saying sorry won't save me.

"What in the…Laurie, what are you talking about? And in front of the boy?"

I stare at him, my heart pounding. I am not backing

down now.

"Did you?"

He shakes his head, then slams his fist onto the table, causing the plates to jump. "No! That is the most ridiculous thing I have ever heard. Why would you say something like that?"

I can't tell him I have been snooping around, reading his messages, so I clam up. Suddenly, he looks like he remembers something, or just figured it out.

"I know where this is coming from."

Please, don't say Vera; please, don't.

"Vera. She's the one who put these ideas into your mind, isn't she? Well, isn't she?"

I shake my head. "No. It has nothing to do with her."

"Then, I don't understand. Where is this coming from all of a sudden?"

I swallow the lump in my throat. I feel like a child. He makes me feel this way—like I am just a foolish kid, and it annoys me. I am not normally like this. I think about telling him how I know…that I know he met with her, that I read the messages, but I know he'll get angry. I think about his hands around my throat the last time I went too far when I asked him what happened in Afghanistan. I don't want to feel that again. It might be nothing. Maybe he didn't have an affair with her after all.

"Dang it," he says and drops his fork. He rises to his feet, pushing the chair backward across the floor. "I've lost my appetite."

He leaves the house, slamming the door shut behind him. I don't know where he is going; I worry he's going to the bar with his friends. I fear he'll come back drunk, or that he'll not come back at all. I worry I have pushed him too far. If he leaves us again, the kids will never forgive me.

It's like I can't seem to do anything right anymore.

Chapter 15

LAURIE PAUSES, then closes her eyes. Jonathan can tell she is getting tired. She keeps fighting those eyelids without much luck. As an experienced FBI agent, he knows there is a thin line between getting your witness to that vulnerable point where she tells all the details—even those that are painful—and then pressuring them to a point where they just tell you what you want to hear. Laurie has crossed that border now, and Jonathan exchanges a look with Detective Grande. She nods in agreement. There's a small knock on the door, and a nurse peeks inside.

"The patient needs her rest now," she says.

Jonathan nods. "We were about to wrap it up."

Laurie opens her eyelids, even though one of them still droops in front of her eye. She looks at them, seeming almost desperate.

"I need to tell you the rest."

Jonathan smiles, then nods. "Not yet. You need your rest. We'll let you sleep for now, then be back in the morning."

They get up and walk to the door when Jonathan hesitates. He turns to look at her, concerned.

"Who is taking care of your children while you're here?"

Laurie sighs. "My sister. I just spoke to Damian earlier this morning."

Jonathan pauses, his eyes scrutinizing her. "And Isabella?"

"Isabella…well…she…she…" she trails off, her eyes looking down at her hands. She shakes her head, and Jonathan knows not to ask anymore. At least not for now.

Jonathan sends Laurie a compassionate smile. He thinks for a minute about his own daughter, Eve, and reminds himself to call her later today. The last time they spoke, they had been in a fight. A stupid one, but aren't all fights silly seen in retrospect? The fact is, he misses her. Ever since she left home, the house has felt empty, and he doesn't know what to do with himself. Is that what retirement is going to be like for him? Loneliness? He doesn't like the thought much. And he doesn't like feeling sorry for himself either.

"You'll be home before you know it," he says.

He looks at Laurie, but she has already dozed off, and her breathing grown heavy. He signals Detective Grande that it is time for them to leave, and they do. He closes the door carefully behind him, even though he knows he could probably slam it shut, and Laurie Davis wouldn't wake up at this point.

"Do you want to go grab a bite?" he asks his young colleague.

She smiles, then shakes her head. "I can't."

He nods. Of course not. She's newly married and wants to go home to her husband. He wishes he would have done the same thing a lot more, said no, and just gone home instead of working till the late hours, never letting go of his cases until they were solved. Maybe he'd have someone waiting for him today if he had done that.

"Well, maybe you can tell me of a place that's good to eat around here?" he asks, holding the door for her as they leave the hospital.

"Depends on what you like."

"Just a good burger and maybe a piece of pie. That'll do it for me."

She smiles. "Then I know just the place."

EVERETT STREET DINER in the heart of Bryson City is everything Jonathan wants it to be. You get the coffee pure black, no hazelnuts, no lattes, no fancy mochaccino, or whatever it's all called today. Just plain coffee served from a pot by a waitress named Joanne, who calls you hon and smiles at you in that way that makes you want to stay longer just to get another one. Jonathan likes the place so much that he returns the next morning for breakfast. In the middle of biscuits and hash browns, sausage, and eggs, Detective Grande enters. She looks tired, and her pretty brown eyes don't have the same spark to them as the day before. She's holding a folder under her arm as she comes up to Jonathan at the counter and sits down.

Joanne doesn't even ask; she pours her coffee and slides it toward her with one of her smiles.

"Anything to eat, hon?"

Detective Grande shakes her head while Jonathan finishes his eggs and washes them down with coffee before Joanne refills his cup.

"Good morning," he says. "Got out on the wrong side of the bed?"

She nods. "I was called out to the cabin early this morning."

"Really?" he asks surprised. "Any news?"

"Yes," she says as she sips her coffee. She reminds him of a small bird the way she delicately drinks. She seems so fragile, but he has a feeling she's a lot stronger than she looks. He hopes she is, or she won't last long in the job.

"And then I received a call from the lab. They've been going through Laurie Davis's phone. This is what they found."

Detective Grande opens the folder and pulls out a couple of photos. Jonathan wipes his fingers on a napkin, takes them, and flips through them one after another. It doesn't take him long to figure out what she's trying to tell him.

"You see why I'm a little off this morning?" she asks.

Jonathan nods.

"This does change things."

She finishes her cup, and Jonathan pays for both of them. They walk outside into the gloomy day that has just begun. Beautiful mountains surround them, and as always, the tips are hiding behind a light cloud cover. A car with kayaks on the roof passes them on its way to the river. Jonathan is not much of a watersports man himself, but his wife was. She'd always try to make him go with her, but he was very good at coming up with excuses. He always had work to do. Now, he wishes he could go with her again—just once. He'd do anything to be able to spend another day with her.

In the distance, he can hear the old steam train as it blows its horn to mark its departure. The city offers tourist train rides through the mountains, and it is supposed to be gorgeous. There's also some old train museum that Joanne told him he ought to visit while he is in town.

He hasn't told her why he is really here.

"I think we need to take a different approach to her," Detective Grande says as they reach their cars in the parking lot outside the diner. There are a few puddles of snow left on the side of the road, but most of it has been washed away in the recent rainfall, as is the custom when spring makes its arrival. Grande is standing on the other side of her car, and he can barely see her as she opens the door. She pauses and looks up at him.

"Laurie Davis has been playing the victim's act all along. I don't think she's as much of a victim as we have believed this far."

Part II

Chapter 16

SHE IS JUST DONE EATING her breakfast when they knock on her door. The nurse takes her tray, and Laurie looks at their faces. Jonathan can tell she already knows just by looking at them. The nurse leaves, and he closes the door behind her.

Jonathan sits down. Detective Grande remains standing with the folder clutched tightly in her hand.

"Good morning," Laurie says.

"Feeling better today?" Jonathan asks.

She nods. He can tell that she knows they're not happy. She has tension in her shoulders, and her fingers are fiddling with the bandage holding her arm in place. The doctor had told them she was lucky. The bullet had only caused some muscle and tissue damage—nothing fractured and nothing vital damaged. Now, she just needs to keep it calm so she won't rupture the sutures.

"Much better, thanks. Probably also due to the drugs," she says with a light laugh.

Jonathan glances at Detective Grande, who obviously doesn't have the patience he possesses. He chalks it up to her lack of experience. He once was as eager as she is. Now he knows it won't get you very far in an interrogation situation. Patience is your friend. With patience, the story will be revealed; with patience, the witness opens up and tells it in her timeliness. Experience has taught him that you can't pull a story out of someone. It has to be revealed, and for that to happen, you need time. You can't be in a rush, or essential parts will be left out.

Grande opens the folder and places the pictures in front of Laurie.

"Care to explain these?"

Laurie stares at them. She doesn't have to look long to know what this is about.

"These pictures were taken on the phone—your phone, just a few days ago. Who is the man in the pictures?" Grande asks.

Laurie looks at them again. It can't be because she doesn't know who he is, he concludes, but for some other reason. Maybe because she longs to go back to that moment when they were taken?

"The thing is, Mrs. Davis," Grande adds. "You've been going on and on in here, telling us how you suspected your husband of having an affair, and this, to me, looks like you're the unfaithful one. It doesn't take a detective to conclude that from these pictures here—where you're kissing one another. And if you look closer, it becomes pretty obvious that he was with you in the cabin. Our technicians also say they found a lock of hair in the bed, black hair, and as far as we were told, your husband is bald."

Laurie Davis closes her eyes briefly and nods.

"Why have you been lying to us?" Grande asks.

She smiles. "I haven't. I was getting to this part."

"So, who is he?" Grande asks.

Laurie sighs and leans back on her pillow. "That is Frank."

Jonathan lifts his head and looks at her. "As in Vera's brother? The guy who works at the military forensic lab?"

She nods. "Yes, that's him."

AT THIS POINT, I feel like an awful mother and an even worse wife. Ryan hasn't been home for three days, not since I asked him if he had an affair with Sandra, and I am about to lose it. My kids are angry at me; they think I drove him away—that he is not coming back because of me, and I am beginning to think they're right. My husband is a combat-wounded and highly-decorated war veteran, and yet I can't seem to honor him with something as simple as trust.

I again fear he has killed himself. Do you know what it is like when they're away? When they're deployed? You're constantly worried, terrified. You feel sick from morning till evening—when the phone rings—if someone comes to your door, you want to throw up. Your stomach crumbles. All the time, you wait for that message, you wonder how they'll say it and imagine how their eyes will look. Will you even hear what they say? Will you be able to hear the words?

Then, finally, when they do come home, you think it's all over. Everything will be fine now; the hard part is done. But no.

I am not a model wife. I know I'm not. And I never will be. I get angry. I get frustrated. I yell at the kids and then at him when he doesn't help or when he doesn't show up. To be honest, it was probably easier when he was away. We had our routines. I knew I was alone in handling everything. There was no question as to who did what; I had to do everything. Now that he was back, I expected him to help, to be there. And those expectations weren't fulfilled. I was disappointed. Did I drive him to run away? Was it because of me and the pressure I put on him that he couldn't bear staying under the same roof with his own family? That his children had to miss their dad and feel abandoned? Is it because of me that they will have to wonder if they weren't enough for the rest of their lives? No matter how much I love him, it's not enough. It's never enough for him.

Now, I worry even more than before because I don't know where he is or what he's doing. Is he in so much pain that he wants to end it all like Sandra? None of us knew what she went through because she hid it well.

So, yes, I call Frank. I don't know where else to turn. Vera is in training to become a pilot, so she's gone a lot of the time. My parents have taken a trip to Georgia to visit old friends. I am all alone at the base—just me and the kids, and I am in pain. I am so scared. I call Frank and ask him to meet me. I tell him I want to talk about his sister, about Clarice, that I might be doing a story on her since I kind of promised their parents I would. Damian is at home with a cold, and Frank tells me he'll stop by. As I shower and put on makeup, I wonder why I am doing this. Am I trying to punish Ryan? Am I hoping he'll hear about Frank's visit and get jealous? Perhaps. Or maybe I just really want to tell Clarice's story and help her poor parents. Either way, I am getting myself dressed up real nice. As I wait for him, I keep checking myself in the mirror.

Chapter 17

WE SIT IN OUR KITCHEN. I have made a light lunch for us, a salad that I barely eat any of myself. I don't want to get anything stuck in my teeth. I want him to find me attractive because I am angry with Ryan. Does that make any sense?

I'm not sure it does to me.

But I do have the feeling that I am heading for disaster.

He eats and smiles, then leans forward, placing his elbows on the table, getting closer to me. He's eight years younger than me, and I don't understand why he is interested in me at all.

"So, you don't think Clarice committed suicide either?" I ask, pulling away and trying to stay on subject. I feel guilty already, even though I haven't done anything wrong. I can't stop thinking about Ryan and worrying that he'll get hurt. I immediately regret having invited Frank over. Luckily, Damian is in his room, playing on his computer. There's no chance he'll be down unless we lose wi-fi for some reason.

Frank shakes his head. "I saw the autopsy. She was bruised."

"Your parents said she had a broken nose?" I ask.

He nods. "And a lot more."

"What does that mean?"

Frank sighs. His expression grows serious. I can tell he's heartbroken over losing his sister. Talking about it doesn't come easy. I realize at this instant that I care for him more than I thought. Seeing him like this hurts me deeply, and I reach over and grab his hand in mine.

Our eyes meet.

"There were things I never told my parents," he says, then pauses. "Because I don't think they could have handled it. She was…in the autopsy…it showed there were signs that she…"

He pauses again to breathe. I get a feeling I know what is coming and prepare myself for it.

"She was…raped?" I ask.

He looks up, then nods. "There were teeth marks on her shoulder and mutilation of her…you know."

"Mutilation?"

"Someone had poured acid on her private parts. It's not unusual in rape cases, to remove any DNA. But the signs weren't conclusive enough, the report said. The investigators decided it wasn't important. There was also a trail of blood indicating her body had been dragged across the ground, but that too was deemed inconclusive and never considered in the conclusion. The Air Force keeps telling us it was suicide."

I lean back in my chair, my heart quickening. You don't have to be a former reporter to realize that there is a story there somewhere, a great one, an important one. But I don't work anymore and have no outlet for it.

"There's more," he says.

I clear my throat, pushing back the dreadful feeling his information has left me with. How much does Ryan know about this, I wonder. How much does he know about what happened to Clarice? Does he know who raped her, and is he covering for this person? Are all of them? Is that what caused Sandra to kill herself? Because she knew and didn't tell?

Is that what is bothering Ryan?

"And that is?"

"Clarice wasn't very liked by her colleagues."

"I heard she wanted to complain about their interrogation methods?" I ask.

"Yes, she saw them use methods that she didn't want to be a part of. We're talking cramped confinement, stress positions, sleep deprivation, insects placed in a confinement box, and waterboarding. She refused to participate in this and went to her superiors to file a report. She was then placed on guard watch to guard the gate and put on suicide watch. They claimed she wasn't well mentally."

"And her report?"

"Gone. I've tried to get it, but it's gone, they say. They say it never happened."

"But you're certain it did?" I ask.

"Clarice wouldn't lie about something like this. Why should she? She knew that she'd become unpopular with the others. She stood up for herself, and it cost her her life; that's what happened if you ask me. And, of course, the Air Force doesn't want that to come out, so they call it a suicide. It all happened so far away, so we have no way of proving they're wrong. My parents have tried to engage reporters from the big TV stations, CBS and ABC, but they won't run the story. I guess it's all up to you. Anything you can do will be of great help."

Frank leans over and touches my hand, taking it in his just as the front door slams shut, and Ryan steps in.

RYAN STOPS as he sees us, then looks down at our hands. Seeing this, Frank pulls away, but it's too late. The damage is done. Ryan has seen it.

I leap to my feet, blushing. "Ryan, I…you know Frank, right?"

Ryan stares at us, his fists clenched. Then, something changes, and he smiles. "Of course. Hi, Frank. What brings you here?"

I look at Frank, and we exchange glances for just a few seconds too long. I don't know what to say to Ryan. I can hardly tell him I am digging into Clarice's death; he'll only get angry at me for messing with his world, sticking my nose where it doesn't—and never will—belong.

"No?" he asks and throws his keys on the counter. "No one can come up with an explanation? Not even a lie?"

Frank gets up. He grabs his phone from the table, then walks to the door. "I should…probably."

"Yeah, you should…probably," Ryan says.

I nod and force a smile. I am staring mostly at my shoes, feeling like a child caught in a lie. Why does Ryan always make me feel like I am the one letting him down?

Frank sends me a last concerned smile before he walks out the door, leaving me alone with Ryan.

Chapter 18

THE SILENCE IS SO thick it almost hurts. I don't even look at him as I turn around. Ryan is staring at me, hands on his hips.

"Well, that was embarrassing," he says. "You even think about what people might say? Seeing him come here while I'm not home?"

"Is that what you're worried about?" I ask and look up. "What the neighbors will think? What your war buddies might think? Because I am way beyond that already. They've been talking about us since you got back. You don't think they notice you're never home? You've been gone three days, Ryan."

"Oh, and that gives you permission to have an affair? We had a fight. I left because I was afraid of losing my temper. I am trying to keep myself together here, Laurie. You're not exactly making it easy on me. First, you accuse me of having slept with Sandra, and now you're with him? I don't know what's happening around here. How long has this been going on?"

"I am not having an affair," I say. "We were just talking."

"With your hands?"

"I was comforting him. He was sad. We talked about his sister; you remember her? You remember Clarice?"

Ryan's smug grin is gone. His eyes go blank for a second. Then he points his finger at me, moving very close.

"Don't you dare mention her name."

"Why not? Why can't I talk about her, huh?" I ask. "Why doesn't anyone talk about Clarice? Or about Sandra, for that matter?"

He shakes his head with a scoff. "You just don't get it, do you?"

"No, I don't. Please explain it to me," I say.

He pauses. The finger comes down. He turns away from me for a second, then faces me again.

"Don't make this about me. I just caught you with a guy, and now you want to put the blame on me?"

"That's not what I was doing," I say

"That is exactly what you did. And you always do this because there can never be anything wrong with perfect little Laurie, can there?"

"You're making no sense any more, Ryan," I say. "I don't understand what's going on with you."

He is biting his lip. I can't tell if he is angry or ready to cry. It seems to be either-or these days. There is no in-between.

A tear escapes his eye, and he wipes it away. I shake my head and want to walk past him, but he blocks my way. I gasp as he stares down at me. I am scared he'll grab my throat again, and I can barely breathe. He grabs my face between his hands and stares into my eyes, his look piercing through me. I feel my heart rate go up and fear he's going to hurt me.

But he doesn't. Instead, he leans over and kisses me. He presses his tongue in between my lips and holds me in a tight grip. The kiss is awkward and a little too demanding, but I kiss him back.

"I love you so much. I hope you know this," he whispers. "I can't do this without you. I'm struggling here. I'm scared of myself and what I might do. That's why I go. That's why I can't stay. But I'm trying to get better. I really am. Don't leave me, please."

I can barely breathe as he looks into my eyes, holding my face tightly between his hands. I can feel his warm breath on my face, and the tears are streaming down his cheeks. His veins are popping out on his neck, and he is shaking.

"You hear me, Laurie? I can't get through this without you. Don't give up on me. Please."

I kiss him back, and we hug awkwardly. I am crying too now, my heart beating so fast.

"I'm trying," he whispers. "I'm trying to get better."

"I'm not going anywhere, Ryan," I say, wiping away my tears. "I'm here. Just stop running away from me. Please, stop running."

THAT NIGHT, Ryan stays with me, and we make love in our bed again. As he falls asleep, I lie awake, staring into the ceiling, wondering about what Frank has told me. I get up and check my email, then find one from him. Smiling to myself, I open it.

Hi, there, lovely lady,

Thank you for a wonderful lunch. I truly enjoyed spending time with you. I hope I didn't cause too much trouble? Are you okay? Here is the material you asked me to provide. If you choose to use it, remember not to mention any names. I still want a job, at least for now.

I hope to see a lot more of you soon.

Love,

Frank.

I smile again, then look at Ryan, who is still heavily asleep. I click the files Frank has sent and open them, then read through all the devastating material. The autopsy, in particular, makes me sick to my stomach. I don't understand most of what is written since you have to be a forensic expert to translate, but I get the gist of it, and then there are the pictures. They alone are enough to make anyone feel sick.

I close the files, then close the lid on my laptop and sneak back into bed just as Ryan turns in his sleep and places his arm around me. I close my eyes as the words to my article are already shaping in my mind.

I know exactly how to write it. I also know it is going to create quite a ruckus when I do. But at this point, I don't care anymore. The truth has been buried for way too long.

It's time for it to get out, even though it is going to hurt.

Chapter 19

I WORK on writing the story whenever I have the time, which isn't much these days. I am busy taking care of my family, running errands, shopping, and doing laundry. You know, the usual stuff, the things no one notices gets done, but think just kind of happens on its own.

Ryan is home with us, staying the night. Every time he leaves the house, I fear he won't come home, but so far, he has come back every time since the day he found me with Frank in the kitchen, and we enjoy every second we have with him. But I can tell even the kids have that anxious look in their eyes, asking, *how long will it last this time?*

My parents are back from their trip and keep calling, wanting to see the kids. I invite them for dinner that same night, feeling like I have been keeping them from their grandchildren, and so I make a second run to Publix, thinking I can still make it back before the kids come home. I buy everything my parents like, including my dad's favorite beer, but also make sure there are a lot of vegetables with the chicken, so my mom can see how healthy I am keeping my family.

I don't know why. I just do it out of reflex. I am sure my parents are way more concerned about my marriage than our health right now. Yet, this is what I can control. I can't fix my marriage before tonight, but I can make a healthy meal and make us look like we're doing well.

I rush back through town and drive onto the base, praying I won't be picked for a random inspection. Luckily, the car in front of me is picked out, and I can go straight through. With the groceries clinking in the back, I drive past the landing strips, toward the living quarters. We live in the south housing area, but I promised Vera I'd buy her some toilet paper and take it back to her place, and she lives in the north housing area, so I go there first. I place the pack outside on her doorstep as I know she won't be home till later, then get back into my minivan and drive down her street, hoping the ice cream in the back hasn't melted.

I turn a corner by the end of the street when I suddenly slow down to almost a stop. I stare at a driveway and the truck parked there in particular. It's black and has a sticker on the back that says, US AIR FORCE inside of an American flag, and next to it, one that says, GUNS SAVES LIVES. I know both stickers and the truck a little too well.

Ryan.

I stare at the house behind it. I don't know who lives there, but wonder if it is one of his war buddies and drive on. I pause at the end of the street, then look at my phone, unable to escape a nagging thought in my head.

Is it a woman he's visiting? Another affair?

I grab my phone, heart pounding in my chest, then dial his number. He picks up right away.

"Hi, babe. What's up?"

"I was wondering when you'd be back today?" I ask. I

listen to his breathing. It sounds ragged—like he is in the middle of something. Do I hear voices? Another person breathing in the background? "My parents are coming to dinner, and I was wondering if you had time to make your famous spareribs? I'm also making chicken, but maybe we could grill some ribs for my dad's sake? You know how much he loves them."

Boy, I can lie about spareribs!

"Uhm, I don't know. Around three o'clock, I think. I can make spareribs if you want me to. I'm at the medical center right now and don't think we'll be done till then, but there will still be time when I get back if I'm not too tired, that is. Jimmy is being tough on me today."

"Okay," I say, my heart dropping. Another lie. Is it really that easy for him now? How much can I trust what he has told me? Is everything he said the other day about him trying to get better a lie too?

"Jimmy wants me to go; we got work to do, but I'll see you later," he says, then hangs up.

I sit in my car, staring at the phone, a lump in my throat, wondering how long this has been going on. How long has he been lying to me?

HE COMES home at three o'clock exactly, almost like he has planned it. He seems distraught and stays in the garage for a long time after I see his truck arrive. I am peeling potatoes and chopping carrots as he finally enters the house.

I don't know what to say to him. I've been thinking about it all day, coming up with a thousand ways to confront him. I want him to know that I saw him and that I read the messages to Sandra. I want to ask him what he is up to. But I am not sure of exactly what to say because the fact is, I don't know who lives in that house, and the more I think about it, the more I realize that he could come up with a million excuses to explain why he was there and not at the center where he claimed to be. I wouldn't know whether it is true or not. I am not properly prepared for a real confrontation. I need more ammunition. So, I decide not to say anything as he comes through the door.

Not yet.

He stops and stares at me, and I finally look up. I try to avoid his eyes because I am afraid he can tell something is up, but my eyes meet his anyway. I feel a pinch of anger in my stomach but manage to suppress it.

"So…how was your physical therapy?" I ask, thinking he can see straight through me. He can hear it in my voice, can't he? Or see it in my eyes?

He doesn't answer. He looks away. Something is off with him; he's different somehow, in another place in his mind. He barely looks at me, just goes to the fridge and takes out the ribs. He rubs them with barbeque sauce and goes outside to light the grill. I keep looking for lipstick marks on his shirt or a different smell on his skin, but I don't find any convicting clues. As he disappears outside with the grill, he leaves his phone on the counter, and I stare at it for a long time while preparing the salad, then pick it up and open it. I glance toward the sliding doors leading to the yard, making sure he's not coming. I tap his password and am happy to realize he hasn't changed it. I open his texts and scroll through them. He's been texting his friends a lot. I recognize Chip and Ted and then some others, Sonny and Seth, among others. They mostly goof around, sending each other stupid gifs and making plans to go out for beers or a run on the beach. It all seems very innocent. Nothing unusual. I open the most recent text message he has sent, and it is to Ted. He tells him he's gonna come by today to pick up his stuff, and thanks him again for letting him sleep on his couch while he got himself together.

I read it three times, feeling like such an idiot. Here, I had thought he was having an affair with someone when he was, in fact, just picking up his stuff after sleeping at Ted's place for the past three days while calming down so he wouldn't hurt me or the kids.

I stare at the door, then put the phone down, feeling all kinds of emotions rush through me. I am so confused right now. Am I just seeing things here? Sandra? This visit today? Is it all just me being super paranoid?

Maybe Ryan is actually just struggling to get better, and that's why he kept leaving? It isn't because he has some other woman he is seeing on the side?

I smile, relieved, as he comes back inside for more barbeque sauce. I hand him the bottle, then pull him into a deep kiss.

"What was that for?" he asks. "Not that I'm complaining."

"I'm just so happy to have you home; that's all."

Chapter 20

MY PARENTS ARRIVE, and I can tell they're worried. When they see Ryan, my dad's face lights up, and he goes to the grill with him, where they each get a beer. Meanwhile, my mom helps me with the food, putting it out on the table in the yard. The kids are fighting about something stupid, and I have to tell them to stop. Isabella helps set the table, while Damian goes into the yard to throw his ball. My dad goes to play with him, and soon they are tumbling around out there, laughing loudly. I enjoy watching them and turn to look at Ryan. He is smiling at me while drinking his beer. I smile back.

We eat, and it all feels really good and amazing and just the way it is supposed to be. Me and my family. All together. Even Rosie, our dog, is enjoying this, sitting by Ryan's feet, probably hoping some food will drop.

My dad and Ryan talk football while my mom tells me about a book she read recently that I really ought to read.

I'm not really listening. I'm trying just to enjoy the moment. It's harder than I thought, and I wonder why. It's because of that thought that won't stop nagging me.

Why did he lie? He could have told me he was picking up his stuff at Ted's. He didn't have to lie.

"So, you're doing well again? You and Ryan?" she then asks.

I smile. "We are."

"That's good. You don't seem very happy, though," she says. "You're distant. Is something wrong?"

"No, no, everything is just fine. I'm just a little tired; that's all."

I smile again, wider this time, trying to seem sincere. Ryan and my dad are discussing loudly now, and I can tell Ryan is getting agitated. They have moved on to politics, and they never can agree on that. Ryan is drinking more beers and seems to get more and more tense. I worry this might end badly. I don't want it to. We were doing so well.

By the time they finally leave, Ryan is drunk and can barely stand still on his feet as we say our goodbyes. As soon as they're gone, Ryan goes back into the yard and sits on a chair, then continues to drink. I start cleaning up, then put the kids to bed. I know he's just drinking more while I do all this, and as I come back out, I am worried.

"I'm going to bed now," I say. "Are you coming?"

He pauses for a long time, then places the bottle in front of his lips and takes another sip.

"Why did you call today?"

"What do you mean?" I ask. "Am I not allowed to call you?"

"You called me while I was at the center. You never do that. Were you checking up on me?"

I shake my head. I'm tired, and I sense he just wants to fight. I don't want to. I want to sleep. I want to get by for one day without us fighting.

"No. I wanted to make sure you had time to do the spareribs," I say.

"Your parents think I'm cheating on you," he says.

I frown. This sounds odd in my ears.

"They said that?"

He drinks again. "No, but I can tell. The way they look at me. Did you tell them I've been cheating on you?"

I shake my head again. "No. I would never say anything like that to them."

He stares at me, beer bottle clutched in his hand. I feel like he's getting himself worked up, and I want to end it. I fear he's gonna get in the truck and drive somewhere in his condition or that he'll go out drinking all night with his buddies. I fear he'll leave and not come back for days again.

"I'm…I'll go to bed now," I say.

"You do that," he answers, pointing the beer bottle at me. "Go to bed and get your beauty sleep."

I turn around, closing my eyes briefly. I want to ask him if he's coming. If he'll be up later, but I don't dare. He's in that mood where he's just looking for a chance to hurt me or get angry. I am not giving it to him.

So, I leave without a word.

I WAKE up to the sound of a truck roaring to life. I jump out of bed just in time to see him take off in his black truck. I feel awful. The man is plastered. He might hit someone.

I have to stop him.

I go to Isabella's room and wake her up. I tell her I need to leave for a few minutes and to watch out for her brother.

"Where are you going?" she asks.

I give her a look, and she knows not to ask anymore. I

rush out of there as I open the app on my phone and hope it'll tell me where he's heading. It does. It tells me he's driving toward the north housing area, and I follow him in the minivan. He stops at an address, and a minute later, I drive up in front of the house. I stay out there for a few minutes, wondering what he's doing, who he is visiting. It's the same address where I saw him earlier in the day. He's in there for at least fifteen minutes before he comes stumbling out and almost trips over his own feet in the grass before he takes off. I debate whether or not to follow him again, but then curiosity gets the better of me. I've been wondering about this all day, ever since I knew he was in there. Who lives in that house? Is it Ted? Or is it someone else?

I get out, then sneak up to the front door and look for a name. It's not hard to find. Kenopensky, it says, right by the doorbell. I breathe a sigh of great relief. It *is* Ted's house. So, Ryan was actually just picking up his stuff earlier, and he was probably just asking Ted if he wanted to go out just now. I am so relieved I can feel it physically as I turn to walk back to the car. But as I do, out of the corner of my eye, I see something that makes me stop.

I move closer to be certain I am not just imagining things and look in through the window. In there, in the middle of the living room, I see something that stops my heart.

A pair of dangling legs.

Chapter 21

I CAN'T BREATHE; I struggle to stand still while waiting for the Security Forces to arrive. I've called them, but don't know what to say once they get here. I am freaking out.

What do I do?

They arrive less than five minutes later. Two SP officers on night duty come up to me. I tell them what I've seen, that there's a set of dangling legs in the living room, and they look inside for themselves. They grab the door handle and realize it's open, then rush inside. I follow them, bracing myself for what I will find in there.

As I lay eyes on Ted dangling from the ceiling, I break down and cry. Tears well up in my eyes as I stare at his face while they struggle to cut him down. His lifeless body slumps to the ground, rag-doll limp. One of the SP officers feels for a pulse but doesn't find it. He shakes his head at his colleague, and they call for the ambulance.

They take my statement. I'm not even sure what I'm saying anymore. I tell them I was out driving and saw there was a light on in the house, then spotted the legs. I'm lying through my teeth, or at least withholding vital information, and I don't know why. Why don't I tell them my husband was in there just a minute before I called? Why don't I tell them I followed him here?

Do I still believe in his innocence?

They let me go, and I drive home, crying so hard I can barely see the road in front of me. I park in the garage, then sit there for a very long time, how long I don't know. I just sit there, trying to calm my pounding heart.

I'm pretty sure my husband just killed someone. I don't know what to do. It's the only explanation, right? It can't be a coincidence that he was with both of them right before they died, allegedly killing themselves, right? I mean, I'm not just being paranoid anymore; I can't be.

Something like this doesn't happen twice.

Does it?

I CRAWL into Isabella's bed and try to fall asleep. I sleep with her for the rest of the night, or at least until I hear the garage door open and the truck come back. My heart is hammering in my chest as I hear him downstairs. He tips something over, and it falls to the tiles, shattering. I'm guessing it's a glass or maybe a beer bottle. I hear him open the fridge and rustle something, probably eating leftovers. The stairs creak, and then I hear the footsteps outside the door. They stop right on the other side. I stare at the door, praying it won't open.

It doesn't. The footsteps disappear, and I hear the door to our bedroom click shut. I breathe and lie completely still, hoping Ryan is too drunk to realize I'm not in our bed.

I close my eyes, telling myself that I'll tell the investigators the truth tomorrow. I'll tell them he was there, just like he was there right before Sandra killed herself. I need to tell them the truth. I can't live with myself if I don't.

I finally doze off as the house grows silent, and I sleep for an hour or so before I wake up with a gasp. I open my eyes and realize the door to Isabella's room is open. I turn to look and see Ryan sitting in the chair by the bed, hands folded, eyes glaring at us. He looks angry.

"R-Ryan?" I say and sit up. "What are you doing here?"

He reeks of alcohol even from where he is sitting. I think he's still drunk.

"Why are you not sleeping in our bed?" he asks. His speech is slurred. "I came home, and…you weren't there?"

"I…Isabella needed me. She had a nightmare," I lie and try to keep my voice low. "Let's talk in the morning, okay? I don't want to wake her."

He gets up and walks closer, then sits at the foot of the bed. He grabs my hand in his, then caresses it. I hope he won't notice how badly it is shaking. Can he hear my shuddering breath? Can he hear my galloping heart?

"I'm sorry if I acted badly tonight," he says, suddenly a lot calmer. "I think I had too much to drink."

I just want him to leave. I don't know if I'm looking at a murderer or what the heck is going on. I need time to think this through. I need rest. I find it so hard to believe. I have known this man since I was twenty. He's been my entire life. Everything I did was for him. Could my Ryan have murdered someone?

I can't wrap my mind around it.

The only explanation for it is the war. He went away and came back changed. Maybe he really had lost it over there? Could it be his PTSD? Maybe he isn't even aware of his actions? Maybe he doesn't even remember killing them? Is it possible to have a blackout and then kill someone and not remember afterward? Is it possible to be that sick?

"It's okay," I whisper, calming down. Yet, I still can't help it. I begin to cry. I feel so hopeless and scared.

"Hey, hey," he whispers. "What's going on with you?"

"I'm just…I'm just so tired is all," I say. "It's been a long day, with my parents and all that. And the fact that I never know when you're going to leave us again. It wears on me, Ryan. It really does. That and then the drinking and…" I am about to say more, but I stop. I can't say what I saw. Not now. Not here. I need time to think it over; I need time to figure out how to handle this. I don't know what to do. I don't have a clue.

He pulls me closer and starts to kiss me—first my forehead, then my lips. His kisses are soft yet insistent.

"Come back to our bed," he says between kisses. "It's so empty without you. I don't want to sleep without you. I miss you terribly in there. We've been apart enough. I don't want to sleep apart anymore."

I look into his eyes, not knowing what to do, what to think. It's all so chaotic in my head. All the many thoughts rushing through it. It's like it won't stand still enough for me to think properly. It's just all those images of Ted and Sandra, and then Ryan. My beloved Ryan. I have loved this man all of my adult life, as long as I can remember. He has to be in there somewhere, doesn't he? I can't just give up on him.

I search my brain for any logical explanation but don't find one. He was there, and then they both turned up dead. And I am the only one who knows.

"Come," he whispers, then pulls my hand. I let him and follow him back into our bed. I lie down, and we cuddle all night, me constantly trying to remain calm and not freak out. I finally fall asleep right before sunrise, and he lets me sleep in, then gets up and makes sure the kids aren't late for the school bus.

I pretend to be sleeping, but instead, I write to Frank. I ask him about Ted and whether he can give me any insight into the body they found. And then I ask the question that I want answered most of all right now:

What is the time of death?

I close the lid of my laptop right as Ryan comes into the bedroom, carrying a tray with coffee and toast. He has even taken a flower from the yard and placed it in a small vase. He smiles gently and crawls under the covers with me. I shiver lightly when he brushes against me. After we have eaten, his hands crawl up under my dress, and his fingers play with my panties. He smiles and leans in over me, then pulls them off forcefully. I gasp lightly as he enters me with a groan. I pray he doesn't realize my entire body is trembling in fear as he makes love to me. As I close my eyes, all I can see is Ted's eyes as they cut him down and the small broken blood vessels around them. I had seen enough dead bodies in my line of work to know those were an indication of asphyxiation.

As Ryan kisses my breasts, and later my lips again, I can't stop wondering if he strangled him before he hung him up or if Ted died while hanging.

Chapter 22

TWO DAYS GO by before I hear back from Frank. He texts me that he needs to talk to me. He comes over as soon as Ryan leaves for his doctor's appointment. Ryan is almost back at one hundred percent, he says, and he hopes the doctor will give him the all-clear to get back to work. Not having to go every day is driving him nuts, he says. He needs to have a reason to get out of bed. I wish him luck, and as soon as he leaves, I text Frank that the coast is clear.

He arrives a few minutes later, and I make him coffee. He smiles gently as we sit down at the dining table. I have a basket of laundry sitting on top of it, which I put on the floor first.

"How are you doing?" he asks. "You look a little…flustered."

"I'm okay," I lie. Because I am not. I am anything but okay. I am worried and scared out of my wits. I feel like my world has come crumbling down and that I am disappearing into a deep darkness that I can't drag myself out of. I keep seeing Ryan as he kills Sandra or Ted. I keep imagining it and dreaming about their dead bodies. I can't help it.

"And is everything okay with Ryan? He looked a little…tense the last time I was here. I hated to leave you like that."

I am biting my lip anxiously. I think I hear a car on the road and check to make sure it isn't Ryan coming back because he forgot something. But the car continues on and doesn't stop, and I breathe, relieved again.

"Did you have time to look at that thing I asked about?" I say, sipping my cup.

"Ted Kenopensky," he says, nodding. "Why are you asking about him?"

"I need to know when he died. And how. It's very important to me."

Frank looks at me, a frown shaping between his eyes. I can tell he's wondering about my motive for this, but he doesn't dare to ask. He doesn't want to make me mad at him. I fiddle nervously with my cup as he pulls out some papers from his briefcase.

"I was able to print out the autopsy without anyone seeing me," he says and pulls out a stack of papers. "But I'll have you know that what I am doing is illegal, so you can't tell anyone who your source is."

"Of course not. It's not for anyone else but me."

He spreads out the papers, and once again, I am looking at Ted's dead eyes. "He was found hanging from his ceiling," Frank says. "And that is the cause of death, according to the autopsy."

I look up, and our eyes meet. I like sitting here with him. Frank makes me feel safe. It's the first time in days I feel remotely calm.

"But…" I say and grab a photograph. "The tongue

isn't thrust out of his mouth. Isn't it usually when people hang themselves?"

Frank gives me a look. "That was the first thing that made me suspicious. You're absolutely right. Usually, when people hang themselves, the tongue is thrust out of the mouth, and the jaws are clenched. Once, back when I was an EMT, I was called out to a suicide where the jaws were clenched so tightly that they had to be pried open forcefully, so we could pursue lifesaving measures. Three times I have worked scenes where a person hung themselves, and each of the victims had a thick foam around their mouths, and they had soiled themselves. Their hands were clenched into fists—what they call 'posturing.' This happens when the brain begins to die. Also, they all had claw marks around their necks from desperately trying to free themselves, thrashing about violently as the body instinctively tries to survive. None of these indicators were present in Ted's body, at least not according to the autopsy."

"And not in real life either," I say, thinking back to the night when he was taken down. I had seen no tongue thrust, no clenched jaws, and definitely no foam. "But there are broken blood vessels," I say. "Around his eyes. That means that the cause of death was asphyxiation, right?"

Frank nods. "His neck is unbroken, but his hyoid bone is broken, which indicates he was strangled."

I look up at him, holding the picture between my hands. It is shaking violently, and I try to make it stop, but I can't. "So, what you're saying is, you don't believe he hung himself, is that it?"

Frank swallows, he sips his cup again, then sighs. "It doesn't look much like a hanging to me, no."

"And the marks around the throat? Are they from a rope?"

He shrugs. "Could be a rope or hands. It's hard to tell when I'm just looking at pictures. I'd have to examine the body myself in order to determine this, and even then, it might be difficult to tell the difference."

I exhale and drink more coffee while my hands shake nervously. I know coffee probably isn't what I need right now, but I can't help myself. I haven't slept properly for several nights, and this is what keeps me from passing out.

"And the time of death?"

He looks down at his papers. "They determined it to be between midnight and five after two a.m. when the SPs arrived."

I stare at him, barely blinking.

Ryan was there at two a.m. Or ten minutes to, to be exact. I still remember the time because I looked at the clock in the car right when he left Ted's house.

"And they can't be mistaken?" I ask. I can hear how bad my voice is shuddering, but I can't make it stop.

"It is an approximate time, but the body was examined pretty soon after death occurred, so it can't be off by much. They can be pretty certain, due to body temperature, degree of decomposition, blood pooling, rigor mortis, and so on."

"So, he did definitely die at night and not earlier in the day?"

Frank nods. He pauses and drinks more coffee. I finish mine and look out the window, worried, wondering when Ryan will be back. None of what Frank has told me has made me calmer. Nothing is giving my husband the benefit of the doubt, only confirming my suspicions.

Frank exhales. His eyes are scrutinizing me. It makes me nervous, the way he is looking at me.

"What's going on here, Laurie?" he asks. "First, you ask about Clarice, and now this? I'm concerned about you;

you seem a little out of sorts. Could you please let me in on what you're working on? Is it for a news story? Because if you are working on a story, then I have to tell you, it makes me slightly nervous. I'm risking everything by giving you this information. The least you can do is let me in on what is happening."

***

IT TAKES me a while to get to the conclusion that I need a friend in this. I walk to the kitchen and pour us both some more coffee, then grab a couple of Oreos and eat them while I'm out there. Frank comes out to me, brushing up against me while the coffee machine is brewing, the smell of fresh coffee filling my nostrils. I have always loved that smell; it reminds me of my grandmother's house. I miss her and am suddenly overwhelmed with deep sadness. Tears roll down my cheeks, and I try to hide it from Frank, turning away from him, but of course, he notices. He grabs me by the shoulders and tries to turn me back around.

"Hey, what's going on, Laurie?"

I lower my head and hide my face in my hands, then cry. "I…I fear that Ryan is in trouble," I say.

"What do you mean, trouble?"

I look up at him, and our eyes meet. I feel warm inside and hopeless at the same time. I feel so stuck in this house like I can't get out, but I know it's not the house. It's my life and my marriage I'm thinking about. I feel stuck in a situation I can't resolve, and I'm afraid it's gonna end in disaster.

"I mean that I…he was there, Frank. Right before Ted died, he was in the house. I saw him leave."

"So, what? You think he…no, Laurie, come on."

"Then, why didn't he call the security force? If he

didn't kill him, he must have seen him hanging there. And now you tell me that you don't believe he was…that he killed himself, that maybe he was already dead when he was hung up."

Frank sighs. "I know what I said, but going from that to…to think that Ryan has…"

I turn to face him. We're standing really close now, and I can almost feel his breath on my face. He smells good, and I like being close to him. I miss being close to someone I don't fear.

"He was there at Sandra Mulcahey's house right before she died too. I saw a message where he wrote that he would stop by for coffee. I thought he had an affair with her…that maybe she killed herself because he wouldn't leave me and marry her or something like that, but now this thing happened with Ted, and I don't know what to think anymore."

Frank closes his eyes briefly. "So, wait a minute. You're telling me that Ryan was in Sandra Mulcahey's house right before she killed herself? And he was there on the night that Ted killed himself?"

I take a deep breath. It feels good to share this information with someone and not be alone with it anymore. But only for a few seconds. Then I am filled with guilt. I feel like I have just terribly betrayed my husband.

"Does the OSI know this?" Frank says.

I shake my head and cry. "I can't get myself to…"

He grabs me by the shoulders and looks into my eyes. "You need to tell them, Laurie. You need to go down there and tell them what you know."

I bite my cheek. I know he is right, but it still pains me so much. "What if I'm wrong? What if it is just a coincidence? What if it just happened twice? Lightning can sometimes strike the same place several times. I read of a guy who was struck by lightning twelve times and survived all of them. Coincidences happen, even odd ones."

He shrugs. "That's your defense for him? This is what you've been telling yourself? Tell me this, has Ryan been violent with you? And tell me the truth. I saw the way he looked at you that day when he came home. Has he hurt you? What about the kids?"

I swallow. He's getting a little too close for comfort now. I look away and am about to grab my coffee cup when he pulls my shoulder and forces me to look at him.

"Laurie, tell me the truth here. Has Ryan been violent with you since he came back?"

I look up, and our eyes meet. Frank doesn't need my answer anymore. He knows. He pulls back, cupping his mouth.

"Oh, dear Lord, Laurie. I thought something was off between you guys, but this...you have to go to the Office of Special Investigations, the OSI. You can't live like this. Promise me you'll talk to them. Promise me."

Chapter 23

I PROMISE HIM, even though I'm not sure I'm going to keep it. When Frank leaves, I rush to the kitchen to clean up after breakfast. I think about what I'd say to the investigators. They'll ask me why I didn't tell them anything earlier. What is my excuse? I can't come up with one that sounds plausible. Will it be enough if I explain I wanted to protect my husband? That I still don't know if it is all just a coincidence? What am I going to say? They don't even think there's been a crime committed. And maybe there hasn't. Maybe I'm just making things up in my mind.

Frank is a forensic technician. He knows what he's doing. He told you that Ted didn't die by hanging. It doesn't look like suicide.

"Then why are they calling it suicide? Why does the OSI claim it is?" I ask into the empty kitchen. Only Rosie is with me, and she doesn't even seem to care. "Maybe Frank is the one who is wrong? He could make mistakes, too, right?"

"Who could make mistakes?"

I almost drop the bowl I am holding between my hands as I hear Ryan's voice behind me. I turn to see him. He is smiling. He grabs a grape from the counter and eats it, chewing with his mouth open.

"You scared me," I say.

"I'm sorry. I didn't mean to. Who were you talking to?"

He looks around like he's expecting to find someone.

I smile nervously. "Just Rosie. We like to have a little chat now and then."

He grins. "You're talking to the dog now?"

"She's the only company I have all day," I say.

"That's a little sad," he says.

"How did it go at the doctor's?" I ask. "You look happy. Was it good news?"

He smiles widely. "I got it—the old all-clear. I'm ready to get back to work again. I'll start Monday."

I gasp happily. "That's awesome news, honey. You've worked so hard for this."

He grabs another grape and pops it into his mouth. "Yup. Gonna be good to get back in the saddle, you know?"

I nod and put the bowl back on the counter.

"As a matter of fact, I think I'll go for a run," he continues. "I need to get in better shape to keep up with the others come Monday."

He leaves to get dressed for his run, and I continue to put away plates, emptying the dishwasher when I see the two cups sitting on the counter next to me. I stare at them, then wonder if Ryan saw them. I pray he didn't. Maybe he was too happy to notice.

I grab both cups and put them in the dishwasher, then close it up as Ryan returns. "Say, where is my shirt? The white one I always run in?"

"Ah, I haven't had time to wash," I say. "I'll do it later. Can you maybe wear another one?"

He pauses, then tilts his head slightly to the side. "You

haven't had time to do laundry? Don't you usually do the laundry in the morning after the kids leave?"

"Y-yes."

He frowns, still smiling, but the smile is stiffening slightly. "So, please tell me, what have you been so busy with all morning that you didn't have time to do the laundry? And that you aren't cleaning up after breakfast till now?"

I stare at him and feel the blood leave my face. I don't know what to say to him. I realize now that he could have seen those two cups; he probably did, and now he's waiting to see if I'll lie to him.

"Vera stopped by," I said. "Just for coffee."

"Vera, huh?"

"Yes, Vera. I know you don't like me seeing her, but she needed my advice on something with a boy she met."

The lie is so thick; I fear he'll see straight through it.

"That's strange," he says.

"What is?" There's a tremor in my voice, and I worry he'll hear it. Sweat is springing to my forehead, and I can't hold my hands still.

"Well, first of all, you just said you had only been talking to Rosie all day. And second, I saw Vera an hour ago when I stopped by to tell the others the great news that I'll be back next week."

I look away and feel his eyes on me. It's like they're burning on my skin.

"Well, she was only here briefly."

I close the dishwasher, then walk past him, holding my breath. I can feel his eyes are on me as I walk up the stairs. A few minutes later, I hear the front door slam shut, and I look out the window from upstairs to see him running down the street, taking long, determined, and—what seems to me like—aggressive strides.

"YOU NEED TO TELL THE OSI."

Frank's words keep ringing in my ears as I put the laundry in the washer and turn it on. My heart is beating fast with fear and worry. I know he's right; I'm just not quite sure what will happen afterward. Will Ryan realize I'm the one who told them? Do I need to get away? I don't want to have to take the kids out of their familiar surroundings and go into hiding. Because that will be the result, won't it? I'll have to hide from him. And then what when he finds me?

Will he make it look like I killed myself when he murders me?

Will the kids have to grow up alone with a father who's a murderer?

I am spinning out of control, and I know it. I am losing my grip and allowing my active imagination to run away with me. I know this, but I can't stop it.

He'll tell them I am crazy, that I was slowly losing my mind. He saw it coming long before it happened. That there was nothing anyone could have done. I was depressed.

I can even hear him saying the words to my family and my children. And they believe him. Of course, they do. Ryan can be very persuasive when he wants to.

I shake my head and fold the towels I had left in the dryer from the day before when I hear the door slam shut and hear him enter the house. He is panting heavily, and so am I as I wonder how this is ever going to end well.

Chapter 24

IT TAKES me a week to get the courage to go to the U.S. Air Force Office of Special Investigations. It's the federal law enforcement and counterintelligence agency for the United States Air Force and United States Space Force. This is where they investigate criminal activities that happen on base.

But even on the day I finally decide to go, I keep losing my nerve. I turn the car around at least three times and am on my way back home, but eventually, I end up parking outside the tall beige building. I take a few deep breaths, telling myself it's the right thing to do, that I am not going to destroy my family, even though I know that's exactly what will happen. I say this over and over again and walk inside and ask to speak to Investigator Rick Thibodeau. I remember him from when Sandra died, and I like him. I have a feeling he will understand my story and forgive me for not coming in earlier.

Rick Thibodeau comes out to greet me. He's a tall man with light blue eyes, who looks like he works out a lot, which he probably does. He's also very young, and I wonder if he has solved many cases if any. I worry that it's not often these people are involved in murder investigations.

"Mrs. Davis?" he says and holds out his hand. I shake it nervously. "I'm surprised to see you here? How can I help you?"

"I'd like to talk to you somewhere private," I say. "It's kind of a delicate matter."

He smiles curiously. "Of course. No problem. Come with me."

We walk down a hallway, and as we pass other men in uniforms, I lower my eyes, worrying they might be friends with Ryan. There are only about fifteen-thousand people on base, and only around four-thousand of those are active military personnel; the rest are contractors or medical personnel, or children and spouses, like me.

Rick takes me into an office and closes the door, then points at a chair.

"Go ahead."

I sit down. I can hear my heart pounding in my ears. I am terrified and want to run away, but it's too late now. I have to do this. I have to get it off my chest, even though it'll cost me dearly. Frank convinced me to let Vera in on it as well, so I have. I told her everything during a lunch this past week. She too encouraged me to go to the OSI, and to be honest, it was probably her words that finally made me go.

"You at least have to do it for your own conscience. You can't live with yourself knowing this. What if he is a murderer? What if he killed those two people? Can you live with him, knowing he got away with it? Knowing he is still free because of you? Because you didn't tell?"

Of course, I can't. Any way I look at it, this is the only solution that makes any sense even if it hurts. Even if it is devastating to go behind my husband's back like this. I feel like I am betraying him. It's the worst feeling in the world.

"Coffee?" Rick Thibodeau asks, and I shake my head. I've had three cups already while gathering my courage, and it's barely ten o'clock. My heart is pounding so fast in my chest, and I don't know if it's because of where I am and what I am about to do or the caffeine. It might be a little bit of both.

Ryan is at work, so he won't worry where I am, which I am pleased about. We haven't been doing well lately. There's this tension between us that is very uncomfortable. I've been avoiding him at the house, making sure to keep myself occupied with chores, and I have spent a lot of time in the laundry room lately. But I can't avoid him constantly. And when I do spend time with him, I feel so awkward, and he senses it. He can sense something is off. He's being extremely suspicious of me and keeps asking me where I have been and with whom. Even when I tell him the truth, I feel like I'm lying. He looks at me as though I am, as though he doesn't believe a word I tell him. So, I try to talk as little as possible to him, and that makes him even more suspicious of me. Just the day before, he asked me what was wrong with me.

"Nothing," I said. "I'm just tired."

"You're acting weird."

The thing is, he's right. I am acting weird, but I don't know how not to anymore. I don't remember how to act normal around him. The more I think about it, the worse it gets. It's like this circle that I can't escape. I just can't relax around him enough to seem normal.

Luckily, getting back to work has given him other things to think about, and I am off the hook, at least until he gets back later in the day. Tonight, he will ask me what I have been doing all day, and I am ready to tell him. I have a list in my mind of things I have done that won't arouse any suspicion—things he will approve of and hopefully believe. I don't like to lie to him, though. But lying has become my life now. I feel like it's all I do. I don't like how good I am becoming at it.

"You don't mind if I have a cup, then?" Rick Thibodeau asks, and I shake my head again.

"Of course not."

He leaves and comes back with a cup in his hand. He sits down across from me. "So, what can I do for you, Mrs. Davis?"

"It's about Sandra…I mean Mrs. Mulcahey," I say. I look down at my hands, and they're trembling. I keep them clasped together in my lap, so he won't see.

He nods and sips his coffee.

"What about her?"

"I…I fear it might not have been suicide."

Rick Thibodeau lifts his eyebrows and leans forward, folding his hands on the desk. "And just what makes you say that?"

I exhale deeply. This is it; this is the moment. There's no turning back now. "My husband…he was with her right before she died."

Rick Thibodeau nods. "And?"

"Well, he met with her right before she died. I read a message from him on Facebook, where he told her he'd stop by."

"Okay," Rick Thibodeau says. "I can understand from your perspective how that seems suspicious, and maybe it was, maybe they were having an affair, but how does that involve me or the OSI?"

I am shifting in my seat, unable to sit still. "Well…the

thing is, he was there when Ted Kenopensky died too. Right before he was found hanging."

Rick Thibodeau grabs the cup, then slurps his coffee while watching me intently. He puts the cup down slowly like he has all the time in the world.

"I see. And this is what you came here to tell me?"

"Yes."

He nods again, moving slowly. He grabs his cup, then asks before he takes another long sip, "And just how are things in your marriage, Mrs. Davis?"

Startled at this, I frown.

"What do you mean?"

"Are things good? Are you happy together?"

"I don't see how that has anything to do with…"

"Oh, I think it has everything to do with that. Why else would you come here to incriminate your husband?"

I can feel my face flushing. What is this? Do *I* need to defend myself now?

"Listen," I say. "I don't find this especially pleasant, and I certainly take no joy in saying these things. But no matter what happened, the fact is, he saw Ted hanging in the living room, and he didn't do anything. He didn't even call the security forces. Who does that? Who sees a guy, a good friend, dangling from the ceiling and doesn't tell anyone, not even his wife? Does that not seem suspicious to you? I can't explain why he would do that unless he has something to hide."

Rick Thibodeau exhales, then leans back in his chair. "You're forgetting something here. Your husband has been to war, Mrs. Davis. He has seen death up close before. He might have panicked when seeing Ted Kenopensky; he might have been scared to death, and it might have ripped up some bad memories in him, seeing his friend like that. Maybe he's afraid of what he might do to himself. Did you ever think about that? There are many reasons why he would do just what he did. And maybe, just maybe he was only drinking coffee with his good female friend, Sandra. Maybe they were even talking about stuff they experienced in the war that could lead to her committing suicide. Or maybe it was an affair gone wrong. Sad as it may be for your marriage, I don't see anything suspicious, and either way, both cases were deemed suicides. There's nothing more to it, Mrs. Davis. No active murder investigation. Just tragic suicides, which we, unfortunately, see way too often. Do you know how many soldiers kill themselves?"

I shake my head, feeling like a child at the principal's office. Rick Thibodeau seems annoyed with me now.

"No."

"Twenty-two veterans per day, one every sixty-five minutes. That's a lot."

He sighs and leans back in his chair. "Now, I don't know what's going on at home, in your marriage, or why you feel the need to hurt your husband. But I suggest you put your energy into saving your marriage instead of running to me with accusations against your husband. I think you're just mad at him, and that's why you're busy claiming these things. I have nothing here telling me anyone was murdered or even a crime committed. I am sorry, but I can't really help you."

I feel defeated. I wonder for a second if I should tell him about what Frank has said, about how Ted's death didn't look like suicide, but then I decide against it. He'll ask me how I know this, and I'll only compromise Frank, and I promised not to tell anyone. I have nothing. I realize I am not getting anywhere with this guy, then get up, fuming with anger. If there is one thing I can't stand, it's being talked down to.

"This was a mistake," I say, then leave while shaking

my head, once again reminded of what my mother always used to say:

If you want anything done in this world, you have to do it yourself.

Chapter 25

I TIPTOE around Ryan for yet another two days, making sure I don't anger him or draw any suspicion to myself before Vera and Frank both come over for lunch. Frank says he has news to share with us. Vera is on a lunch break and decides to stop by and eat with us. I make them sandwiches, and we eat them in our kitchen. I tell them about my visit to the OSI, and how investigator Rick Thibodeau had brushed me off.

"I think I'm going insane," I say. "I don't know what to believe anymore."

"Maybe if she went to the police outside of the base?" Vera says, taking a bite of her chicken sandwich.

"They'll tell her to go to the OSI," Frank says. "It's their jurisdiction. Plus, there are no open investigations into those two deaths, so it's gonna be hard to make anyone look into it."

"So, that's it?" Vera says. "She's on her own? No police will help her?"

"If they don't believe there has been a crime..." Frank

says and trails off. He sips his iced tea. "They're not easy to dance around with. We know. I tried so hard to get them to reopen Clarice's case, based on what I saw in the autopsy report, but they refused. It was deemed suicide, and that was the end of it. They won't listen."

I look at him with a sigh. I genuinely fear that one day, my parents will be trying to get the military officials to reopen the case of my suicide because they desperately want to know what really happened. Because they believe Ryan killed me, but they're the only ones. The thought saddens me, and a wave of fresh fear rushes through my body. I have been weighing my options the past few days, wondering what I can possibly do.

"You said you had some news?" I ask Frank.

He nods, wipes his fingers clean on a napkin, then pulls out a folder that he places so that both Vera and I can see it if we skootch closer on each side of him.

"I took another look at Sandra Mulcahey's autopsy report; actually, I went through the entire death report, and this is what I found. Look."

He pulls out a sheet, and we both look at it but don't really understand what it is. Frank knows this, so he translates.

"The cuts on her wrists. They were deeper on her right side than on her left side. That would usually indicate that she was left-handed."

"But she wasn't," I say, my eyes growing wide. "I know because I more than once talked to her about Joe, Jr., her son. When she realized he was left-handed, she worried it would make things difficult for him."

"In her files, it doesn't say anything about being a lefty either," he says. "That's why it had me wondering."

"So, she didn't cut her own wrists?" Vera asked. "Is that what you're saying?"

"That could be the explanation," Frank says. "It would have been the other way around if she did. The cuts would have been deeper on the left side instead. But it's not exactly evidence. Not enough to reopen her case." Frank pauses and finishes his sandwich, then wipes his fingers again.

"There's more."

"I was hoping you'd say that," I said, still wondering about the two coffee cups on the kitchen counter in Sandra's kitchen. I should have told the investigator about them on the day she was found. Then it would have been in the report; then, they would have looked for that person, at least to know if Sandra mentioned anything about wanting to end her life. But I didn't think it was important then, and now, it's too late.

"Her toxicology report states her blood had an exceedingly high concentration of fentanyl. She had sixty-nine micrograms per liter. This drug has been proven deadly at much lower rates than that. They found huge amounts in her liver and her stomach as well."

"So, she overdosed on painkillers?" I ask. "Before her wrists were cut?"

Frank nods. "Looks like it."

"Still sounds like suicide," I say.

"Of course," Frank says. "And that's what they'll tell us if we point it out. But what I found odd was that the exact same thing was found in Ted Kenopensky's blood. The same drug and almost the same amount."

"Which can also still be argued as being a way to commit suicide," I say.

"Definitely. But it could also be used to make a victim unresponsive or unable to fight back before you kill them," Frank adds.

"Makes it a whole lot easier to put them in a tub or hang them from the ceiling," Vera says.

I sigh. I don't like where this is going. "Are you both seriously suggesting that these two were drugged and then murdered?"

I think about the coffee cups on the counter again. Of course, I do. Is it possible to dissolve painkillers into coffee without anyone tasting it?

It's not Ryan. He's your husband!

I finish my iced tea, trying to calm myself.

"I don't like that you're here in the house with him. Not till we know more. You should leave," Frank says to me. "Get off base. Take the kids and leave. Maybe go to your parents' place."

I shake my head. "I have thought this over a million times. He'll come for me. He'll know where I am and will come for me. He'll take the kids, have me declared mentally unstable, and take the kids away from me. Me showing up at the OSI, blabbering on about a murder that hasn't been committed and accusing my husband probably didn't help my case. All his war buddies will willingly say how I've lost it, and their wives will chime in too. Look at how they've turned their backs on Vera because she questioned her sister's death. They all think she's crazy; that's what Ryan told me. You were right about them. It's like a cult. Either you're with them or you're against them. They'll have me locked up somewhere and take the kids."

Or he'll kill you and make it look like suicide.

I touch my throat, remembering that day he almost did. I am conflicted, so darn torn inside between loving him, hoping I am wrong, and wanting him to go to jail for the rest of his life, so I never have to see him again.

Frank shakes his head slowly while looking at me. "I

don't like it. I'd prefer to have you out of here, as far away as possible."

I place my hand on his arm and exhale. I force myself to sound as convincing and reassuring as possible and not let my deep anxiety shine through.

"I've got this. Trust me."

Chapter 26

THE NEXT DAY, I get the kids ready for the bus and send
them off. I kiss Isabella and wave at Damian, who doesn't
want me to kiss him in front of his friends anymore. As the
bus hisses, satisfied, and leaves, I walk back into the house
and find Ryan in uniform, drinking his coffee and eating
toast, standing by the counter. He's looking at his phone,
scrolling.

"Good morning," I say.

He stops scrolling, then leans down and kisses me.

"You smell good this morning," he says, taking a deep
breath. He smiles and touches my hair, looking at me
intently. My stomach is in knots. I feel like he can see
straight through me. I'm scared he can somehow read my
mind and see that all I'm thinking about are the things
Frank told me the day before. I keep pondering the details,
like how did he get the Fentanyl into his victims? Did they
pass out right away, or did he chat with them till they
slowly dozed off?

"So, what are you up to today?" he asks.

I shake my head. "Nothing much. I'll clean out the

bunnies' cage and maybe do some yoga. Isabella has cheer this afternoon, so I'll drive her there and bring Damian too. He usually plays around with some other kids there while she practices."

Ryan scoffs.

"What?" I ask.

He shakes his head. "Nothing. You have it easy, do you know that?"

He places a hand on my neck. It's gripping me like he's holding me, so I won't run away.

"You get to hang out at the house and then with the kids all afternoon. I hope you appreciate how good you have it."

I nod. "I do."

I try to pull away, but he's not letting me go. His grip on my neck gets tighter until he leans over and speaks close to my ear, "What we have is so precious. We don't want to ruin that, do we?"

"N-no. Of course not," I say. I wonder what he is refer-ring to. Does he know I have been meeting with Frank and talking about him? Does he know I was at the OSI? Did someone see me and tell him?

"Good, we agree then," he says. He studies me. His glare is running up and down my body like he is sizing me up. Then, he leans over and kisses my cheek and then my shoulder. "You're so delicate, so fragile."

"You're gonna be late," I say. I grab a dishtowel and start folding it, praying he won't see the goosebumps on my arms and neck.

He leans up against me.

"Maybe I'll be late today then. You don't mind, do you? It's not like you have anyone who expects you to show up, do you? You're not seeing anyone today, are you? Just like you didn't see anyone yesterday, right?"

I swallow. Does he know about my lunch with Frank and Vera? I think like crazy; I go over all my messages with Frank and wonder if he might have seen any of them. No, it can't be. I've been careful to delete everything. Every time Frank emails me or texts me, I delete it.

I stare at my phone on the counter where I left it when going to send off the kids. Did he have time to go through it? Has he found something I missed?

I scoff. "Of course not. But Chip might be pissed if you don't show up."

He laughs. "What's with the potty mouth? You never talk like that."

I laugh a fake laugh, and, as he kisses my ear, his hand finally lets go of my neck. His hands are on my breasts next, and he's moaning, pressing me up against the counter. I close my eyes and pretend to enjoy it, but I want him to leave. The thought of him touching me, his hands groping me, makes me want to scream.

"Honey?"

"Mmm."

"You're gonna be late now. Seriously."

He looks up at the clock above the window. "Shoot."

He kisses my cheek, then drinks the rest of his coffee before he rushes out the door. I smile, relieved, and wave at him, then exhale deeply as I close the door behind him, my beating heart threatening to explode.

I've got to do something, I think to myself as I wave to him, smiling eagerly, while he is driving out of the driveway.

This can't go on.

I CLEAN THE HOUSE, running the vacuum cleaner across the floor aggressively, then pick up Ryan's pants from a chair and hang them back in the closet. I'm putting his shoes away when my hand brushes against something at the bottom of his closet. I pull it out. It's his thermos bottle —the one he usually takes with him in the truck or when going for a run. I frown while I wonder what it is doing there. I also wonder if it needs to be washed, so I unscrew the lid and look inside to see if there's any liquid in it that may have grown old and gross. I wonder why it is rattling when I shake it. I peek inside.

Then, my heart stops.

There's no liquid inside it. But there is something else. I turn it upside down, and out fall at least three orange bottles of prescription pills. I pick one up and look at the label.

Painkillers.

Fentanyl.

I stare at the label, blinking to make sure I am not just seeing things. I can't breathe. I can't hear anything over the sound of my pulse pumping in my ears, and it makes me dizzy.

I rise to my feet, holding the pill bottles between my hands. I then decide to place them back inside the thermos, so the kids won't see them when they get back and take the thermos with me downstairs.

I start cooking dinner, preparing everything while planning how to deal with this properly. I know he'll be angry, but I'm done. This is it. I'm done being a victim. I need answers now. A plan has been brewing inside of me for days now, and as the afternoon progresses, I pop open a bottle of wine, then have a glass before the kids come home from school. I am very good at pretending like nothing happened, and they both grab a snack, then do their homework, and we take Isabella to cheer. Once we're back, a few hours later, Ryan isn't home yet, so I drink another two glasses while finishing dinner. When I hear his truck drive into the driveway and the garage door open, I place my phone in my pocket and turn on the Dictaphone Voice Recorder app I used to use for work. My plan is to confront him and then record his response. What I'll do with it depends on what is on it. If I find it incriminating, I'll go back to the investigator. At least, I think I will. If it's not enough, then maybe I'll just keep it and use it in case I need to fight for my children in court. No matter what, it is time to face the music.

I am done pretending.

Chapter 27

I POUR myself another glass of wine, then down it fast before putting the empty bottle away. I am washing the glass when I hear his steps in the garage, and he opens the door.

"I'm home."

I take a deep breath, then grab a mint from the drawer, so he won't smell the wine on my breath.

"Honey?"

"I'm in the kitchen," I yell back. He comes out to me, whistling happily.

"Today was a good day," he says, smiling. I turn to face him, and he sees it on my face immediately. I am not even trying to hide it.

"What's wrong?"

I grab the thermos and place it on the counter. It rattles as I put it down. "I wanted to wash this, but when I opened it, guess what I found?"

Ryan stares at the thermos. His smile is gone, so is the light in his eyes. He doesn't say anything, so I open it and pour out the pill bottles. They roll onto the granite countertop.

"Care to explain?" I ask.

He stares at me, then takes a step closer. I regret drinking all that wine since it makes it harder for me to evaluate the situation properly. I thought I needed it in order to confront him. I should have stopped earlier.

He shrugs. His eyes change as he stares at me. He gets that expression on his face, the one that makes my skin crawl.

"Do *I* care to explain? Me? You want me to explain these?" he says as he grabs a bottle and throws it at me. I duck, and it hits the stove behind me with a loud clang. "How about you explain why you're snooping around in my closet, huh? How about you explain that?"

"No," I say, staying firm. "Not this time. I'm not letting you make this about me. I asked you a question, dang it. Answer me. Why do you have these?"

He scoffs. "I was injured, remember? They gave me a medal and everything. Called me a combat-wounded war hero, remember that, do ya? Yes, they gave me pills for it, and yes, I have been taking them. I still do. I can't seem to stop, even though the pain is gone."

"Why didn't you tell me?"

"Why didn't I tell you? Are you freaking kidding me? It's not something I am particularly proud of, Laurie. It's quite simple. I didn't want you to know because I didn't want you to worry. You've had that look in your eyes for months now, and I can't seem to shake it. You act weird around me like you're afraid I might break or something."

I stare at him. Now, I'm worried. I'm very concerned that I'm mistaken. Once again, I doubt my own judgment. I shake my head. No. I can't let his words get to me. I saw him run out of Ted's house. I saw the messages to Sandra. I know he met with her. It's not just in my head.

"Okay, so tell me this," I say. "Why did you meet with Sandra right before she died? And don't say you didn't because I know you did."

"What on Earth are you babbling about now? I swear I don't know what you're saying half of the time these days," he sighs.

"You were at her house, weren't you? On the day she died. You were over there, having coffee with her, am I right?"

He pauses. He's biting his lower lip like he always does when he's pondering something serious—like when we got the news that Damian had a cleft palate and needed surgery at the age of only eight months.

But he's not talking yet. I try one more punch.

"I know you were at Ted's house too."

"Excuse me?"

"On the night he killed himself. You were there both in the afternoon and then again later. I followed you when you left our house, drunk, and I know you went inside Ted's house. When you left, I looked in through the window and found him dangling from the ceiling in his living room. Yes, that's right. I was the one who found him. I never told you about it, but it was me."

I stare at him, scrutinizing him. I can't seem to read his reaction properly. Is he regretful? Is he surprised? I can't tell.

"We…we went to the funeral and everything, and you didn't even tell me this?" he asks, again trying to make it about me, but I'm not taking the bait. He wants me to be the small one because he knows I have the upper hand now.

"You have no idea what you're talking about, Laurie. Do you hear me? I'm telling you… Back off now."

I shake my head. "It's too late. Cat's out of the bag. There's no way back now. And let me ask you this, Ryan because it has had me wondering for days now. If you went in there…if you were in Ted's house and he had already killed himself, why didn't you call the security forces? Why didn't you call for help?"

He is staring at me, his fists clenched. I can hardly hear anything over my beating heart, knocking against my ribcage. I have no idea where to go from here, what to do or say next. I wanted to confront him because I thought he'd tell me the truth. I thought he'd come clean, and we would clear everything up. It was naive, yes, but somehow, that's what I believed would happen.

Why doesn't he at least try to defend himself? Why doesn't he even plead his innocence?

But, of course, he doesn't. He doesn't say anything. Instead, he takes the wine glass I just washed into his hand and throws it against the wall with a loud growl. As the glass rains onto my kitchen floor, he turns on his heel and walks out the door, slamming it shut behind him.

<hr>

THAT NIGHT, I am alone in bed. Ryan doesn't come back, which is no surprise to me. I dream about Sandra for some reason. She's alive and waving at me from the driveway across the street. I wave back but can't understand what she's doing here, how she is not dead after all. So, I go to see her, but as I cross the street, a car hits me. And as I turn to look at who is driving it, just before it hits me, I see Ryan behind the wheel, a grin on his face.

I am sleeping so deeply that I barely hear the footsteps

as they come up the stairs and approach my bedside rapidly. I think they're a part of my dream, and they move so fast that I don't have time to realize what's happening. I don't react until a hand grabs my arm, and I am being pulled forcefully out of bed.

Startled at this, I let out a loud scream as I am being dragged across the floor before he finally lets go of me. Ryan bends down and is hovering above me now, placing his face close to mine as I sit up, trying to gather myself. He's very obviously drunk. His eyes are blank, his breath stinks, and his speech slurred.

"You think I'm a murderer, huh? You think I killed my friends? You think I killed Sandra and Ted, huh? Is that what you think?"

I don't speak. I am scared, terrified, and I don't know what to say. He is yelling at me as he says next, "How can you think that, Laurie? We love each other."

The blood is leaving my face fast. "Ryan...I..."

He has tears in his eyes. "All this...us...is it all just a lie?"

I shake my head. "N-no, Ryan."

"Because I love you. And I am fighting to get back to being the husband you deserve—to be me again. And all this time, I thought you were with me, that you were on my side, and then I realize that you...you think I'm a murderer?"

I swallow. I can't think straight.

"Is that what you think, Laurie? Is that what you think about me?"

My breathing is shuddering; I have no idea what to think or say. I feel so confused.

"Tell me, Laurie. Because that's what you were implying earlier, wasn't it? That's what I heard clearly. You think I killed them, or at least drove them to suicide, don't you? But how, Laurie? How could you possibly think that about me?"

"I don't…I don't know, I just…well, you were hiding things, and when you left Ted's house and didn't call the police, I…"

"You wanna know why I didn't call anyone?"

"Yes, please."

Ryan snorts. He is so angry that he's spitting when he talks now. I recognize that anger in his eyes from the day he tried to strangle me. He's out of control, and it scares me like nothing else. I want to cry, but I'm too afraid even to do that.

"I thought I had dreamt it," he says. "That's why. I was in a bad place, Laurie. I had been drinking. I was very drunk and out of my mind. When I woke up the next morning, I thought it was something I had dreamt about. I blacked out that night and have no idea what I had done or where I had been. I had these images in my mind of Ted, but I was so sure it had to be something I had seen in a dream because it didn't feel real. I pushed it back and didn't want to think about it anymore. That's why I didn't go to the security forces. I was too drunk, Laurie. That's all it was. Once I realized it was true that Ted was dead, I couldn't tell anyone I had seen him. I could have lost everything if they found out I was driving around drunk in my truck. Don't you see?"

I stare at him. He's crying, his mouth frothing. I don't know if I believe him. It makes sense, yes, but can I trust him?

I shake my head.

"No," I say.

"No, what?" he asks, surprised.

I push him away and get up on my feet.

"You don't believe me?" he says with a scoff.

I am standing in front of him. He can barely stand still and is swaying from side to side. "What about Sandra?" I ask.

That sets him off. I see it immediately in his eyes as a spark of fire that is lit. His jaw is clenched, his teeth gritted. He doesn't take the time to answer; instead, he pulls out his gun. He points it at me, his hands shaking.

"I thought we loved one another. I thought we trusted one another. But I guess I was wrong."

I stare into the barrel of the gun, thinking, *this is it. He's gonna pull that trigger and then end me.*

"Please," I say, trying to calm him. "Please, don't…"

I don't get to say anymore. A voice stops me. It's coming from behind Ryan.

"M-mom?"

It's Isabella. She's woken up from our yelling and is standing in the doorway right behind Ryan. Ryan is taken by surprise and reacts the way a soldier with PTSD would. He screams loudly, turns around, and fires a shot.

Isabella doesn't even realize what's happening. The bullet hits her in the stomach, and she goes down immediately. Her body tumbles to the carpet with a thud.

I scream.

"ISABELLA!"

I rush to her and take her in my arms. She's just lying there, lifeless, while blood gushes out of the wound, soaking her shirt. I lift my gaze, completely in shock, and look at Ryan. I am struggling to breathe, a scream caught in my throat. He stares down at her in complete shock as well.

"Oh, dear God. No. Please…please…" he mumbles under his breath as he approaches her. He reaches out his hand toward her.

"My...my baby…"

"Don't you dare touch her," I yell at him. "Don't you dare touch her!"

I am screaming at the top of my lungs, spitting, tears and snot running down my face. Ryan looks startled, then says, "You made me do this…if you hadn't…"

"Get away," I yell at him while holding my bleeding daughter in my arms, rocking her back and forth.

"GET AWAY FROM US!!"

Chapter 28

"I'M SORRY, but it's soon lunchtime, and then the patient needs to rest."

The nurse comes in just as Laurie wipes away a tear from her cheek after telling them about her daughter. Jonathan sends her a smile, even though he is annoyed that they're being interrupted at this very moment, just as Laurie was getting somewhere with her story.

"We'll take a break then," he says and looks at Detective Grande next to him. "Maybe go find ourselves a lunch?"

Detective Grande looks at her watch. "Sure. Why not?"

"We'll be back later in the afternoon," Jonathan says and sends Laurie a reassuring smile. He can tell she is exhausted from talking about all this, and even though he would have liked to dig in a little deeper, he's sure rest will be good for her right about now.

They leave her room and walk out into the parking lot of the hospital through the sliding doors. Detective Grande sighs deeply as they go back to the Everett Street Diner and sit down in a booth. Joanne is still there, and she still smiles at Jonathan in that way that makes him want to order more food than necessary just to get to see it again. He decides to leave her a rewarding tip afterward when they're done. Jonathan has always been a firm believer in tipping well.

"I'll have the soup of the day and the Reuben sandwich," he says.

Grande orders a salad. She sighs, annoyed, as she hands Joanne the menu.

"I take it you're not satisfied with this morning's testimony," he says and leans back in his seat.

"I feel like we're not getting anywhere," she says. "I would like to get to the point."

"She'll get to it in her own timing. Don't be in such a rush. I know you're young, and you think you're in a hurry to get somewhere, climbing the career ladder, or whatever young people dream of these days. But it'll all come, don't you worry. In due time."

"Well, I'm not sure I have that much time. I mean, she hasn't even told us what she was doing in the cabin with Frank yet."

Their drinks arrive, and Jonathan sips his Coke. Not surprisingly, Grande has ordered a club soda with her salad. Always keeping up the perfection like so many of the young girls Jonathan runs into on the job, and just like his own daughter, wasting their youth away, trying to reach what is impossible. Always in such a hurry. It's a shame. Jonathan was guilty of the very same thing in his young days, starting out at the beginning of his twenties—always rushing along, always going somewhere. Now, he is at the end of the rope, at least as far as the FBI is concerned. There is no more for him there. He's had the career he wanted, but then what? Was it worth it? He lost his marriage in the process and the relationship with his daughter that he wanted. He is trying to fix it now, but it's hard to do in retrospect. He wants to explain all that to young Grande, but he knows she will not listen. He wouldn't have when he was her age.

"So, I take it you're still suspicious about our witness?" he asks as the food arrives, and they dig in.

That's another thing that is different when you're at the end of your fifties from the beginning of your twenties—the ability to appreciate something as simple as a good meal. These days, it is worth looking forward to in ways it never was before. Jonathan used to eat whatever was within reach, eating from snack machines, or old leftovers he had forgotten in the fridge as he came home late. When he was still married, his wife would leave a plate out for him that he could heat once he got back. He never properly appreciated the gesture and wishes now he had done that. Nothing beats a good homecooked meal. Jonathan rarely gets that anymore.

"I don't know about her," Grande says, crunching her salad. "There's something that rubs me the wrong way."

"Well, it is only her side of the story we're getting, so it will, of course, be quite biased," Jonathan says and pours ketchup on his plate then dips a fry in it. The fries aren't half bad. He's had better, but he's also had worse.

"You know why we called you down here, right? Because she said she had information about a serial killer."

Jonathan nods.

"I didn't know she was just trying to incriminate her own husband," Grande continues.

"You don't think he did it?" Jonathan asks.

Grande scoffs. "It's all a little blurry, isn't it? She suspects he has killed these two people because her friend tells her they might have been killed. To me, it sounds like they committed suicide; that's all."

"The friend is, after all, a forensic investigator," Jonathan says, dipping another fry in ketchup. "I think she's telling us all this to paint a picture and to let us know all she has been through. I, for one, think she's one tough cookie..."

"But isn't this forensic guy also interested in splitting her and her husband up?" Grande says. "He's obviously in love with her."

"There are other ways," Jonathan says with a grin. "To get a woman. I don't see why he'd go to these lengths."

"But come on. The investigators don't even believe her at all."

"Because he makes it look like suicide?" Jonathan says.

"I say she's full of it," Grande says. "She's obviously crazy-paranoid."

Jonathan chuckles. "The cynicism of youth. Her daughter was shot. The man is definitely ill."

"That's true," she says, drinking pensively. "I still don't think he killed those two from his unit. Do you think he did it?"

Jonathan chews and swallows, taking his time. "I don't think I know enough to make any assumptions. And maybe whether or not he did it isn't the point. Maybe it's what they've been through. What she has been through. The fear she's been enduring, and now her daughter getting shot. It's a lot."

Grande is tapping her nails impatiently on the table. "I just wish she'd get to the point, you know? We have a dead body and still don't know exactly what happened."

Jonathan finishes his drink and food, then leans back, satisfied.

"You both done with these?" Joanne says and grabs

their plates as they nod. She's wearing red lipstick today, and it makes her look good, Jonathan thinks. "I'll bring you your checks, then."

"I think she's getting there," Jonathan says as he pays and leaves a fifty-dollar tip, wishing he could see Joanne's face when she gets it. But he prefers to be gone by then since he doesn't want her to feel awkward or feel like she needs to thank him. She's doing a great job, and he wants to reward her; that's all. And maybe see one of her smiles next time he comes in. He'd really like that.

They get up, grab their phones, and leave. The bell on the door rings as they walk outside into the cold mountain air. He takes a deep breath, then sighs, looking at Grande.

"I also have a feeling we'll be quite surprised at the conclusion once we get there. We think we have it all figured out by now, but I bet we don't even have a clue."

Part III

Chapter 29

WHEN THEY GET out of their cars and walk into the hospital, full from a rock-solid lunch, Detective Grande gets a call. She picks it up.

"Talk to me."

Jonathan lifts his eyebrows at this. No *hello* or any other greeting. Just *talk to me*. Right from the get-go. They walk into the elevator, and Jonathan presses the button. Grande is very quiet as they travel up to the third floor, and the doors open. All he hears from her are small grunts of confirmation to let the person on the other end know she's still listening.

They walk down the hallway, and Jonathan greets a couple of nurses he recognizes from earlier. They smile warmly, and he compliments one on her hair, another on her necklace, a third on her smile. Grande walks by all of them, barely noticing anyone, phone pressed against her ear.

As he is about to open the door to Laurie's room, she grabs him by the shoulder and stops him. He turns to look at her. She has hung up and is putting the phone away. He smiles, happy to have her attention.

"When we get in there, let me do the talking to start. There has been a new development."

Jonathan sends her another smile. "Oh, you mean because they found another body?"

She stares at him, startled.

"How did you know?"

He shrugs. "Call it a hunch. I had a feeling we might find more than one."

She gives him a strange look, then opens the door and bursts inside. Laurie's face lights up when she sees them like she has been expecting them. Jonathan likes her. She seems like the type of woman he might date if he was fifteen years younger and not still hung up on his ex-wife. Laurie has that quality about her of being just a genuinely good girl, one that might get herself in trouble, but always does everything out of a good and decent heart. The kind of woman who'd do anything to protect her children.

Grande doesn't seem to see what he sees, and she stands by her bedside, looking angry. Jonathan sneaks inside and sits down, waiting to see what Grande wants to do next.

"Laurie," she says, making her voice deeper than usual.

Laurie's smile freezes. She can tell something is wrong. She bends her head slightly. "They found him, didn't they?"

"In the river, yes. This means we now have two dead bodies and only one survivor, you."

The fact that she doesn't try to avoid this confrontation makes Grande ease up on her slightly. Her shoulders come down, and she pauses, leaving room for Laurie to explain. Laurie exhales deeply, and tears spring to her eyes.

"I was going to tell you about him," she says. "But I

wanted to tell the story first. It's important you get the entire story. I want to make sure you understand the background for all that happened. I promise you; I was going to tell you about him."

Detective Grande lifts both her eyebrows. Jonathan nods calmly. Grande sends him a look of impatience, and he mimics for her to calm down. He reaches over and squeezes Laurie's hand lightly.

"We have all the time in the world, sweetheart. We appreciate you telling us everything, Laurie; we truly do. Take your time. We know it can't be easy."

AFTER ISABELLA IS SHOT, everything is a little blurry to me. I walk around in a haze I can't escape. I spend night after night and day after day in the hospital. I have no idea how long I'm there, and if you ask me to tell you what the doctors tell me at this point, I won't be able to recollect it. There are so many faces, so many words, and so much fear in those days; I can hardly believe I survived it.

Isabella has suffered a gunshot wound to her abdomen, and it came dangerously close to her vital organs. She goes through so much surgery you wouldn't think a young girl could possibly endure it. Every day, it's something new—a fracture here, a piece of bone there. It is like her body has completely shattered. She is breathing through a tube; she's unable to talk and communicates with us through blinking. Yes, it sounds crazy, but that is all we have. I am being told so many things; I hardly know what to believe. One day, they say she'll never walk again, the next that she will walk but not be able to utilize her hands. But then she suddenly starts moving both legs and arms, and soon she is sitting up in the bed. After more surgeries, she's slowly getting better, even though we're told she'll need physical therapy afterward to learn how to walk properly, and until then, she'll need crutches. I am struggling to keep it together and sleep most nights in her room, while Damian stays at my parents' place. They make sure he gets to school every day and then bring him out to me in the afternoon, where we hang out by Isabella's side, just praying for her full recovery and reminding ourselves how blessed we are to still have her here with us.

Our prayers are answered as we are able to take her home with us a month later. I take her to my parents' place, and we stay there for a few days until it finally gets too small for all of us, and I rent an apartment in the condominium building next door. This way, the kids can hang out with their grandparents as much as they want to, but we won't have to get on each other's nerves. The apartment is expensive, and I don't know how long I can continue to pay for it, but my parents have given me money to help me out for now. They don't want me to worry about getting a job at this point when things are still so new, and Isabella still needs my care.

I haven't heard anything from Ryan while all this has been going on. After the incident, he was arrested by the SPs, and he told them it was an accident, which I couldn't tell them wasn't true. The incident is still under investigation, and he has been released for now. Meanwhile, he has promised to get therapy and to stay away from us. I have gotten a protective order out on him, just in case, so he can't come near any of us, which makes me feel slightly safer. My biggest concern is him showing up, demanding to see us, trying to get us to come back home. I fear he might be able to persuade us, and then we're back in that prison it was living with him, always worried we might anger him or trigger his anxiety somehow. I still wake up, bathed in sweat at night, and I dream about him shooting Isabella most nights, but I also often dream about him crying and telling me he never meant for it to happen. I am filled with guilt during the day, wondering why I didn't move away earlier before things got so bad but also fighting this feeling deep inside me that I somehow pushed him this far. That if I hadn't started asking him all these questions, accusing him, he wouldn't have pulled the gun.

Frank and Vera both tell me I can't think like that, that something like this would probably have happened anyway; it was just a matter of time—that every day, women are killed by their abusive spouses, that I was lucky no one died. And they're right, I guess. No matter what, I couldn't keep living like that, continually fearing my own husband. The good part is, I can now see them both as much as I want to. No one can stop me, no one can tell me not to, and no one can get jealous. Vera doesn't have much time since she is still in training, but I am seeing Frank almost every day. He stops by, bringing flowers or things he believes we might need, like milk or eggs or maybe a vase. He uses it as an excuse; I know he just wants to see me, and I let him. I accept his gifts and tell him he's a lifesaver, that I just needed this. He de-clogs my shower drain for me and fixes my doorbell, and he puts up smoke detectors all over the condo, even though the owner has already put some up. Frank doesn't believe it is enough. He wants to make sure we are safe. We spend a lot of time drinking coffee and talking about everything and sometimes nothing at all, and it feels good. After a few more weeks like this, I can't keep it at bay any longer.

We're sitting in the living room of the condo, over-looking the ocean beneath us, when he leans over and kisses me. I don't protest; I don't push him away. I enjoy feeling his lips against mine. I enjoy hearing his heartbeat next to mine. I don't know whether I am in love with him or not; it's too early to tell, and I am pretty broken at this point. All I know is that I enjoy being with him, and I like that he likes me.

But as soon as his lips part from mine, I can't help feeling a pang of guilt. I am, after all, still married to Ryan, and I feel like I just cheated on him. I turn away from Frank. He sees it and gets worried.

"I'm sorry," he says. "Was that not okay?"

I look at him, my heart bleeding.

Here I am with the sweetest guy, who is totally into me. And I can't even kiss him without feeling bad about it. What is wrong with me?

"Oh, no, it was. It's just…it's been so long, and I am technically still married."

"But you'll be getting a divorce, right?" he asks.

I look down at my ring. I am still wearing it, and I don't know why. I nod. "In time, yes. I just can't…not yet."

He smiles, but it doesn't seem genuine. "Okay. I'll wait as long as it takes."

I grab his hand in mine, feeling relieved.

"Thank you. That is all I can hope for. You're such an angel."

Chapter 30

OUR HEALTH INSURANCE is still through Ryan and his work, and Isabella's physical therapy is taking place on the base, so I go there every day with her. I drive through the gates like I used to and show them my ID at the guard-house, but now it fills me with such dread and fear. I am so scared of bumping into Ryan or any of his war buddies.

One of the days, it was a Monday, I think, while Isabella was going through her physical therapy, I drive down to our old house and pack a bag of things. I don't know if Ryan has been back there at all, but I have a feeling he hasn't. I walk upstairs, my heart pounding when remembering what happened on that awful night. I stop and look at the blood on the carpet, then try to calm myself just enough to focus on why I am there. I promised Isabella I'd get her iPad and Damian's Nintendo Switch. I also pack some more clothes for all of us and some makeup I have missed terribly and my favorite yoga outfit.

I pass the blood once again on my way back out, then stop. I can still hear my own screams as I hold her in my arms. The thought quickens my pulse, and I am barely breathing. I feel dizzy, and I can't hold back my tears anymore. Since I am alone, I allow myself to cry. Tears gush down my cheeks, as I, for the first time, allow myself to think about what happened.

I wipe my tears away, then walk down the stairs and look around. I have a feeling I'm never coming back unless it's to grab more stuff. At some point, I have to get a truck and move everything I want to keep. It's not much. Everything in there reminds me of Ryan and my life with him. And I want to forget. I don't want to be reminded that I ever loved him. I never want to live here again, I realize. I am done with this place.

I rush out the door, slamming it shut behind me, then walk to my minivan, put my bag in the back and drive off. I am relieved that I haven't seen Ryan at the house. I have been thinking about it all weekend, worried he might be there. But it doesn't look like he has been in there at all since the incident.

I wonder for a second where he is staying, and, like an old habit, I worry about him. I worry he's drinking too much and that he has sunken into that deep darkness that has threatened to swallow him for so long. I worry he won't be able to pull himself out of it this time.

I also think about Sandra and Ted and the pills I found in his thermos. I have talked with Frank about this a lot, but we haven't exactly decided what to do with this knowledge. I have thought about going to the police outside of the base. But what I have isn't enough. Not even close.

I park in front of the medical center and walk across the parking lot toward the front door when I suddenly see something that makes my blood run cold.

Ryan's black truck.

It is parked close to the entrance, and there is no one

inside. I lift my glance and look at the building, my heart throbbing.

Isabella!

Panic-stricken, I start running and push open the door. I rush down the hallway, panting and agitated, my heart pounding in my chest.

Ryan is here? He is here, close to Isabella? And I'm not there to protect her? How could I have let my guard down like this? How could I have let this happen?

When I walk inside the room where the doctor is working with Isabella, I see him. He's sitting on a bench, looking directly at her. My heart is beating so fast; it makes me feel sick. I hurry to her, and the doctor smiles as she sees me.

"She's been making real progress today," she says. "I am so proud of her."

"How long has that man been here?" I ask. I can hear the desperation in my own voice, even though I am trying to suppress it. "The one sitting on the bench?"

She looks over toward the benches, where relatives can sit and look in on the training. It's where I usually sit and wait. There are maybe ten other people in the middle of their training right now. All of them are soldiers who have been wounded in combat.

"Who are we talking about?" she asks.

I turn to look, but now Ryan is gone. Of course, he is.

I breathe again, yet I can't escape the eerie feeling that he is still here somewhere. Is he still watching us?

I turn around to look, but I don't see a trace of him.

"Who was it, Mom?" Isabella asks.

I look into her eyes. I don't know what to tell her. I don't want her to worry. We haven't spoken much about what happened yet, or how she feels about her father. She hasn't wanted to, and every time I try, she walks away from me, angry. I sense she's struggling with accepting it as anything but an accident. And rightfully so. It was an accident. Ryan didn't want to hurt her. It was me he was after.

"No one, sweetie," I say, smiling, pushing my anxiety back. I don't want my daughter to see how concerned I am, even though I know she can detect it just by the small shiver in my voice.

"You're making amazing progress, huh? That's wonderful."

ONCE WE'RE HOME, I call the local Dundee Beach Police Department and speak with an officer on duty. I tell him my situation, how I have a protective order, and now Ryan has shown up. I want to know what to do if he shows up where we live or if he approaches us somewhere. The officer tells me the protective order I have is issued by a commanding officer on base, and they can't enforce it outside the walls of the base. I'll need a separate restraining order, issued by the state court. But it will be nearly impossible to serve the order to him, he adds since local law enforcement does not have the authority to serve documents on military installations. It'll have to be done at a time he's off base.

I hang up, realizing Ryan probably knows this. This means he can get to us out here without getting in trouble —at least until I get the restraining order against him. I wonder how he knew we were there today. I'm guessing one of his friends alerted him; maybe they have even told him we go there every day. He might even have come several times; I just never saw him. He could have watched us from outside the windows or watched us from somewhere else. I suddenly feel very unsafe and afraid.

I have promised myself not to, but I do it anyway. I open the app I have always used to track my family members. It doesn't always work to perfection, but I can usually see where they are within a certain radius—enough to guess and give me a picture of where they are and what they are doing. I used to use it a lot for Isabella when she'd leave the base with her friends and sometimes spend the night with someone in town. I have also used it to track Ryan when he was gone for days. I would see him go to bars downtown, and sometimes it would tell me he was at the beach, and I assumed he was down there sleeping because he didn't know where else to go.

I look at it, and then my heart freezes. I see his small icon, with a little picture of him inside it, an old one we took one day when goofing around, taking silly pictures of one another. It was from about a year ago before he left for deployment.

A lifetime ago.

I see he is moving. But I also see something else that terrifies me to the core.

He's off base and not very far from us, moving closer at a steady pace.

Chapter 31

I STARE at the small icon, worrying that he has somehow found out where we are and that now he's coming for us. I stare at it, and I see him come closer and closer still. I tell myself there is no way he can know where I am since only my parents and close friends know I have moved into this apartment.

After a little while, the icon stops moving. Ryan has stopped somewhere. I stare at it for a very long time, making completely sure he's not suddenly moving closer. Sometimes, the app is slow to react, and it is delayed. I also briefly fear he has found out I am tracking him via this and maybe shut it off. But no. That can't be it. Then the icon would disappear completely. He truly has stopped, and the icon isn't moving at all.

I breathe, relieved, and lean back on my couch, trying to calm my throbbing heart. I stare at Damian, who is sitting by the window, doing his homework. Isabella is in her room, resting, I hope. Physical therapy takes a toll on her body, but I am so glad she's making progress.

"Mom, I don't get this one," Damian says and shows me a math problem.

"Let me take a look," I say, putting down the phone and my obsession.

I help him solve it, even though my math skills are almost nonexistent. I can still do first-grade math. It's worse when Isabella asks me about algebra since I am at a total loss there. Her school has signed her up for virtual school, so she can try to catch up on some classes and hopefully pass her grade, even though she has missed more than a month. Luckily, Isabella is a bright girl, and she is also a hard worker. If anyone can do this, it's her. I just worry it is too hard on her, that it's too much with everything else she's going through. She must be struggling more than she tells me. Being shot by your father must make some scars on the soul. I only pray that she'll get out of this all right.

"I'm done," Damian says and packs up his stuff, then runs to his room to play. I have placed the Nintendo Switch on his bed and hear him scream victoriously when he sees it. He yells, "Thanks, Mom," through the door.

I open the app again on my phone and see that Ryan still hasn't moved. I keep staring at it, wondering what he is up to now. If he isn't coming for us, then what on Earth is he doing? I stare at the address and realize it's a house on the corner of A1A. I wrinkle my forehead when I realize I know this address. I have been there to visit someone.

A pilot from Ryan's unit, Duke Marchant, lives there. He's one of the few that lives off base.

Ryan is probably just visiting his friend. He's not on his way here. You're fine. He doesn't even know where you live. You're safe.

Still, I can't stop staring at the icon and the address, wondering what he is up to now. Duke was not one of his favorite people while they were deployed. As a matter of fact, I remember Ryan often telling me how much he *couldn't stand the guy*. The one time we went to visit him was because he had invited all of the unit to a barbecue, but Ryan had a ton of excuses for us not to go.

"I don't want to," he kept saying. "I hate the guy, okay?"

We went anyway, and Ryan spent all night talking to everyone other than Duke, avoiding him at all cost.

Why is he suddenly visiting him?

Has he run out of places to crash?

I shake my head. No, not Ryan. He always had so many friends offering their guest bedroom or couch for him to sleep on when he was too drunk and didn't want to come home to me, or after he left, after the time he almost strangled me. I know they all offered to take him in. They stay together like that—take care of their own.

"Why are you there, Ryan?" I ask like I expect the app to answer me. "What are you up to?"

Finally, I can't stand it anymore. I am worried. I have this deep unnerving sensation inside my stomach that I can't escape. I call my mom and ask her to come to look after the children. I have put them to bed, so they won't cause any trouble. When she asks me where I'm going, I tell her I'm meeting up with a friend for a drink. She buys it and comes over, and I rush out the door, bringing my purse with the gun that I bought after Isabella got hurt. I have spent many afternoons at a shooting range lately, learning how to shoot and not miss.

I DRIVE TO THE ADDRESS, and there's a truck parked in the driveway. I park by the house across the street, hoping not to be seen. I can't see if it is Ryan's truck since I'm not close enough, and it's dark out. But I assume it is his. I check the app, but can't see the icon anymore. It has suddenly completely vanished like he has realized I was tracking him and shut it off. It could also be that his phone ran out of battery. That would have the same effect. Concerned about this, I look at the house. I am about to leave, thinking I should get back to the kids in case that's where Ryan is heading next. I need to be with them if he shows up.

But then I see someone moving inside the house. The light is turned on in the living room, and I can see someone in there. I can't see who it is, though. The shadow moves across the floor, first leaving, then returning into my field of sight. I stare at him, wondering if it is Ryan or maybe Duke. They're similar in stature, seen from afar. I am certain it looks like Ryan. Is he still there? Is it his black truck in the driveway? It could be, but I'm not sure. I wonder if I should get out of my minivan and get up close to see if it has the stickers in the back or to read the license plate.

But I don't dare. I fear Ryan might come out of the house and see me. I wouldn't know how to explain myself out of that one. I don't want to have to.

I keep staring at the shadow moving around inside the house when I realize something is off. Something is very much off. This person is lifting another person and dragging his lifeless body across the floor.

Chapter 32

WHAT IS it exactly I am witnessing here? Is it a buddy helping another buddy who is too drunk to walk and get to bed on his own? Or is it something else? Is it something so terrible I don't even want to finish the thought?

I have a deep feeling of dread inside me, and I can't leave this alone. I have to know what it is. I get out of the minivan and walk up to the house, gun clenched in my hand. I look through the window, hoping he won't see me, and I watch as the body is dragged toward the stairs. I can't see the face of the one dragging him. There are no empty bottles on the floor or scattered across the countertops, nothing to indicate this person—whom I can now see is Duke—has been drinking heavily.

He's being dragged to the stairs and now upward. I think about Sandra and the water she was in, and I can feel her coldness as my finger touched her skin while feeling for a pulse. I shiver as a chill runs down my spine. Panic starts to rumble in the pit of my stomach.

If you had a chance to save Sandra, you would have. This is your chance.

I see Duke disappear up the stairs, his legs bumping against each and every step. Then, I walk to the door and grab the handle. It is open, and I walk inside as quietly as possible, heart hammering in my chest. I try to control my breath, to keep it as calm as possible, given the situation.

I walk to the stairs, gun clenched in my hand and lifted in front of me. The first step creaks, but it's not loud, so I continue. I can hear the water from the bathroom upstairs as it is being turned on.

I can't escape the images of Sandra in the tub as I continue upward, my hands shaking terribly, wondering what I am about to see up there. I worry if I have what it takes or if I'll freeze. I'm not a trained soldier; I'm not even a police officer. I'm just an ex-reporter turned housewife, who has taken a few lessons in shooting.

If it is Ryan is in there, will I be able to pull the trigger? Will I be able to shoot my own husband? The father of my children?

I don't want to think about it. I have to move on; I have to keep going. I was too late for Sandra. I was too late for Ted. I can't miss this one too.

I walk as cautiously as possible, trying not to make a sound, then walk to the bathroom door that is left ajar and look in through the crack. I am breathing heavily now and barely able to hear anything over the sound of my beating heart. I can hear the water, though, and I can see Duke as he is plunged into it. Then a pair of hands grab his wrists, and a knife is placed on the skin.

That's when I make my decision. I can't wait anymore. I push the door open forcefully and hold the gun out in front of me. But the man is gone, and I can't see him. Duke is still in the water, and before I can react, a gloved hand reaches out from behind the door and grabs the gun. My hand is pulled forcefully sideways and slammed against the door until I drop the gun. Then, he lunges at me, grabbing me by the tops of my arms. I am wrestled to the floor. My head hits the tiles and is pressed down, the weight of this person heavily on top of me, a knee in my back. He grabs my hair and pulls my head backward, then smashes it into the tiles one, two, three times, so hard I can see nothing but flickering stars. I taste blood in my mouth right before I black out.

WHEN I WAKE UP, he is gone. I'm not where I am supposed to be either. I'm sitting in my minivan, slumped over the steering wheel. My head is pounding, and I can barely lift it. I sit back, trying to remember what happened. I then open my eyes and touch my face. I look at myself in the rearview mirror and see my bloody face. The blood has been smeared all across the steering wheel as well. It looks like it has come from my nose. It is swollen and painful. I have a cracked lip as well, and my head feels heavy but other than that, I seem fine. I suddenly remember what happened and turn to look at the house across the street. There are police officers there and ambulances. The black truck is gone.

Duke!

I see him as he is being rolled out on a stretcher and into the ambulance. My heart drops at the sight.

I messed it all up. Instead of saving him, I messed it up.

I stare at the two-story house, wondering if I should go over there and tell them I was there, that I saw someone in there. But then my phone makes a sound in my purse, and I pick it up.

I WOULDN'T DO THAT IF I WERE YOU

A frown grows between my eyes as I read the text. The

sender is not a number I know. I write back: WHO IS THIS?

THEY'LL FIND YOUR BLOOD IN THERE AND YOUR FINGERPRINTS ON THE DOOR.

I read the text over and over again, wondering if this is the killer…if this is the guy who knocked me down. It has to be, right? How else would he know these details?

WHO ARE YOU?

He doesn't answer me, and I can't seem to make up my mind. Should I go over there and tell the police what I saw, what I know? Will they believe me? Or will it look like I am the guilty one? Is this person right? I grab the phone, then call the number, but he doesn't answer. My hands are shaking in frustration and confusion as I try again. No answer. No voicemail. Nothing.

I text him again.

IS IT YOU, RYAN? IS IT? ANSWER ME! I AM GONNA TELL THEM EVERYTHING!

I sit still, my heart beating fast, waiting for him to answer. An officer has had his eye on me for a little while, and now he starts to move toward me. I'm freaking out. I'm terrified he's gonna ask me questions, so I start up the engine, then wait.

Another sound comes from my phone. It's him again.

IF YOU TALK TO THE POLICE, I'LL COME FOR YOU AND THE KIDS!

I look at the words, my hands shaking. The officer is close now, and I can tell he wants to talk to me. I don't even think about it. I push the accelerator down and roar past him, praying it's too dark for him to see my plates.

Chapter 33

I SNEAK back into the condo. My mom is sleeping on the couch, snoring lightly. I am relieved to find that everything seems calm. I hurry to the bathroom, then wash off all the blood, my heart still racing in my chest. On my way back, I circled the neighborhood a few times, just to make sure no one followed me. I have seen it in movies and thought it was a good idea.

The blood comes off, but my nose is still big and swollen, and my lip is double its normal size. I don't know how I am going to explain this to my mother when I wake her up and tell her to go home, but then I realize it's past midnight, and it's too late for her to walk home anyway. I decide to let her sleep and put a blanket on top of her, then walk to the front door and check the locks are properly locked a second and a third time. I go to the kitchen and find the ibuprofen and take two to get rid of the excruciating pain in my head. I then go to the kids' room and check on them both. The condo is only two bedrooms, so they have to share, which they are not all too happy about, especially not Isabella. Her crutches are leaning on her bed, ready for when she needs them. Soon, she won't need them as much anymore, I hope, as she is making great progress—at least physically. Mentally, I fear it's an entirely different story.

I sigh and go back to my own room, where I turn out the lights and go to sleep. I get at least two or maybe three hours before I wake up bathed in sweat. I am certain I heard a sound and jump out of bed, heart knocking against my ribcage. I don't have my gun anymore since Ryan took it when he attacked me in Duke's bathroom. I have no way of protecting us if he is coming for us now.

I stand next to the bed, listening, but the noise is gone now. I calm myself by trying to breathe properly. I sit on the bed, my legs shaking, and then I bend my head and hide my face between my hands while I cry.

I CALL Frank the next day, and he comes over on his lunch break. When I open the door, he gasps.

"What on Earth happened to your face?"

"I'll tell you everything. Come in."

He is still staring at me like he isn't even quite sure it is me. My face does look awful. My nose is so swollen, it fills half my face, and it makes my eyes look narrow, not to mention my lip. On top of it all, I am in deep pain. My head is pounding despite the pills I have taken, and the light from outside bothers me, so I keep the curtains closed.

"How did the kids react when seeing you like this?" he asks.

"I had my mom take care of them and drive Damian to school and take Isabella to her physical therapy. My mom has begged me to take her for days because she wants to be there for her and see how well she is doing. I didn't tell her what happened. I don't want her to be sad or worried about me. I told her I had too much to drink and that I couldn't get out of bed, speaking through the door, so she wouldn't see me. I'll have to deal with the kids later since they will see this at some point. I just couldn't deal with it all this morning. I needed time to figure out what to tell them."

"Can I get you some water? Or coffee?" he asks.

I nod. Frank is always so nice to me. "Coffee would be great, thanks."

He pours me a cup and one for himself, and we sit down. I swallow another pill to subdue the pain, then sip my coffee.

Frank sighs. I can tell he is upset. Seeing me like this makes him concerned; of course, it does.

"I take it Ryan did this to you?" he asks. His nostrils are flaring lightly, and I can tell he is getting himself worked up.

I nod and look into my cup. "I mean, I didn't see his face. It all happened too fast, but I am pretty sure it was him. He knocked my face into the tiles when I tried to stop him from killing another guy from his unit."

Frank almost choked on his coffee. "There was another one?"

I nod. "This time, I actually saw it happen. I saw him drag the guy up the stairs and prepare him in the tub. I even saw the knife being placed on his wrist. There's no doubt anymore. He's killing his way through the unit, getting rid of these people for some reason."

"I take it you told everything to the police?" Frank asks.

I try to avoid his eyes.

"You didn't talk to the police?" he asks. "Why the heck not?"

"I was knocked out, and I woke up in my car, blood

smeared everywhere. The police will find my blood and fingerprints all over the place. I didn't wear gloves, but he did. I can still feel them from when he touched me. And then…well, there was this."

I pick up my phone and show him the texts.

"He threatened the kids. I couldn't risk it, Frank; you have to understand. I simply couldn't."

"Hey. Hey, take it easy," Frank says and grabs my hand in his. "No one is blaming you for anything, okay? You want to protect your kids, of course, you do. It's just that… well, if you don't speak up soon, then he'll get away with this. And since he knows that you know what he is up to, he might come after you anyway. He knows that you have identified him. I say you need to get the police all over him right now."

I sigh and lean back, grabbing my forehead, closing my eyes briefly because it hurts so badly. I realize Frank is right. I'm in trouble either way. It's only a matter of when.

"The police will probably come for me soon anyway," I say and fiddle with my cup.

"How so?"

"First of all, I'm pretty sure they saw me drive away from there and probably also got my license plate. Second, I was the one who called nine-one-one. Before I went into the house, I called and told them someone was about to be murdered, then gave them the address, and hung up. I just couldn't wait for them to arrive; I was scared they'd be too late. I had my gun. I thought I'd be able to defend myself. But he must have heard me on the stairs or maybe when I was by the door. Boy, he moved fast."

"Plus, you wanted to be sure it was Ryan, am I right?" Frank asks. "A highly skilled soldier with PTSD who can kill you with his bare hands. Didn't you think about that at all? You completely disregarded your own safety to play a silly Miss Marple or whatever their names are."

"If I am anyone, it's Hercule Poirot," I say, trying to lighten the mood. "Annoying and stubborn."

Frank laughs, but he isn't happy. He's mad at me for not taking better care of myself. I can't blame him. I would be mad at me too.

Chapter 34

FRANK DOESN'T GO BACK to work. He stays with me, and we order a pizza for lunch, then eat together. I also order a smoothie since I can't really chew much with my lip, so I stay mostly on a liquid diet. After finishing up, Frank makes a couple of phone calls while I clean the kitchen from this morning. I feel overwhelmed as I put the bowls in the dishwasher. I am not just in physical pain. I feel broken inside and can't wrap myself around the fact that my husband isn't the man I once knew. Not only has he changed drastically, but he's become a murderer like the ones you read about in novels or watch on TV. It's hard for me to believe that a man could change this much. Especially Ryan. But you hear the stories, right? How some women refused to see their spouses for what they really were, even some who were married to serial killers. Or stories about those who live in an abusive relationship who continuously makes excuses for them, even when they isolate them from the world and hurt them. I don't want to end up like one of those numbers in the statistics who were killed by their husbands because they refused to see the signs. I really don't.

Still, it is hard for me to believe it.

Look at Isabella. He shot her! Look at your face. Isn't that proof enough? How much more do you need?

I shake my head as Frank returns from the balcony, holding his phone in his hand. He closes the sliding doors behind him, shutting out the soothing sound of the waves. It's getting hotter out now, and the AC can barely keep up inside. I haven't been out there all day since the bright sunlight hurts my head.

"Okay, so I spoke to the ME's office on the mainland," he says, looking at me pensively. "I have a colleague who works there. He told me something interesting. He said they never received Duke Marchant's body."

I want to grimace, but my face is in too much pain, so I sit on a dining chair instead and look up at him. The place was furnished when I rented it. I don't care much for the flowers on the back of the chairs, but who am I to complain, right? I'm just glad to have a place to stay—a place that hopefully remains safe for the kids and me.

"What does that mean?"

"That he didn't die," Frank says and sits down across from me. "I then called the hospital, and a nurse told me they have him in the ICU. His wrists were cut, and he lost a lot of blood."

I stare at him, barely blinking. "So…what you're saying is…he's alive? He didn't die? I was so certain…I guess I just assumed he did because the paramedics didn't look like they were rushing, but I could have misinterpreted that. Ha. So that means…he can talk to the police, right? He can help them get to Ryan?"

Frank places the phone on the dining table, then gives me a look. His shoulders sag a little. "Hardly. At least not yet. He is not responsive. He hasn't woken up yet, and they are not sure he will."

"Oh."

Frank grabs my hand in his and looks down at it. "But it does mean you saved his life. If you hadn't called the cops or even disturbed Ryan when he tried to kill him, he probably wouldn't be alive."

"Dang it," I say and bite my lip.

"I know you were hoping that this guy, Duke, could talk to the police about Ryan for you, but I am afraid it won't be the case. You're not off the hook, Laurie. I still think you should go to them and tell them that you were there."

I shake my head, feeling distressed.

"No."

"Why not, Laurie?" Frank asks, getting impatient with me. I can hear his breathing, quick and shallow.

"Because he will come for the kids," I say. "And me. It'll put us all in danger. I can't do that. I'm not doing it. End of story."

WHEN HE LEAVES, I sit back alone behind heavily locked doors and wonder what to do next. A big part of me is happy that Duke is still alive; of course, I am thrilled. I feel like I have finally had a win over Ryan. But the rest of me is in deep pain. Not just because of my face and the possible concussion I am suffering from, but because I know that Frank is right. For the relatives of the people Ryan has killed to get closure, I have to help them. If we're to stop Ryan from killing more people, I have to be the one to step up and speak up.

The door buzzes, and I press the intercom. It's my mom.

"I'm bringing the kids back," she says. "They can walk up on their own, right? I need to get home. Your dad hasn't seen me since yesterday, and I have to get him to his doctor's appointment at four."

"Of course, Mom. Thank you so much for all your help."

"No problem, sweetie. The kids were both wonderful."

I hear her giving them kisses when I buzz the door open and let them in. I wait by the door, feeling anxious because I have to tell them what happened. When I hear the elevator ding, I open the door to greet them. They both stare at me like I am a ghost.

"What happened to you?" Isabella asks, humping along on her crutches. She seems almost angry at me.

I stare at her. I have been going over this in my mind all day, what to say, how to tell them that their dad did this to me, but when I look into their faces, I can't get myself to do it. So, I come up with a lie.

"I fell down the stairs, clumsy, huh?"

Damian looks up at me, mouth gaping. "Were you running? Because Grandma always tells me not to run on the stairs."

"Yes, sweetie, I was," I say. "I was in a hurry, and so I fell."

I bend down so Damian can touch my lip. He smiles as he runs a finger across it. He touches some of the dried-up blood that I haven't been able to wash off, then says:

"Cool."

Damian takes off to play with his toys, satisfied with my little story, while Isabella still looks at me like she doesn't buy a word of it. I close the door behind me and lock both locks, then shake it several times to make sure it is actually locked. I turn around and find myself face-to-face with my daughter. She lifts her eyebrows.

"Fell on the stairs, huh? If you want me to buy that, you'll have to at least say you were drunk."

With those words, she turns around and leans on her crutches into the bedroom and closes the door. I feel heavy-hearted. I don't like having to lie to them, but I guess I did it because I felt it was necessary. Right now, I just can't deal with more broken hearts. I know more are bound to come once their dad is put in jail, but right now, I hope to have just bought us a little time.

Chapter 35

I SIT in my car for a few minutes, finding strength. The gray two-story house in front of me looks like it is accusing me of something. I'm scared of what I'm about to do, but I feel this is the only way. It is Saturday, and I have left Damian with his grandparents. My parents wanted to take them both to the beach, but Isabella didn't want to go since it is hard to walk on crutches in the sand, and she has a lot of homework to catch up on. She is determined to pass her grade even if it means she has to do work every day, also on weekends, in order to do so. So, I have allowed her to stay at the condo alone for a few hours while I do this.

Meanwhile, I have been speculating like crazy over the past few days about what to do. I know I can't just do nothing and pretend like I don't know what my husband has been doing. I can't go to the police since he has threatened to come after the kids and me if I do. So, I don't dare to do that. But there is something else I can do, and now I am sitting in my minivan, parked on a street on base. Technically, I still live in my house further down the street, which I passed on my way here. That way, I still get to keep my ID card and still have access to the base. It was no problem getting past the guards at the gate. I drove up there and passed the card out the window. Active duty military cards are called CAC cards and have microchips in them. Mine is civilian and has a barcode on the back. A guard at the gate uses a handheld scanner to check it before I drive onto the base. Being here again doesn't make me feel very good. Passing my old house made me feel sick, to be honest.

You can do it, Laurie.

I take a deep breath and decide now is as good a time as any. I get out of the comfort of my car, then walk up toward the house. I check the driveway to make sure Ryan's truck isn't there. I've been trying to track him via the app the past few days, but he must have turned the location tracking off or deleted the app because his icon is gone. This means I have no way of finding out where he is or what he is doing. It scares me.

I ring the doorbell, then wait.

I touch my nose gently. It isn't swollen anymore, and neither is my lip. I still have a crack in it, and my nose is still sore like crazy, but I no longer look like a monster, which pleases me.

The door opens, and a face appears. My heart drops for a second as I prepare myself for facing this woman again.

"Laurie?"

I smile, trying to seem genuinely happy to see her. "Hello, Lotty."

"W-what brings you here? We haven't seen you in forever."

"I would like to speak to your husband, actually. Is he here?"

She nods. "Yes. Yes, of course. Come on in."

She steps aside and lets me in, then closes the door behind me. I can tell she is puzzled and slightly uncomfortable about me being here, but I choose to ignore it. She smiles; it comes off as awkward and forced.

"He's in the backyard, mowing the lawn. I'll get him for you."

I follow her out to the back patio. Their backyard is fenced in, unlike most of the houses on base. Base housing is managed by a private company, and they run things pretty much the same as most rental property management companies, including taking care of your lawn—except when you have a fenced-in backyard like Chip and Lotty do. Then, you have to mow it yourself.

The sound of the mowing tractor that Chip is riding drowns out everything else, and he doesn't see Lotty till she is up close. I can hear her yell, and Chip finally stops the machine. They talk, and she points in my direction. Chip gets off the machine, then walks toward me.

"Laurie?" he says as he approaches me.

I smile and nod. There's an uncomfortable silence. I know they're waiting for me to say something, but the words don't come yet.

"I'll get us some iced tea," Lotty says and disappears inside.

WE SIT down on the soft patio furniture. Chip is sweaty, and his forehead is glistening. He wipes it off on a towel, then grunts tiredly. His wife returns with a tray between her hands. She smiles nervously and serves me a glass of iced tea. I take it and drink.

"How have you been, Laurie?" Chip asks after

downing an entire glass for himself. He is crunching the ice while he speaks.

"Yeah, how have you been?" Lotty says. She sits with her hands in her lap. "It's been a while. How are the kids; are they okay?"

I nod. "They're okay, given the circumstances."

Lotty nods, looking down. "Of course. They must miss their dad."

I scoff. "Of course, they do. But he's not himself. And that is actually why I have come."

"Oh," Lotty exclaims, then shifts in her seat.

I focus on Chip. He's the guy I need to tell this to. He's the guy who should know. I put my glass down. Chip grabs a small silver case he always carries in his pocket and pulls out a long black e-cigarette, then starts to vape. The smoke filling my nostrils is nauseatingly sweet.

"We need to do something about Ryan," I say. "Now, I hate to come here, going behind his back, but we need to stop him."

"What are you talking about, Laurie?" Chip asks, looking at me like he's already determined that what I am going to tell him will be ridiculous—that he is above having to listen to all this nonsense. He doesn't have the time for it.

The way he looks at me makes me nervous, and the words are more difficult to find now.

"I think…I believe…I don't think Sandra killed herself."

Chip rolls his eyes. "Not this again. We've all heard how you tried to incriminate Ryan for this to the OSI. Please, don't humiliate yourself again."

"But it's not just her," I say, losing confidence by the second now. "It's also Ted and the other night…Duke."

Chip shakes his head at me. "All suicides. I really don't

appreciate you coming here and using these tragic deaths to…"

"Look at my face," I say and point at my lip and nose. "He did that to me. Ryan did all that." I fumble with my phone and find the picture of me that I took on the day after my meeting with Ryan in Duke's bathroom. "Look. This is what I looked like right after. Ryan did this, Chip. In Duke's house. I was there. He was trying to kill him when I tried to stop him. I am not making this up, Chip. You're the leader of this squadron; you're his leader. You can do something."

Chip stares at the photo, then at my face. He hands it back to me, still shaking his head.

"Listen, Laurie. I know things aren't well with Ryan. I have known this for quite some time. He comes here now and then; he sleeps on the couch, and I hear him scream at night. I can see in his eyes that something is wrong. And I am sorry if he did this to you; it's truly awful."

My eyes light up. Finally, we're getting somewhere. "So, you know I'm right?"

"Let me finish," he says and leans forward. "With that being said, yes, I know Ryan has PTSD. I have seen this a lot, and I even struggle with it myself after what happened. We were in the same truck on the day that Ryan saved my life. So, of course, Ryan struggles. It's only natural. But for you to take that, and in your desire for vengeance for him hurting you, or whatever it is you want to achieve, to accuse him of having…killed someone. That is just taking it too far, Laurie. Even for you."

I stare at him, mouth gaping. I can't believe this. I can't believe him. "He shot Isabella, Chip. For crying out loud. He shot his own daughter."

Chip slams his fist onto the table, and it makes me jump. "It was an accident, Laurie. A tragic and terrible one, yes. But he didn't intend to hurt her. And you know this. Ryan didn't hurt her on purpose. Don't you understand? Do you have any idea how hard it is on Ryan? He's a mess. He loves his kids as much as any dad. And now he can't see them. I'm this close to placing him under suicide watch."

"But…Chip, even you must see that with three suicide attempts within a unit, that something is awfully wrong here."

"Suicide clusters are actually very common after coming back," he says, rubbing his hair. "They say they sort of inspire one another. And it is so darn hard to stop once it has started. I'm struggling, seeing my close friends take their own lives like this, and frankly, I can't have you coming here and accusing my best friend, the man who saved my life, of murdering them. It's just too much, Laurie. You need to stop this."

"You even went and got a protective order on him, Laurie," Lotty chimes in. "You need to stop. All these accusations, all this nonsense, it's driving him over the edge. It's like you don't even care about him."

I stare at them. I'm getting desperate now. "He was there. Before Sandra died, he met with her. He was in her house. Same goes with Ted. Ryan was there, drunk and out of his mind. I saw him come out of Ted's house myself, then walked up to the window and saw Ted's feet dangling in the living room. I was there when he attacked Duke. I saw him drag him up the stairs and place the knife on his wrists right before he attacked me."

They're both shaking their heads now simultaneously. Their eyes are avoiding mine. They won't even look at me. I am that embarrassing to them. I stare at them for a few more seconds, then get up.

"Fine. Let him kill everyone in his unit if that's what you want. What do I care?"

I'm looking down at both of them. I still hope to get at least a reaction from one of them, but none comes. I can't believe those two had once been among our closest friends. Lotty used to be so sweet to me when we moved here, and she'd tell me she'd help with any need I might have.

Well, now I have one. I need you to believe me!

"Maybe it's what happened to Clarice as well. Maybe he killed her over there, and you all refuse to see it."

Chip gets to his feet now too, anger springs to his eyes, and his fists are clenched. "You don't know what you're talking about."

"Maybe you should leave now," Lotty says, speaking with a small, still voice. She reaches out a hand to hold back her husband. I send him one last look of defiance to let him know I don't let myself intimidate that easily, then turn around and leave.

Chapter 36

AS I DRIVE BACK to the condo and let myself in, I feel defeated. I am so tired of having to fight these people, and I am sick of not being able to tell the truth. That's when it occurs to me. I do have a weapon. I really do. I have a way, an outlet to let the world know—one that doesn't involve talking to the police.

I grab my laptop and open the document I started a few weeks earlier. It's almost done; it just needs a few more paragraphs that I can easily add. So, I write it. I write the story about the Air Force covering up a possible murder as suicide. The story of Clarice's family searching for justice for their daughter, making sure you can feel their pain dripping off the pages. It's the story of the many closed doors they are met with when asking simple questions, and how the forensic evidence speaks to their case. I write the rest of the entire article the way I initially wanted it but then tie in the stories of Sandra, Ted, and Duke as well. I don't mention Ryan, but just place a question mark to the conclusions made in the death reports. The fact that Sandra's wrists were slit deeper on one side than the other when she wasn't left-handed. The fact that Ted had drugs in his blood and that he was most likely already dead when he was hung up. I raise all the questions that Frank, Vera, and I have asked one another. I don't mention any names, so they won't get into trouble. I end the article by letting the reader know that there is a witness who has seen a man run from Ted's house and seen a person inside Duke's house, dragging him up the stairs. I don't mention that the witness is me.

Is the Air Force covering up all these deaths? I ask. *If so, it leads us to several other questions. Like why? Is it because they're afraid of a scandal? Are they protecting someone?* And then the inevitable: *How many murders have been covered up as suicides in the past several years?*

I read through it after I'm done, then send it to Frank. He emails me back a little later and tells me he thinks it's great. He sends me two things he thinks should be corrected, two technical forensic things, and then I decide it is done. I look at it and feel proud. Then I pick up the phone and call my former editor at *USA Today*. She says she'll take a look at it. That's all she can promise, and I send it to her, then go to the kitchen and make myself a snack. Damian comes back from spending the day with my mom and dad, and he is all sunshine and happy tales about all the sandcastles he has built and all the waves he has ridden on his boogieboard. His nose is slightly sunburned, but it looks cute, and he seems so happy, which I am thrilled about. He has been missing his dad a lot lately and crying for him at night before bedtime, asking if he'll come and tuck him in soon, or play ball with him. I don't really know what to tell him. I don't intend to let Ryan see either of the children anytime soon, if ever. How do I tell a six-year-old child that? He idolizes his daddy. He doesn't understand why he can't see him. He'll think it's my fault.

He'll end up resenting me for keeping them apart. I'm kind of hoping he'll be able to understand better once he grows a little older, but I fear he won't.

"Can I have a popsicle; can I, Mom?" he asks.

"Go ahead, buddy," I say and ruffle his sun-kissed hair.

"Thank you again," I say, addressed to my mom. My dad has walked into the kitchen with Damian and is grabbing a popsicle for himself. He helps Damian with the wrapping.

"He needed this cheering up," I say, speaking with a low voice so the boy won't hear me. "Last night, he kept asking for Ryan, and I don't know what to tell him. He was crying so badly that I had to take one of the bunnies out of the cage and let him pet it till he calmed down."

"Kids cry," my mom says. "They'll get through it."

"I'm not so sure," I say. "I fear this will end up haunting him for the rest of his life."

"You're exaggerating," my mom says, almost laughing at me. We never did agree much on children or how to raise them, so this was no surprise to me.

"He is, after all, just a child."

Damian grabs the popsicle from his grandfather's hands, then runs to his toys on the floor that he left out from the day before.

"See?" she says and points at him while he is playing, forcing the cars to crash into one another with a loud noise. "He has already forgotten. Besides, he didn't mention anything about his dad all day today. I'm sure he'll be just fine."

Easy for you to say. You're not the one who needs to comfort him tonight when he cries because he misses his daddy, and you simply aren't enough.

My dad approaches us and stops to look closer at my face. I can tell he is wondering about my bruises. We haven't talked about it, but of course, they have noticed. I look away, but it's too late.

"So, when are you going to tell us how you got those bruises?" he asks.

"Maybe we shouldn't…" my mom says, but my dad isn't giving up now.

"Was it Ryan?" my dad asks.

I don't answer; instead, I pull away. I know they resent him already for all he has put us through, not to mention shooting Isabella, even if it was an accident. But for some reason, I don't want them to hate him. Maybe I just don't want them to worry. My dad has high blood pressure, and I don't want it to go through the roof because of me. My dad is clenching his fists, and his eyes grow darker, angrier.

"Dad. It's fine," I say. "I've got a restraining order out on him. If he comes near us, he'll be arrested."

"But surely you told the police what he did to you?" my mom asks. "He should be arrested for that, for bruising you like this, shouldn't he?"

I look away. I know this won't go over well.

"I didn't report it."

My mom's eyes grow wide and big. She looks appalled like when I told her I only wash my hair twice a week because it's better for the hair and the environment.

She puffs herself up and snorts as she speaks, "Why on Earth didn't you report it?"

I sigh. I don't want to have to explain myself. "Because I couldn't see him. I couldn't see his face when it happened. I can't prove it was him."

"But surely, you could…they must take your word for it; I mean, look at that face. Is your nose broken? Did you even see a doctor about it?"

I want to direct the conversation onto something else. I don't want them to ask more questions about how it happened. I don't want to have to lie to them. I need a distraction, fast.

As if she had read my thoughts, my editor, Selena calls. I grab the phone and walk out on the balcony.

"We'll run it," she says.

"Really?" I ask, surprised. I was prepared to have to fight for this. I had an entire speech ready to convince her to publish it. Not many newspapers want to run negative stories on the military.

"Don't be so surprised," she says. "It's a well-written piece. It's an even better story. I think it might shake up some people around here, and you know I love that. I'm sending you the few corrections I have, and then we'll put it in Monday's paper."

She hangs up, and I stand back, looking out over the ocean, feeling slightly overwhelmed, knowing I have crossed a line now.

After this, there is no way back.

FRANK COMES over when he's done at work, and we drink a glass of white wine on the balcony. Damian is getting ready for bed, and I have promised he'll be allowed to play with his cars for a few more minutes after he has put on his PJs, while Isabella is busy in her room, doing her schoolwork. I feel terrible for her, having to do all this extra work with what she's been through, but this is what she wants. And I have to admit I am proud of her for fighting and not just giving up.

Frank puts his arm around me as we sit on the patio swing together. The sun is about to set, and the shadows are growing long on the beach. I like to feel his arm around me and to feel him close. But I don't know why.

Am I in love with him, or am I just glad to have him here because I'm scared to be alone?

"I think you did great today," he says with a soft smile. "I'm really proud of you for writing the article. I know my parents are going to be very pleased too."

"It's not gonna get Ryan, though," I say and sip my cool wine. "He's still out there, roaming, planning God knows what. And to be honest, I'm kind of scared of what he might do once he sees this article. He's not gonna be happy about it."

Frank pulls me closer. My head is touching his cheek now, and it makes me feel safer. "He still doesn't know where you live, does he?"

I shake my head. "I don't think so. Yet, I fear he'll find out somehow. That's why I lie awake at night, listening to every darn sound this place makes, worrying it's him trying to get in somehow. I even bought a new gun, so I can protect us all in case he does show up."

Frank nods. "I can't blame you. That's why I don't understand why you didn't mention Ryan's name in the article."

I look up at him. "I can't do that."

"Why not?"

"You can't incriminate someone without him even being a suspect in the eyes of the police. You can't make a man a criminal in the eyes of the public based on circumstantial evidence. That's not ethical."

He shrugs. "But it's the truth, right?"

I don't answer. I stare out at the ocean as it grows darker still. The fact is, I don't know for sure if it really was him that night in Duke's house. I curse myself for never seeing his face properly.

He was there. You saw him in the app. It looked like his truck in the driveway. Stop making excuses for him.

"I'm sure he'll be put to justice if it is him," I say. "I still have faith in our justice system."

Frank scoffs. "So did I. So did my parents until we lost Clarice, and no one would be honest about what happened to her."

I nod and think about Sandra's relatives, and especially her son Joe, Jr. How are they coping with all this? Do they believe the Air Force when they say it was suicide? And Ted's family? He had a girlfriend living up north who he was about to marry later in the year. She was going to move down here and begin a new life on the base. I met her twice when she visited, and I really liked her. How's she coping with all this? And Duke's wife? She was out of town with all three of their kids when he was attacked in his house. She came home to a man in ICU. How's she taking it? I had looked into the eyes of Frank's parents and seen the despair, the grief. They knew they were being lied to. How do you move on from that? How do you ever trust again?

Chapter 37

I HEAR my daughter scream in her room. I run in there and see the roach sitting on the wall next to her bed. It's the length of my finger and is moving fast. It's crawling toward her, its antennas moving. Isabella shrieks and moves away, while I think about what to do. It has always been Ryan who took care of spiders and roaches. I hate those nasty bugs more than anything, especially how fast they shoot across the floor once they realize there is danger. One could survive a nuclear war, they say. I never understood what that meant until I tried to kill one myself.

"Please, Mom, get it away from me."

I grab my shoe and lift it in the air, then let it fall onto the roach, closing my eyes. I smash it against the white wall. I slam my shoe against it over and over again, heart in my throat. I was in my bed when she screamed, and I got up a little too fast, thinking something terrible had happened. Now, I can't seem to calm myself. I sit on her bed, panting and agitated, unable to relax.

The roach has fallen to the tiles and is still moving its legs as I pick it up with toilet paper, wincing. I throw it in the toilet bowl and flush. I watch as it spins in the water and is sucked down into oblivion.

The kids come into the kitchen, and I serve them breakfast, then run down to the mailbox and empty it. I grab my copy of *USA Today* and open it. My story is on the front cover, and seeing my byline under it makes my heart rate speed. It's been a while since I last saw my name in a paper. I feel proud for a few seconds, then run back up and eat breakfast with the kids. I drive Damian to his school and drop him off, then continue to the base, where I show my ID to the guard and drive on toward the medical center where I park outside the yellow building.

I hand Isabella over to the doctor, and she leaves with her, while I sit down on the bench to watch her. My phone rings and I walk outside to pick it up.

It's Frank.

"My parents are thrilled. They told me to thank you for telling their story. Their phone has been ringing off the hook all morning with reporters who also want to hear it. They're going to be on *Good Morning America* tomorrow morning. This is truly what they needed. We hope that this might persuade them to reopen her case. Thank you, Laurie. You have no idea how much you helped us."

I hang up with a sigh and look at Isabella through the window to the training room. She is taking a few steps on her own without anyone holding her, and the doctor looks excited. I bite my lip. Things seem to be clearing up now. I am even getting paid well for this article, and that should help me out financially, at least for a little while. My parents are on my case, pressuring me to get a divorce from Ryan so he can start paying alimony. They want to hook me up with a lawyer they know, to make sure he pays up. I'm not sure I am up for any of that just yet. I can't really think very far ahead. I am just surviving today.

Isabella spots me through the window and waves at me proudly. I wave back and give her a double thumbs up. I feel better today; I feel like I might actually get through this. I have done my best, and now it is beginning to pay off. The story is out there, and the media is throwing themselves at it. The ball is rolling, and it is out of my hands from now on. Hopefully, it means they'll look closer at the three deaths. Hopefully, this means Clarice's parents can finally get the closure they have wanted for so long. And, hopefully, I can begin to look ahead and plan for a future soon. For the first time in months, I actually feel okay; I feel like things could be okay.

LATER, I pick up Damian and take him to Publix with me. I let him pick a few items he wants, and he grabs a bag of candy and a toy F-16 fighter jet. It's big and a little too expensive, but I tell him he can have it anyway, letting my guilty conscience control my spending. *It's not even his birthday*, my mom would have said. He is playing with it while I throw food in the cart, then go through the cash register and pay. My boy is happy, playing loudly with the fighter jet, and the lady behind the register smiles at him. He does look cute with his tanned face and sun-made highlights.

I take him to the car and drive home to Isabella, who is yelling at the computer because the online school system is lagging, and she can't watch the learning video she's supposed to go through today because she has to take the test tomorrow. I hate it when computers act up because I have no idea what to do about it, and again, I miss having a man in the house. I consider calling Frank, but then she suddenly tells me it's working again, and I relax while unpacking the groceries. My parents call and check in on me, like usual. I can hear my mother is worried by the way her voice trembles lightly when asking how I'm doing. I can also hear that she is desperately trying not to sound worried. I assure them I am fine, and not just that, I am actually doing pretty good today.

They don't mention the article, even though I know they read it. I'm sure it just filled them with more worry and concern, so I don't say anything either. We hang up, and I prepare what to cook for dinner, then go out on the balcony and drink a glass of white wine while listening to the ocean and enjoying the cool breeze. Temperatures are in the upper seventies now almost every day, so that ocean breeze is a great help. I never did well with intense heat, especially not the moist heat, and Florida sure is both hot and humid.

I make spaghetti and meatballs, and we eat together, the three of us. Rosie is by my feet, looking at the door. She has been staying close to me since we moved. She's kind of moping around, looking sad most of the time. I know she misses Ryan since he is her favorite, but the dog belongs to the children, and it goes where they go.

After dinner, I take her for a walk on the beach. Damian comes with me, and we throw a ball for Rosie to fetch. It's a beautiful night out, and as the sun sets, I feel like I never want it to end. Damian is laughing and sticking his feet in the water, then he runs to me and hugs me. I kiss the top of his head and ruffle his hair. I look up toward my condo and think about Isabella. I pray she will be able to walk on her own soon. I want her to come down here and be able to take a stroll with us. I want to see her run on the soccer field again. I want her to worry about normal things, like the prom, or the boy that she likes who doesn't even look at her because he's too shy.

I think about the time when Ryan and I met. I can still feel the sensation deep within me, and it is overwhelming to think about. The way he looked at me, the way he'd kiss me, the way he'd tell me how amazing I was.

Boy, I miss that.

How did we get from that to this?

It seems almost impossible.

"Let's go back up now, Mom," Damian says and grabs my hand in his. "It's getting dark and scary now."

I look down at my boy, then wonder how much he knows about what happened to his sister. We told him daddy's gun went off by mistake, but I sense he knows it was a little more than that. After all, he has tried to sneak up on his father before and seen the result. I know there'll be more questions as he grows older, and I'll have to prepare myself for them. Hopefully, I'll have the answers by then. Hopefully, they'll be better than the ones I have right now.

"You're right, buddy. We need to get you to bed. It's a school night," I say.

"Nooo," he says, whining. "I don't want to go to bed. I'm never going to bed!"

I laugh and grab him by the waist, then swing him around in the air. We tumble to the sand, Rosie jumping on top of us, and lay there for a few minutes, simply laughing, while the darkness surrounds us as the sun sets behind the condominium.

Chapter 38

DAMIAN SEES HIM FIRST. He's standing in front of our door when we walk out of the elevator. My heart immediately stops, and I reach for Damian to keep him close, but it's too late. The boy is already running toward him with his arms stretched out.

"D-A-A-A-A-D!"

Ryan takes the boy in his arms and lifts him. Rosie takes off and runs up to him as well, jumping up at him. Damian throws his arms around his father's neck like he doesn't want ever to let go again. The sight of the two of them together is cute, adorable even, if it wasn't for the circumstances. I approach them slowly, heart in my throat. This is what I feared might happen one day. This is exactly what has been in my nightmares.

Ryan tickles Damian's stomach, and the boy laughs and worms around in his arms. He puts him down, then looks at me.

"What are you doing here?" I ask. I think about the gun in my bedroom. Can I get to it fast enough if I need to?

"I have to talk to you," he says matter-of-factly. Like he is entitled to talk to me whenever he needs to. "Can I come in? It won't be long."

I notice he's sweating and wonder if he ran all the way up the stairs. I can see the muscle flex in his jaw as he clenches his teeth. There's something about the look in his eyes that makes me flinch. He smells like alcohol.

"You're not allowed to come near us," I say. "I have a restraining order out on you. You know you're supposed to keep your distance and not approach us. I can have you arrested just for being here."

I try to sound like I mean it. I don't want him to think I won't call the cops, because I will. I am not afraid of contacting the police, no matter what he writes in those texts he thinks are anonymous. I am afraid, though, of what he might do to us if I do. Now that I know he knows where we live, I am suddenly a lot more terrified.

Damian pulls my shirt eagerly. "I need to show dad my new fighter jet; can I show it to him, Mom?"

I sigh. Ryan smiles. It looks smug like he is enjoying this. I'm sure he is.

"Please, Mom?" Damian begs and drags it out. "Pl-e-e-a-se?"

I look at my son. He knows I can't say no to him. The way he looks at me makes me give in.

"All right. But only for a second. Go to your room and get it." I open the door and let Damian run inside. Ryan walks in with him, moving fast so I can't stop him. This wasn't my intention. I didn't want him inside, but now it is too late. I can't get my heart to calm down. I am on the verge of panic. He's taken me completely by surprise. I didn't think he even knew where we lived. I thought we were safe here.

"So, this is where you're staying, huh?" Ryan says,

looking around. He is edgy. He's moving fast and speaking fast. I wonder if he is on something other than alcohol. Is it just the painkillers, or is it more now? Harder drugs? It wouldn't surprise me at this point.

"I guess it's okay. How do you afford it? Are Mom and Dad paying?"

"How did you find us?" I say.

"I followed you," he says. "This morning, when you went to training with Isabella, I followed you here. I rang all the buttons until someone let me in."

I sigh. Of course, he did. He knew what time I usually go to physical therapy with her. He's known since that day he was sitting on the bench. It's as easy as that, I guess. I was never safe here, was I? He could have found me at any point he wanted to.

Damian runs up to him, holding his plane, looking up at him proudly. "Isn't it cool, Dad? It's an F-16 Thunderbird. Is it like the planes you flew over there, is it? Look, it has missiles and everything, and it can even make a sound if you push there."

Ryan smiles and looks at the plane. He grabs it between his hands and turns it in the light for a few seconds, then pretends to be flying it, making whooshing sounds. Smiling, he hands it back to him. "It sure is very nice, buddy. That is one very cool fighter jet. Just like the real ones. Did Mom give you that?"

He nods eagerly.

"Mom's the best," Ryan says, then looks up at me. "Don't you think so?"

Damian nods. He is biting his cheek like he is wondering about something.

"Okay, cut it out," I say. "Damian, go to your room."

Damian gives me a look of surprise. "But…?"

"Now," I say.

"M-o-o-m!"

"NOW!"

The boy slumps his shoulders, but he obeys. He slams the door to his and Isabella's room to make sure I understand he is not satisfied, but I ignore it. This is what is best for him right now. I can't have him here, listening to what his dad and I are talking about or even risking him getting hurt if things go south. I hope he's not telling Isabella that Ryan is here. I don't know how she's gonna react if she sees him here. She hasn't seen him since the incident. I can't have her see him. I can't put her in that situation. I need to get him out of our apartment now.

I turn to look at Ryan. I am tired of these games. I don't feel safe with him here. I have to find out what he wants and then get rid of him as fast as possible.

"Why are you here? Why have you come?"

He runs a hand across his shaved head, rubbing it. He seems nervous, out of sorts. He is a mess. He has patches of sweat under his arms and on his chest, and his pants don't seem to fit him anymore. As soon as Damian is out of sight, and his eyes land on me, I see the anger in them, and I take a quick step backward, startled.

"Have you lost your mind?" he asks, throwing out his arms violently. "Have you completely lost it?"

I breathe heavily, agitated and scared, and take another step back. I hope the kids will stay in their room and not come out when they hear him yell.

"Ryan, you're not allowed to…"

"I don't give a damn what I am allowed to do," he says, spitting. "You're my wife, and you have crossed a line here. Are there no boundaries, no limits to what you will do to hurt me? To how far you'll go? How could you write that article, huh? How could you put your name on that total piece of crap?"

"Ryan…I'm warning you," I say and take another step back as he leans forward. There is so much anger in his eyes, more than the time he grabbed my throat. "I'll call the police. They'll arrest you."

"You're bluffing," he says, waving his hand at me. "I am the father of your children, goddammit. How could you do this to me? How could you embarrass me like that? You know what happened today after your little article came out, huh? Do you know what happened?"

"I'm warning you, Ryan, one step closer, and I'll make that call."

He doesn't seem to care anymore. He has crossed the line long ago, and now there is no going back. I see it in his eyes; he has made the decision. Harassing me and yelling at me are worth going to jail for. He doesn't care anymore.

"Chip called me in for a little chat. He wanted me to set you straight. Told me to get my wife back in line. Do you have any idea how that felt, huh? Do you?"

Ryan takes another step toward me, and I lift my hand to stop him from coming closer. He pauses, then passes his hand over his mouth, nervously rubbing his chin.

"You have got to stop this," he says. "This harassment. This war you're waging against me. I know I made a mistake, all right? It torments me daily that I accidentally shot our daughter. But accusing me, accusing the Air Force of…covering up murder? Where does all that come from? I'll tell you where…from that twisted mind of yours. You see murder and ghosts everywhere. And it is hurting everyone around you. It has got to stop, Laurie, do you hear me?"

As he speaks, he reaches out his hand and grabs my arm. His eyes are dark, angry. He is holding it so forcefully it hurts.

"Ryan, stop it. Let go," I say, but he doesn't listen.

"You've gone completely insane. It's crazy; can't you see it? You talked to that OSI investigator, didn't you? They told me someone came in and said I was seen at Sandra's house and Ted's house. You're the only one who saw me, Laurie; it could only be you. How could you do this to me? How could you betray me, your husband, like this? I thought we loved one another. Now, because of that article, they've called me in again for further questioning, they say. Because of what you wrote. Because of you! You should be ashamed of yourself!"

"Ryan, let go of my arm," I yell, but he squeezes it harder. He is holding me so tight; I can't move.

That's when the door opens to the children's bedroom, and Isabella comes out. Her eyes grow terrified as she sees her dad holding me.

"Isabella, honey, stay in your room," he says, trying to sound sweet, but it makes him sound even creepier. I can tell she's frightened. This is a little too similar to the night when she ended up getting shot.

He continues, trying to sound like it's nothing…like she shouldn't worry, "Mom and Dad are just discussing something."

"Isabella," I say, groaning, trying to get out of his grip. I can't. He's not letting go. "Call the police."

Hearing this, Ryan suddenly eases up on my arm and finally lets go. I pull away with a loud gasp, then touch my arm in pain. Isabella closes the door and disappears back inside. Ryan is shaking as he turns to face me. I fear he's gonna reach out and grab me once again, so I take another step back.

"You'd actually do that to me?" he says, panting. Disbelief has replaced the darkness in his eyes. He is shaking his head slowly. "You'd really call the cops on me?"

I nod my head, barely able to breathe. "You better

believe it, Ryan. Don't come around here anymore, do you hear me?"

He points his finger at me, snorting angrily.

"This is not over yet."

Then he runs to the door, opens it, and disappears, slamming it shut behind him. I stay behind inside my living room, heart pounding, body shaking. Then I fall to my knees, crying.

Chapter 39

THE LOCAL LAW enforcement comes to my apartment, and I tell them about Ryan coming there and threatening me. They promise me they'll have a talk with Ryan, then leave. I see them out, not feeling very safe or even convinced it's going to help me. I then call Frank, and he comes over as fast as he can. I hear him running up the stairs after I buzz him in. He holds me by the shoulders.

"Are you all right? Did he hurt you?"

I shake my head, then hug him tightly. Damian and Isabella are both sitting in the living room, and they see it. As I turn around, I realize it is the first time Frank and I have been openly physical with one another in front of them.

"How about some ice cream, huh?" Frank says, clasping his hands. He walks to the kitchen and grabs the Moose Tracks ice cream from the freezer. He puts some in four bowls and hands them to us. I am not hungry at all, but I eat it anyway. The kids aren't talking. Isabella is pushing her ice cream around inside the bowl and not eating any.

"Why was he here?" she suddenly asks without looking up from the bowl. "Why did he come?"

I swallow the knot in my throat. "He was angry with me because I wrote an article about the Air Force and his friends."

"So, he didn't come for me?" she asks.

My heart drops. Is that what she thinks? That her dad came to hurt her? "No, sweetie. He is angry with me, not you."

She finally looks up, and our eyes meet. "He was grabbing you. Did he hurt you?"

I shake my head and lift my arm to show her it's fine. "Not really. But it was kind of scary."

"Daddy is mean," Damian says, chewing a piece of chocolate. "I don't want to see him ever again."

We finish the ice cream in silence, and I tuck both of them in, then go back to Frank, who has poured two glasses of Chardonnay for us. I sit on the couch with a deep sigh, then hold out my hands so he can see them.

"Still shaking. I don't think I'll be able to sleep tonight."

He exhales deeply. "I'm so sorry. I should have been here to protect you."

"It's not your job," I say and lift the glass to my mouth. I stare into the liquid afterward, spinning it.

He places a hand on top of mine. "I'm just happy nothing happened to any of you, not like last time."

"You and me both," I say and drink. I think about the day Isabella got shot and shiver. I think for a second about moving again, moving far away so he won't find us. But I know he will find us; somehow, he will.

We sit in silence for a few seconds while I worry about Ryan coming back now that he knows where we are. I remind myself that I have the gun in my bedroom and to sleep with the phone within reach so I can call the cops if he does come back. Then I look at Frank. His eyes are so worried as they linger on me. He looks like a big puppy.

"There is something I have been thinking about, though," I say. "Something I have meant to talk to you about."

"And that is?"

I put the glass down on the table, then face him. "I did some research the other day for my article on suicides in the military and was thinking a lot about Clarice. I then called your dad and had him send me the death report that was sent to him after her death. The official one."

Frank sips his wine and looks at me, an eyebrow lifted. "You did?"

"Yes. And guess what I found?"

He lifts his hands. "I give up. You tell me."

"I've been thinking a lot about a motive for these murders that look like suicides, but I haven't been able to find any. For a while, I believed it was random. That was before I took a closer look at the report."

"Really? You mean to tell me you have a motive?"

"Well, a connection, at least. Besides the fact that they were all from the same unit and deployed to the same base. All of the names are also in the report, in Clarice's death report," I say. "Sandra, Ted, and Duke are all witnesses that the OSI investigators spoke to after her death. They all testified to how depressed she was leading up to the suicide, and all claim to have seen her on the night she allegedly shot herself, and they all say she seemed out of it on that night…like she was in distress. Sandra even says she was worried about her." I grab my laptop and open the lid. I click the mouse on the link, and it opens. "Here, let me show you."

Frank looks at the screen as I show him the names and statements. Then he looks up and smiles.

"You're right. I can't believe I hadn't even thought about that. That's amazing."

"I don't quite know what to do with this information yet, but it is quite interesting to me."

He clears his throat, then lifts his glass. "Here's to our own Nancy Drew."

"Hercule Poirot," I say.

That makes him laugh.

We clink glasses and drink. Then I look at him seriously. "There is one last name left, though. One more person that testifies in the report."

***

THE MEDIA COVERAGE of my story is massive. The next morning, I have the TV running while packing Damian's lunch. I watch Frank's parents as they are on *Good Morning America* and tell their story, then once they're done, I flip through the news stations and see my story mentioned both on CNN and NBC. I feel satisfied, even though I know this will only make Ryan even angrier with me. The heat is on the Air Force right now, and people are demanding answers. Was Clarice killed, and if so, are they covering up a murder, and maybe not just this one, but maybe more?

So far, no one from the Air Force wants to talk to the media, but at some point, they'll have to. I turn off the TV as Damian comes out of his room, dressed and ready to go. I grab his backpack, then open the trash to throw out a piece of paper when my eye catches something inside of it. I put his backpack down, then look at Damian.

"Why is your fighter jet in the trash can?" I ask and

pull it out.

Damian stares at it, then bites his cheek. "I don't want it anymore."

A frown grows between my eyes. I place the plane on the floor. "Why not? What's wrong with it? Do I have to remind you how expensive it was, and how we can't afford it?"

"I just don't want to play with it anymore," he says and walks to his backpack, then puts it on, shoulders slumped, head down. "It's stupid."

"Hey, buddy. What's going on?" I ask, putting my hand on his shoulder.

He looks up at me. "I don't like it anymore."

I exhale. "I see. And why is that?"

He looks down like he's embarrassed. "Because he liked it."

And that's when it hits me. "Because your dad liked it?"

Damian nods. "He was so mean to you."

I sigh and hug him. "I'm so sorry you had to see that, buddy. Your dad isn't well; we've talked about that."

Damian nods again, still biting the inside of his cheek. "Can we go now? I don't want to be late."

"Of course," I say.

Damian picks up the plane, then places it back in the trash. He puts his hand in mine and pulls me toward the door.

"I would like a police car next time. Like the one those guys drove, the ones that were here after Dad…" he trails off like he doesn't want to say anymore, and I squeeze his hand.

"Of course, sweetie. We'll find one."

His eyes grow hopeful as he runs toward the elevator and presses the button, yelling, "A big one."

Chapter 40

I DRIVE DAMIAN TO SCHOOL, then go back to the condo and sit down at my computer. Isabella doesn't have physical therapy today, which I am pleased about since I have no desire to show my face at the base today. She stays in her room, doing online school work, sweating over her math problems.

I sit down in the living room, coffee mug in my hands, then open my computer and go through my emails. I can't stop thinking about what Frank and I talked about the night before, so I read through Clarice's death report once again. The names keep popping up to me, and I know there is no avoiding it anymore. I call Frank and ask him to take an early lunch break. I need his help.

"His name is George Richards," I tell him when he picks me up. "I've met him a ton of times at barbecues and other social gatherings where they would allow them to bring spouses. I always liked George. And he likes me. He would often seek me out in the crowd, and we could talk for hours. He didn't enjoy playing ball or hanging out by the grill, as most of the others did. He went through a bad divorce some years ago, and I was sort of a shoulder for him through those months. He liked that he could tell me everything, he often said. When he was with the boys, he felt like he needed to play the tough guy, to pretend like he was okay. But the fact was, he was hurting, and he missed his ex and the life they used to have. She cheated on him on his first deployment, and he could never understand how she could just leave him. He talked to me about those things, about the deep pain of being left behind. I was his confidante, and I think he'll talk to me, at least I hope so. The only problem is that he lives on base."

"Of course, he does," Frank says.

"Not exactly the place I wanted to go today, as I have made a lot of people angry," I say as we drive down A1A toward the base. "But I thought if we went there in your car, then maybe no one will see me. You work there, at the Medical Examiner's facility. Nothing strange about you coming and going."

"And you're sure you want to do this?" he asks as we reach an intersection and he slows to a stop.

"I have to," I say. "Don't you agree? I have to tell him about what I know. He needs to know. I can't live with myself if I haven't told him."

"I'm just not sure what you expect to get out of it. He's probably not going to believe you," Frank says as the light turns green and he takes off again.

"But at least I'll have done what I could," I say. "That's all that matters right now."

Frank chuckles. "You really are relentless, aren't you? You don't care what they think; you don't care that they call you the crazy lady."

"Not if it means saving a life," I say just as he turns off and drives into the security check. We both show our IDs, and the guy looks at us both. I smile, hoping he doesn't know I wrote that article. He can't refuse to let me in since technically I am still married to Ryan and still live on base, but he can give me a hard time. He can take us aside for a thorough inspection. I feel like his eyes are on me…like he hates me as he stares at my face, comparing it to the ID. His eyes feel like knives to my skin, and I struggle to sit still.

Finally, he lets us go. I sigh, relieved, as the gate goes up, and we drive through, passing the guardhouse. I feel like all eyes are on me as we drive across the base, passing first the landing strips and later the on-base department store, called *The Exchange*. I keep my head down inside the car. I keep thinking I see Ryan every time we pass someone. I pray he won't know I am here.

"George works in Air Traffic Control," I say. "He works in Radar. Now, I don't have access to that since they don't let just anybody in, but I was thinking we could park over there by the tower and then wait for him. They work in shifts of a few hours at a time, and I am hoping we might catch him as he goes out for lunch."

"As you wish," Frank says and parks the car. I lean back in the seat and keep my eyes on the front door. Frank is on his phone, scrolling through social media, while I don't want to take my eyes off the building in case George comes out. I don't know if this is the best idea or if we should have gone to his home instead, but then I see the door open, and I recognize him as he exits along with two others in uniform.

"This is it," I say and open the door. "Wish me luck."

Frank says something, but I don't hear it. I'm already out of the car, rushing toward him.

I approach him, then take off my sunglasses and say, "George?"

He turns to look at me. Immediately, his smile is gone.

"Laurie? Laurie Davis?"

He says it in a disappointed tone. I nod. I try to smile but fail.

"Hi, George."

He looks at me, anger growing in his eyes. Needless to say, it's not the reaction I had hoped for. He's almost spitting as he speaks.

"What the heck are you doing? You have some nerve coming here. Do you have any idea how unpopular you are?"

"I have a feeling," I say, forcing a smile. The way he looks at me makes me feel very uncomfortable and unwelcome. This is not the George I know; this is not the same man I used to hug and chat with about his pain going through the divorce. "But I need to talk to you. It's important."

I can tell by the look in his eyes that he has no desire to talk to me. He shakes his head and narrows his lips. His two colleagues, a young woman probably no more than twenty, and a guy who also looks like he's in training, stare at me from behind George.

George shakes his head. "I don't want to talk to you. No one wants to talk to you. Don't you understand? I think you should leave. It'll be best for all of us."

"Please, George. I wouldn't be here if it weren't important," I say and grab his arm gently. I remind myself about the George I used to care about. He's got to be in there somewhere. "It's not exactly my favorite place right now. Believe me. I know I'm not welcome."

He exhales and looks at me like I am a child he needs to scold. I have never seen him like this, never seen this coldness in his eyes. Like we never shared our deepest fears and hurts. "Just leave, Laurie. Give up. There is nothing for you here. If you're writing another article, no one is going to talk to you. You can forget all about that. You have no friends here anymore."

"It's not for an article," I say insistently. "Please. Just listen to me, dang it. Don't be so stubborn. I will only take one minute of your time. Don't tell me you don't have at least one minute. I need you to listen to me. I am not asking you to say anything. I'll talk, and then you can see what you want to do about what I tell you. You don't have to say a single word if you're so afraid to."

He's about to leave but hesitates and looks at me from the corner of his eye. "And nothing will be in any papers? You promise me this?"

"No, that is not what this is about. Not at all."

He sighs. "I really don't want to."

"Please?"

Another sigh. "All right. One minute and then I'm off to eat lunch, understood?"

I nod. We step to the side where his colleagues can't hear us. I don't want them listening in. He crosses his arms in front of his chest. He makes it very clear to me that he's highly uncomfortable with the situation. I choose to ignore it.

"You know what they call you around here, don't you?" he says.

I throw out my hands resignedly. "What? Crazy Laurie? Laurie, the lunatic?"

He scoffs. "Blue Falcon."

I send him a phony smile. I know he is just saying this to make me feel bad. In the eyes of an airman, Blue Falcons suck. If someone is a Blue Falcon, it usually means they're letting someone take the heat for something. Blue Falcons are the snitches of the Air Force world. They throw others under the bus, and they have no problem ruining you to save themselves. It's pretty much the worst you can be in this world.

I don't really care.

"So, what did you want to tell me?" he asks. "And please, hurry up. I'm on the clock here."

I TELL him everything I know. That I believe the three others were killed because their names were on the death report, and that I think he might be in danger. George listens and seems genuinely interested, which is all I can ask for at this point. When I'm done, he shakes his head and grins.

"And you expect me to believe all this?"

I shrug. "I know it's hard to, but…"

"You're damn right it's hard to. You're telling me one of my colleagues is some murderer and that he's out to kill me because I testified in some report? It sure sounds like you should be writing mystery novels instead of articles, Laurie. Are you certain you're not related to Vera? Because you sound just as crazy as she does. She ran around babbling about her sister being murdered too, and we tried to tell her what we saw. We were there; she wasn't, and neither were you."

"Now, I know it sounds insane. But I can't just sit on this knowledge and not at least warn you. No one seems to want to listen to…"

"And just why is that do you think?" he asks.

"Because it sounds crazy, I know…"

"No, Laurie. No one wants to listen because it's not true. I was there. I saw Clarice grab that weapon and walk away with it. I know she killed herself. It's not something I'm making up or saying to cover for someone else. I heard the noise it made when she did it, right after I had seen her. I looked her in the eyes just minutes before. I could have stopped it. I could have said something or done something, and I didn't. I have to live with that guilt every day because I didn't stop her…because I didn't realize what she was up to in time. Somehow, I can't escape the feeling that I could have done something or said something. No matter how many people tell me I couldn't, that it was her decision, and there was nothing I could have done. I still wonder every day if it's true. It hurts me deeply that you're ripping up these old wounds and questioning all of us. You're basically saying that we all lied when they did the investigation. We didn't. We told the truth, and I suggest you leave it alone. Don't come back here with all your crazy talk about murders and someone covering it up. I know what I saw."

"She had bruises," I say as he is about to walk away from me. He pauses, his back still turned to me. "Clarice was beaten before she died. There were teeth marks on her body. The autopsy showed she had injuries no one could explain. Something happened to her, and you know it."

George stands still for a few seconds, not moving. My pulse has gone up, and I am sweating in the heat. A Hercules is preparing for landing over our heads and roars down above us toward the landing strip. As the noise is gone, George turns to face me again.

"You need to be very careful now. I suggest you get out of here before anyone knows you've been here. Maybe I should call your husband and let him know, huh? Oh, wait, you've put out a protective order on him, so he can't even see his children. What kind of a mother keeps her children from seeing their father, huh? That's the kind of woman you are."

"That's below the belt, even for you," I say. "I came here to help you, to warn you…"

Frank has gotten out of his car and approached us. He grabs my shoulder. "Laurie, maybe we should…"

"Go ahead and get killed," I say, letting my anger run away with me. "I'm only sorry I won't be able to say I told you so because you'll be dead."

George walks away, giving me the finger, while Frank pulls my arm. I snort as he drags me into the car and closes the door.

"He's not worth it, Laurie," Frank says as he takes off. "None of them are."

I am on the verge of tears as we leave the base—tears of anger and frustration. I feel like I *am* Lunatic Laurie, like that crazy person from movies that no one wants to be seen with. And I wonder if any of this has been worth it. Was risking my life in Duke's house worth it? It's not like he's really alive anyway. As a tear escape my eye and rolls down my cheek, I think about the life I used to have. Before Ryan was deployed, back when things were simple, and no one thought I was crazy. Back when we had a bunch of friends and a vibrant social life. How could life change so drastically? Did I let this happen? Is it my fault?

I think about all that, but most of all, I wonder how it will ever be good again. Is there a way back from this?

Chapter 41

I AM WORRIED. I keep checking the news for stories of another suicide on base. I am concerned I might soon see George's name and be told that he decided to end it, that he was known to have been depressed after his divorce. But so far, after three days, there has been nothing. I haven't heard from Ryan or the police. I don't know if they ever had that chat with him, but at least he is staying away. I wake up several times at night, gasping, thinking I hear something, worried it is him coming back. During the day, I fear he'll come to Damian's school or show up at Isabella's physical therapy. There was so much rage in those eyes when he left; I fear he isn't giving up just yet.

If ever.

I stare at my desk and the many photos I have hung up on the wall, then at the small yellow sticky notes and the piles of printouts I have made. I know this looks like a crazy person's, an obsessed person's work, but it's what I have been up to. I have been trying to get myself an overview, trying to find anything that could help me get to the bottom of this. I don't know what I am looking for exactly or what I am hoping to get out of it, but it feels important, and I can't let it go. I guess you could call me obsessive since I think about it all hours of the day and even at night when I am supposed to sleep. Is there a pattern I have missed? A connection that could help me figure out when he'll strike next? Is it on certain dates? Why did he choose to kill them in this order? Why Sandra first? How long till he strikes next? I try to figure these things out but have no success. Every day, I consider going back to warn George again. I have already called him twice, then hung up when losing my courage. Then I write him an email. I tell him that I believe he's in danger, then delete it again. Then I start all over, starting out telling him I know I am the last person he wants to hear from, but he should listen anyway.

I delete that too, then lean back in my chair.

You already told him this. If he chooses not to listen, it's his fault.

I sip my white wine and stare at the wall when my phone vibrates. I grab it from the table and look at the display, then stop breathing.

It's that number again, the one that texted me when I woke up in my car at Duke's house. He has sent me another text. With heart hammering in my chest, I open it.

It says: BACK OFF NOW IF YOU KNOW WHAT IS BEST FOR YOU.

I stare at the message, the phone shaking in my hand. I feel sweaty, and I can hardly breathe. Then I text back: NEVER

I send it, then stare at the phone, hearing the pulse pumping in my ears. A couple of minutes pass, and when I don't get an answer, I text again: I AM ON TO YOU. YOU'RE GOING DOWN.

I look at it, waiting for him to answer, but nothing comes. I want to keep him texting me. I want to know if he really is the killer. Is it Ryan, trying to be clever by hiding behind another number?

Still, no answer. The silence scares me slightly. I stare at the screen, wondering if I should call the number again. It'll probably just go to voicemail like last time. If he wants to talk to me, he'll call me himself.

I stare at the screen, then decide I have lost him. I am about to put the phone back on the desk when it rings. I gasp slightly, then look at the screen.

It's him. He's Facetiming me.

MY FINGER IS SHAKING SO BADLY I can barely swipe it across the screen to accept the call. It slips a couple of times before I finally manage to take it. There is scrambling on the other end; the camera is blurry. My heart is beating so fast that it's hard for me to hear what is going on.

Am I about to see him? Will I see his face and find out if it is really Ryan?

"Hello?" I say. I try to make out what it is I am looking at on the screen. It's defocused and pixelated at first. I squint my eyes to see better.

"Hello?" I say again. "Who is this?"

There is no answer. The camera is moving toward something. "Ryan, is this you? Hello? Are you there? What am I looking at here?"

Finally, the camera stands still, and soon the picture becomes clear. I am looking at someone's face, but it's definitely not Ryan. It's not a man either. It's a woman, and she's crying.

Oh, dear God, no!

As the realization sinks in, my heart drops. I can feel

the blood leaving my face.

"M-MOM?"

I am almost screaming now. The camera moves again, and I am looking at another person.

"DAD?"

"Please," my dad's voice pleads. "Please, don't hurt us."

I realize they're on the ground, both of them are lying on the floor of their condo. I recognize the tiles in the kitchen.

"Dad? What's happening?" I scream.

The camera moves back to my mom. She has a gun pressed against her skin. Her makeup is smeared; she's been crying. She also has a bruise on her cheek.

"Please," she says. "Laurie. Just do what he tells you to. Please."

"Mo-om?" I can hear the desperation in my own voice. It gets shrill and ugly. I can't breathe. "What are you doing to them, you bastard?" I scream at him while I sink to my knees. "Don't you dare hurt them!"

The camera goes closer to my mom's face, where the gun is being pressed against her cheek, hard. I can hear her whimper. It completely paralyzes me.

"Please, don't," I say. "Please, don't harm them. Please."

I stare at the screen through my tears, and I can hear my mother crying out in distress. She's terrified. It's the worst sound in the world.

Not my mom. Not my dad. I need them, God, please.

Tears spring to my eyes, and I can't stop screaming into the phone. "You sick bastard. You sick, sick bastard!"

I hear him cock the gun, and then my mother screams as he grabs her hair and pulls it back, then places the barrel of the gun against her temple. My mom closes her eyes and screams, just as the phone goes dead.

Chapter 42

I CAN'T BREATHE. I look at the screen, then press it, trying to call the number back, but nothing happens. My kids have heard me scream and have come out of their rooms, Damian rubbing his eyes.

"What's going on, Mom?" Isabella asks, visibly worried.

"Take care of your brother, will you?" I ask and rise to my feet. The way I say it makes it sound like I'll never see them again. I don't know how I am even standing now, where I'm getting the strength to stay upright. I am fueled by nothing but fear and anger now.

"Where are you going?"

"Just to Grandma and Grandpa's place," I say and rush to the bedroom, grab my gun, then rush to the door, and open it.

"Lock it after me, okay? I'll be back as soon as I can."

"Did something happen to Grandma and Grandpa?" she asks.

I look into her eyes, trying to sound as calm and

collected as possible, while waves of fear rush through my body, threatening to overwhelm me.

I can't lose them. I can't lose them now, God!

"I don't know yet."

Isabella sends me a concerned look. I know she can tell how desperate I am. I run into the hallway and take the stairs down, taking two, sometimes three, steps at a time. I rush into the street, then run as fast as I can toward my parents' condominium. I cross their parking lot, my heart hammering in my chest, everything inside of me screaming.

No, no, no! Please, don't let them be harmed. Please, let them be alive, God! Please, protect them!

I fumble with the key to the front door of their building, then run up the stairs, running faster than I ever have, fear knocking in my chest.

The door to their condo is left ajar. Seeing this, I stop.

"Mom? Dad?"

There's glass on the floor. The vase they usually have by the door is lying on the tiles, shattered. I am careful not to step on any of the broken pieces while walking inside, holding the gun between my hands.

"Mom?" I say, my voice shrill and high pitched. "Dad?"

There's a trail of blood across the tiles, leading toward the kitchen. One of my dad's woolen slippers is lying by the couch. It has drops of blood on it. The only sound I can hear is the rushing of my own breath. I see the details of Sandra's bloody corpse in the water flashing before my eyes. Images of her, the sensation of her cold skin against my fingers, and I shiver in fear as I move across the living room toward the small kitchen, gun lifted in front of me. I am holding onto it as terror rushes through me in waves.

"Mom?" I cry out. "Mooom?"

I see legs sticking out behind the counter, and brace myself, trying to remain calm, even though my body starts to shake violently.

I approach the legs behind the counter with the gun still pointed ahead of me. I see their faces as I turn the corner. Two sets of terrified eyes are staring up at me, both their mouths covered with duct tape. I sense they're trying to tell me something.

That's when I hear a sound coming from the hallway as something large is tipped over.

***

IT SOUNDS JUST like the umbrella stand that I myself have tipped over a few times when coming to my parents' place. I know exactly where it stands and run back to the hallway just as someone storms out the door. I see nothing but a black figure, someone wearing a ski mask. I go after him. I know he is armed, but so am I. I am not letting him get away. Not this time.

"Stop!" I yell.

But he's out the door faster than I can get there. I continue after him, then run to the stairs where I can hear him below me. I hurry after him, taking several steps at a time, but so does he, and he has longer legs than me. Soon, he's at the bottom, gunning for the door. It's locked, and he's fumbling with it, so I see my chance to catch up to him. I jump down and point my gun at him.

"Stop it right there!"

The figure pauses. He lifts his hands in the air, and I walk closer to see him better.

"Turn around and take off the mask," I say.

He does as he is told, but he is way too fast for me. As he turns around, he reaches out his hand and grabs my gun, then pulls it out of my grip. The gun falls to the floor, and he kicks me in the stomach so hard that I fly backward with a loud scream. I hit my back against the wall, then slide to the floor, the air knocked out of me. I am so dizzy I can hardly see. I manage to raise my head. My head swims, and my mouth is flooded with saliva. I can't think straight; I can barely see. My back is in deep pain, and I am gasping for air. I bite my lip, so I don't lose consciousness. I see him jolt for the exit. Seconds later, he's back by the door, unlocking it, and soon he's running out into the parking lot.

I am still on the floor, moaning, as the door slams shut behind him.

***

ONCE I AM okay to move, and I can breathe again, I grab the gun from the floor and drag myself back up the stairs and into my parent's condo. I find them still lying in there, their terrified eyes staring up at me, their mouths duct-taped, and their hands tied behind their backs. I help them get free. My mom is in shock and can barely speak.

"I'm sorry, Mom," I say, sobbing. I hug her tightly and don't want to let go. My body is shaking, and I am fighting to hold back my tears. "It's all my fault. I am so, so sorry. Are you okay? Are you hurt?"

I look at the bruise on her cheek while she shakes her head. "I'm okay. Help me get up."

My dad is sitting up too while I help my mom to a chair. But as I look at him, I realize something is off with him. He's holding his chest and bending forward. And that is when it occurs to me.

"He's having a heart attack," I say.

I rush to him and fall to my knees by his side while I scream at my mother to call nine-one-one.

Chapter 43

AS YOU CAN IMAGINE, I am completely out of it at this point. My dad is being rushed to the hospital, and my mom is with him in the ambulance while I drive there on my own. We wait for hours till we can see him, and the doctor says he's had a heart attack, as I suspected. The doctors fight for his life and manage to save him. I still remember that smile he sends us as we walk in once they let us see him. My mom is in a state of shock and can barely talk. She sits by his side, holding his hand the rest of the night, while I go home to the kids. I sleep in their room all night, keeping the gun close. I barely sleep at all, naturally, but we make it through the night. We report the attack to the police, and they come to take my parents' statement the next day. They keep asking them what the attacker looked like, but neither of them saw his face. He was wearing a mask when he rang their doorbell and my mom went to open the door. It all happened really fast, she tells the police. He grabbed the vase by the door and hit my mom with it, then dragged her into the kitchen, where he placed both of them with their heads to the tiles.

Laurie pauses and looks down at her fingers. Jonathan nods while Detective Grande looks at her watch.

"You have somewhere to be?" Jonathan asks.

She shakes her head. He knows she is lying. Of course, she wants to get home to her husband. It's late, and she should want to go home. It's a good thing that she feels that way. He wants to tell her to enjoy it while it lasts, but he doesn't want to sound like an old geezer.

"Actually, I am getting kind of tired," Laurie says. "I think I'd like to stop for today."

"Just answer me this," Jonathan says. "Did you ask your parents if they believed it was Ryan? I mean, he is your husband and their son-in-law. They should be able to recognize his voice or his eyes."

Laurie sighs and shakes her head. "As I said, they told me they didn't get to look at his eyes properly."

"And the voice?" Grande asks, leaning forward. "What about the voice?"

"They couldn't say for sure. It all went by so fast, they both said. He was yelling, and they never heard Ryan yell before. My mom leaned toward it being him, while my dad said it was way too vague to be certain."

"Sounds like a scary experience," Jonathan says, then turns off the dictation app and smiles at Laurie. "We'll leave you for now and see you in the morning."

"YOU THINK she's pulling our leg?"

Grande asks Jonathan this as they meet for breakfast at Emmet's Diner the next morning. Jonathan ate his dinner there too, and now he's having the best bacon he's had in many years. Joanne is behind the counter, refilling his coffee, and smiling at him every time she does. Jonathan is beginning to like it in this town. It's growing on him. He loves the small cabins in the mountains, like the one where they found Laurie. One day, Jonathan wants one of those cabins and to wake up to the fog covering the mountain-tops while he's drinking his coffee on the patio, overlooking the valley below, listening to the sound of the rippling creek. Maybe one day he'll see a bear or a wild boar, and once in a while, he'll rent a boat and go sailing on the lakes. Maybe he'll even learn to like fishing. In the distance, he can hear the old steam train as it takes off from the town's center, carrying tourists on the long trail ride through the beautiful mountains. It has finally cleared up after it has been raining for almost twelve hours in a row. Jonathan's shoes are wet at the tips from stepping in a puddle this morning. The creek is overflowing in several places, and they have been warned about the great risk of mudslides.

"You mean she's lying?" he asks and takes a bite of the crunchy bacon.

As usual, Grande is only having coffee. She sips it and looks at him with a smile. Even she is growing on him. There's something to the glint in her eye that makes him want to get to know her better.

"That's exactly what I mean," she says. "I mean this story, isn't it a little too…much? All this housewife-turned-detective routine?"

"But why would she lie to us?" he asks, then sips more coffee.

"Because she killed both of them?"

That makes Jonathan laugh. "Up to now, we don't even know if a crime has been committed in that cabin."

She tilts her head. "Really? The body they found downstream in the river; that's the same man as in the picture on her phone…"

"Frank."

"Yes, Frank. He was found with several gunshot wounds. And you don't believe there's been a crime?"

"It could be self-inflicted. It could be suicide."

"You don't believe that."

"Okay, maybe not. But there are other circumstances that would explain this better than murder. Let's just wait and hear her entire story before we make any conclusions. I can't wait to hear where she's going with it."

"There's something else," Grande says.

Jonathan places his cup on the counter again, then shakes his head when Joanne is on her way to refill it. They're running late and should be going. Jonathan hopes to get the rest of Laurie's testimony today. Hopefully, they can wrap this investigation up soon. Not that he is in any hurry to get away from this town. He will miss it once he leaves. And he'll miss Joanne's dimples when she smiles.

He leaves a bill, enough to make sure there's a huge tip for Joanne included, then winks at her, grabs his jacket, and puts it on.

"Why doesn't that surprise me?" he says and walks outside into the cool wind. He loves the way it nibbles at his skin. He turns to face Grande as she follows him, putting on her raincoat.

"She's pregnant. I talked to the doctor yesterday after we were done, and he said the child is fine, despite the stress her body has been through."

Jonathan widens his eyes and nods. He puts on his hoodie as the drizzle hits his head. The clouds are hanging heavily on the mountaintops, and it'll be raining again in a short while.

"Let's see what Laurie can tell us about that."

"SO, WHO'S THE FATHER?"

Grande goes straight for it as soon as they enter. They have barely said good morning before Grande asks. A little too aggressive if you ask Jonathan. He would probably have chosen a slightly calmer approach, one that would make Laurie comfortable enough to talk about it. But that isn't Grande's style.

"The father of your child, the child you're carrying?" she continues. She's tapping her pen on the notepad.

Laurie gives them a sad expression.

"You knew, didn't you?" Grande asks and takes out her chair, then sits down. Jonathan opens the app and starts recording again. He sits down as well.

Grande continues, "Was that why you went to the cabin with him? Because it was Frank's?"

"We're getting ahead of ourselves here," Laurie says. "Let me rewind a little first."

Part IV

MY DAD RETURNS from the hospital, and my mom takes care of him. I visit almost every day, and my dad slowly grows stronger. Meanwhile, I am a mess, and it gets worse every day. I don't pick up my phone; I stay inside the condo, doors locked, and only leave when I absolutely have to, like to take Damian to school. Isabella is done with her physical therapy and is going to return to her school next week. I am thrilled about that, even though I'm very anxious too. This means I can't keep an eye on her twenty-four-seven like I have since she was shot. I can't hinder her dad from coming to the school and trying to talk to her. I can tell the front office that there's a restraining order out on him, but he could find a way if I know him. The police have told me they spoke to him about the night my parents were attacked, and according to them, he had an alibi. I'm not sure I buy it, though, since it's probably Chip or one of his other war buddies who are covering for him.

Isabella still uses the crutches to ease her walking, but she will soon be able to walk without them, her doctor promised me. She just needs to build up her muscles and keep doing the exercises she has learned. She is all caught up on her schoolwork. So, she should be able to get back with no issues. I just need to get used to the thought of letting her go out on her own again. I have been obsessively protective of her since it happened. I find it natural, but she isn't too fond of it. She keeps telling me to back off and let her live her life. She's probably right, but I am just so terrified she'll get hurt again. It's harder than you think to let go of something like this.

I barely sleep at night. I wake up so many times, it's ridiculous. I sleep with my gun next to me, ready to grab it should something happen. I am terrified of what he might do next. Getting to my parents was a clear signal to me. He can get to me anywhere, and he will. So, I have done what he told me to. I have backed off. I can't fight anymore; I can't risk the people I love anymore. I am no longer trying to warn people, nor am I writing articles or even talking to the police. I simply don't dare.

During the day, I stare at the picture of him on my screen saver, and I am reminded of the warmth he filled me with when we were still together before everything went down the drain. I thought I knew him so well. He was my second half, my better me. I hated being apart. But now I realize I was a fool. It's so obvious he's a killer when you look into his eyes. Even his smile makes me shiver now. He has the smile of a killer, I tell myself. And when I look at him, my stomach crumbles into a hard ball, and my heart rate skyrockets. He's so dashingly handsome, so calm and patient. He can be the sweetest man, so trusting and innocent, but underneath all that, he's really a predator, a vicious killer, a true psychopath. He has been fooling me for all these years, and I feel so stupid for not seeing it earlier. It's so obvious. I see him clearly now.

I just can't stand the thought that he's going to get away with it.

I AM SO CAUGHT up in my fear; I realize too late that I haven't had my period. When I finally buy the test and take it, I am already three months pregnant. I take it in my own restroom and just sit there and stare at it, completely out of it.

What am I going to do?

I call Vera, and she comes over. She brings Publix's sandwiches, my favorites with pastrami and extra mayo, and we eat lunch together when I tell her.

"I'm pregnant," I say, just blurting it out, hoping she won't resent me or judge me for not being careful enough. I need a friend now—more than ever.

She stops chewing and stares at me. She's in uniform since she's just on her lunch break and has to go back to base soon.

Her head tilts forward, and she looks at me, her eyebrows lifted. "Excuse me? Did I just hear you say that you were…pregnant?"

I nod. I don't like the word. I'm thirty-six. I hadn't expected to have more children. This wasn't the plan. The plan was two children—a boy and a girl. We got the girl first, but that didn't matter much. Just one of each and that was it. But then again, there was a lot about my plans that had been modified lately.

"So…?" she asks, waiting for me to say something. I don't know what to say, to be honest.

I shrug. "I don't know."

"But…"

"I don't know," I say. I bite my lip. "Don't judge me."

She throws out her hands. "Hey, no one is judging here. I just…well, it would be great to know if it was my brother's or…"

I give her a look, and she stops talking. This is exactly my dilemma. I have just started seeing Frank. To be honest, I was just seeking comfort with him; at least I think that's what I have been doing. I'm not quite in a state where I can fall in love right now. I like him; I do. But do I love him? It's hard to tell. I am technically still married, and the way things are, it might have to stay that way for a while. I have asked for a divorce, and my lawyer has sent over the papers to Ryan, but he refuses to sign.

"I take it you don't know," she says. "Is there a possibility it could also be…Ryan's?"

I nod, then sip my Coke. I shouldn't be drinking this stuff, I think to myself. I have to start thinking about the baby from now on.

"It could also be his," I say.

"Oh, my word," Vera says, taking another bite of her sandwich. She chews pensively. "If it is my brother's, he'll live up to his responsibilities; you can be certain of that."

"And if it isn't his?" I ask. "Am I about to have another child with a murderer?"

Vera stops chewing again and looks at me. "Shoot. That is bad news."

"I need to find out somehow whose it is. I don't know what I'll do if it's Ryan's."

"Maybe never tell him?"

I look up. "Not quite fair to him or the child. Besides, he'll see it next time he sees me, and he'll start asking questions. If I say it's Frank's, I'll be putting his life in danger."

Vera shrugs. "True. That is quite a dilemma."

"I'm gonna try to get a DNA test," I say and drink more Coke. Last sip, I promise myself. Just like I tell myself

I'll see a doctor about this pregnancy soon. I just keep post-poning it, just like I kept postponing taking the test because I simply can't face this dilemma. I can't have another child with this man.

I don't dare to.

Chapter 45

I ASK Vera to help me get a DNA sample from Frank. I want to try him first, but I can't ask him; I don't want him to be suspicious or even to get his hopes up. We always hang out at my place since he doesn't like me to come to his. He's embarrassed about how small it is, he usually says. He'll be suspicious if I ask to see it, and if I start to poke around looking for hairs on a comb or something like that, I'll only get caught. I don't do sneaking around. It's just not me. I wasn't even able to lie to my parents as a child. I tried once and told them I was going to my best friend Shawna Wyndham's house when I was actually going to a party at Mike Stargill's house. They bought it, but I couldn't stand it, and seconds later, I ran into the living room and told them the truth. I am not good at this stuff, I realized then.

Vera promises me she will get some hair from him somehow, and about a week later, she texts me and tells me to meet her. She's got news, the text says. Then she adds to meet her at the Causeway. I wonder why she has chosen that out of the way place…if she is afraid to be seen with me, then shake the thought. I send the kids off to school, then shower and get myself ready. I feel good today, and for the first time in days, I don't feel nauseous. I look at my naked body in the mirror as I come out of the shower, then feel my bulging stomach. It's still so little that I am the only one who can see it. I never showed much till I was late in my pregnancies, and with Damian, I didn't show until I was seven months pregnant. I know I am not going to be able to hide it forever, but I still have a little time.

I drive past the base on my way there. I feel my heart rate go up as I drive past the entrance, thinking about Ryan and fearing he might see me or know I am here, then tell myself I am silly for being so paranoid.

I drive onto the bridge, going toward the mainland, then take the exit halfway. There's an old bridge there that is closed off now, and a part of it is used today for fishing. There's a small parking area underneath it, where I go. I drive down the narrow gravel road, bumping along, dust whirling in the air around me. I stop by the riverside and put the minivan in park. Vera isn't there yet.

I wait for about ten minutes, then text her, asking where she is.

I AM HERE. WAITING.

She doesn't answer. It annoys me. I hate to wait. There's no one fishing on the bridge today. I get out of the car and walk down to the water. It's a quiet day, and the Intracoastal water is barely moving. I see boats as they rush by, and birds are chirping from the mangroves. I see a row of about ten pelicans as they float above me, then take turns diving into the water, catching fish. It's one of those gorgeous Florida spring days that I used to enjoy so much. But now, it just reminds me of the many times Ryan took us fishing on his days off, of how he used to help the kids and teach them everything about fishing and even how to gut the fish afterward and grill them for dinner. I still have the picture of Damian with the huge grouper he once caught that was almost bigger than himself. It's on the shelf in his room.

I check my phone again to see if Vera has texted me back. She hasn't. It's been almost twenty minutes now. I don't have time for this. I walk back to the minivan, and my hand is on the handle when I see a truck drive up on the old bridge above me. I wonder for a second if it is someone who is coming there to fish, then I am about to open the door when suddenly I pause. The truck stops on top of the bridge, and someone gets out. He's wearing a baseball cap. I can't see his face. He walks to the passenger side, then pulls someone else out. It's the short blonde hair on that person who is being dragged toward the edge of the bridge that makes my heart stop.

Vera?

She's fighting the person holding her, but he's too strong for her. I stare at them, completely frozen, paralyzed.

What's going on? What's this guy doing to Vera?

It all goes by so fast; I can barely react. It all becomes a little blurry. I remember seeing a gun, a gun in the man's hand. At least I think it is from the way he's holding it. I remember Vera screaming, and I see her struggling to free herself from his grip. Then, I see the gun being placed forcefully in her hand, then steered toward her temple. He's the one holding her arm, controlling it.

I don't even have time to scream before the gun is fired. Next, I see her body fall from the bridge toward the water. There are two splashes, one when the body hits the water, and one when the gun does.

I STARE at the water where Vera has disappeared. My breath becomes shorter and shorter until I am not breathing at all anymore. I think I'm shaking, but I'm not sure. I don't know if I'm even blinking. It's like everything has completely stopped. I see the guy get back into his truck and leave; I see the truck drive away, but I don't do anything.

Am I terrified? Possibly. Am I in deep shock? Very possible.

It's not until the truck has completely disappeared that I finally dare to move. I fumble with my phone between my hands, then call nine-one-one. Somehow, I manage to tell the woman at dispatch that a body was just plunged into the water and give her directions. As soon as I have hung up, I throw the phone on the ground, then take off my flip-flops before I walk into the water.

I HAVE ALWAYS BEEN a good swimmer, and it comes in handy now. Luckily, there isn't any wind today, so there are no waves in the river. I push myself hard and realize I am far from the shape I thought I was in. My arms are hurting, and I am panting both with fear and effort. I can't stop thinking about poor Vera, and every time I do, I start to cry, but I can't let myself do that because I am losing momentum when I lose hope. I have to keep swimming if I am to find her; I can't let despair get the better of me now. I simply can't.

I spot something in the water as I swim close to where I saw her being pushed in. But as I come closer, I can no longer see it. Frustrated, I call out her name like she can answer. I keep swimming, and suddenly, I see her. She's lying on the surface, face down. There is blood in the water around her.

"Oh, God, Vera," I pant, then swim to her and grab her. "Please, Vera, please."

I pull her around, then see how badly her face is messed up. There is no way she's still alive. My body starts to shake violently as I realize this, and soon, I break down and cry. I can't stand it anymore; I have to let it out, even though I am swallowing lots of water. I hear sirens approaching in the distance, and soon, I can hear voices yelling as divers are sent in after us.

Chapter 46

THEY TAKE me up on the bridge after taking Vera away in a body bag. They have wrapped me in a blanket and given me a juice box, so I don't dehydrate. I feel like a child as I hold it in my hand. I cry helplessly. I can't control it anymore, and I don't know what to do. Vera is—*was*—my best friend. Gosh, it hurts even to think it. She was the only one I could trust, besides her brother Frank. I can't believe she's not here anymore. It's too surreal.

"So, this is where you saw her?" the detective asks and points. I stare at him, then at the spot. There's blood on the asphalt and the railing. I nod, closing my eyes, trying not to relive it again. I focus on surviving right now, nothing else. I just have to get through this, get through this moment, awful as it is.

If you can get through this, you can get through anything.

"And you say there was someone here with her?"

I nod again. "He forced the gun to her head, then fired it. He pushed her over the edge, and she dropped into the water…I think he wanted to make it look like suicide. That's why he put it in her hand first."

"And why would he do that?"

"Because she's military, and well…suicide is pretty common…it's what he does," I say. I can tell by the detective's face that he doesn't quite understand what I'm saying. He's from the mainland police. He doesn't know anything about the previous murders or about the restraining order, or anything else for that matter. I can't explain it to him. I know he won't listen. I know he'll give me that look that will make me feel like Lunatic Laurie. Besides, I fear this was all Ryan's doing. He wanted me to see it. He wants me to know that he can do whatever he wants, that he'll come for me next if I don't shut up. He's sending me a message, telling me he's serious. He couldn't get my parents, so he found someone else that was close to me. He knew exactly how to hurt me the most and the deepest.

Already, this detective, Reed, looks at me like he thinks I'm rambling.

"Who does this?" he asks. "What do you mean?"

"He makes it look like suicide," I say, trying anyway, even though I know it's no use.

A frown grows between detective Reed's otherwise friendly eyes. "So, you're saying this has happened before?"

I can tell he's exchanging a look with another officer who is taking pictures of the scene. I know that look. I don't want to stay here anymore. I want to leave. I am broken to pieces. I have called my mom and asked her to pick up the kids at school today. I told her I'd have to explain later. She could tell I was in shock, so she naturally asked me if I was okay. I am not, I told her. Then I broke down and cried.

"Yes," I answer. "Something similar. Not the same."

"And how do you know this?"

I tell him everything anyway, just in case. As I do, he nods along like he knows what I am talking about.

"I think I read about this in the paper," he says.

I stare at him, wondering if he is actually taking me seriously. He seems to be.

"Yeah, I did," he says. "There were a lot of unanswered questions. But it's on Air Force grounds, so the cases are investigated by their people. I think they reopened some of the cases, though. I'll call and have a chat with them. Now, what can you tell me about the car this guy drove?"

"It was a truck. A big blue truck."

As I say the words, it occurs to me that Ryan's truck is black, and when I think about it, it didn't look like his at all. This one was only a two-seater; Ryan's is a four-seater. But I think I have seen this truck before. I just can't recall where. It's not until the detective leaves me to talk to someone else, and I spot something on the ground that I fully realize whose truck this is.

The very thought causes my blood to freeze.

THEY TELL me to go home. They tell me to get some rest, and then they'll ask me to come in for more questioning later. Detective Reed even hugs me and tells me it'll be okay, that they'll get this bastard, but it doesn't make me feel better. I don't tell him what I have found on the ground. Why not? I can't say. Maybe because the realization shocks me so deeply, I have to deal with it myself.

So, I don't do as he tells me. I don't go back home, even though it is late, and I need to get back to my children. Instead, I go to the base, show my ID, then drive in. I drive past the landing strips, past the big playground that is empty now due to it being so late, past the community pool, and into the south housing area. I drive onto a small street and look at all the houses on each side, warm lights oozing out of them as the families are doing their routines inside, enjoying that the workday is finally over and they now have time for what they really love, who they really love. I remember those days when I just couldn't wait for Ryan to come home…when hearing the truck drive up in the driveway was the biggest highlight of my day. Once he was inside, and we had kissed, everything would be calm again. He'd take the crying kid in his arms and change the diaper, or he'd take over the cooking while I'd set the table, handing him a much-deserved beer, enjoying his downtime from a long day. He'd tell me stories about flying if he'd been in the air that day, which were his favorite days. He'd tell me fun stories someone else had told him or what someone did, and we'd laugh together. We'd eat together, and everything was right with the world. I'd worry about him being deployed soon or about the kids getting sick, but those were my biggest troubles. Back then, they had seemed so big and overwhelming, but compared to now, it was a walk in the park. I'd go back to that time any day now if only I could.

But it is too late for that.

I park in front of the house, then kill the engine. I hold the object tightly in my hand and look at it one last time before I leave the car. I know this is risky. I know I should have let the police take care of it, but this has gotten personal.

I wipe the tears away and let the anger fuel me. I walk up to the front door, then ring the bell, taking a couple of deep breaths to calm myself enough to muster the courage

I very much need. I have the gun in my pocket and am just so relieved I wasn't taken aside for random inspection on the way in. I couldn't do this without it. I couldn't catch a killer without being armed.

Chapter 47

HIS BLUE EYES stare at me from behind the screen door. He opens it and steps outside, running a hand across his bald head, rubbing it nervously as the door slams shut behind him. I can hear cicadas singing somewhere close by. I used to love that sound, but now it annoys me; it's like a drill in my head.

"Laurie? Is that you? What are you doing here?"

I can barely breathe. I haven't seen Ryan since the day he was in my condo. I have been so angry with him, so frustrated and mad, but now, as I am standing right in front of him, looking into his deep blue eyes, all those emotions seem to melt. Gosh, I miss him. For some reason, I can't stop thinking about the cute way he curls his lip when he concentrates. Like he's doing right now as he steps toward me.

"Laurie," he says my name so softly it almost rolls off the tongue. "Listen…about the last time I came to see you…I was… Well, I haven't been well, Laurie. I know it's no surprise to you, but that day, it was bad. It's no excuse, but you have to know something. After I read that article, and after everyone was on my case about it, I did something I wasn't proud of. I took some…something I wasn't supposed to. I got my hands on some…cocaine. It messed me up."

He whispers the last part since he's afraid someone might hear. Doing drugs could get him kicked out of the Air Force, and he knows it very well. There's something different about him today. There's a different tone to his voice than the last time we spoke, and it is haunting me. Today, both his voice and eyes are saturated with guilt.

"What you did," he says, clenching his fist swiftly, then easing up again. "Writing that article made me so angry, and I still think it was wrong of you. You could have come to me; you could have talked to me about those things instead of making all these accusations, claiming those awful things. You didn't think about the consequences, and you did a lot of harm around here and made me very unpopular. But that being said, it didn't give me the right to…" he trails off, his jaw clenched before he continues. "What I am trying to say is that… The man you saw on that day, the man that came to you, it wasn't me, Laurie. You know it wasn't. You know me, and that day, I was someone different. I'm embarrassed to tell you this, but…I think you deserve to know the truth. And I can tell you it won't happen again. I promise you this. I have stayed off the drugs since. I have meant to tell…"

"Save it, Ryan," I say. Tears are stinging the back of my eyes. I can't grasp any of what he is saying. I try so hard not to think about Vera, but the images of her falling from the bridge and lying on the stretcher as they close the body bag, keep flickering in my mind. I don't want to hear all of Ryan's excuses and explanations. I am not here for them.

He pauses, then looks down at what is in my hand. A

deep frown grows between his eyes, and he gives me a puzzled look.

"Where did you get that?"

I lift the silver case. The e-cigarette inside of it rattles.

"I found it."

He looks at me expectantly, waiting for an explanation. "So, you brought it here to give it to Chip? He can't live without this stuff. I don't know how he can get himself to vape…"

Ryan stops. He sees my eyes as they fill and takes a step toward me. The softness in his voice gives way to a slightly more doubtful tone.

"Laurie, are you okay?"

I shake my head while biting my lip excessively.

"He killed her."

Ryan looks worriedly at me. He is getting small red spots on his cheeks, as he often does when agitated. The way his upper lip curls tell me he's trying to hide his skepticism. He doesn't want to push me away, so he is really trying to sound compassionate.

"Who? What are you talking about?"

I swallow the growing knot in my throat. I lift the case. "This. This is why I'm here. For Chip. He killed her."

"Now, you're not making any sense at all, Laurie…" The pitch of his voice is raised a little.

"He killed Vera, Ryan. He shot her and pushed her off a bridge. He placed the gun in her hand first to make it look like suicide. I saw him do it. I saw… I saw… Vera plunge right into the water. I was there when they pulled her out and took her away. She's gone…Vera is dead. And Chip did it. He probably killed Clarice, Sandra, and Ted too, and tried to kill Duke. It was him all along."

Ryan pauses. He looks at me, and I can tell he's at a

loss for words; he's debating within himself what to say, what to believe.

"Laurie, you're beginning to sound crazy again. I don't think you're well... Maybe I should take you home," he says. "Come, let me drive you home; you shouldn't be driving in this state."

Ryan is about to grab me when the door opens behind him, and Chip comes out. "Ryan are you goi..."

He stops when he sees me. "What's she doing here?"

I am crying heavily now, even though I'm fighting to hold it back. Seeing Chip makes me lose it, and my torso is bouncing violently as I try to hold back the sobs. I see Vera fall over and over again. I hear the plunge; I see her face on the stretcher over and over again, and I want to scream. The air is so hot and muggy; I can hardly breathe.

Chip steps out with a smug smile on his face. He leans on Ryan's shoulder like they're best buddies, making sure I understand that they'll stay together, and I can't come between them, that they'll protect one another no matter what.

"What's going on here?" he asks, looking from me to Ryan, then back at me. "You bringing any more lies and crazy stories?"

"Did you kill her?" I ask and hold up the case with the rattling e-cigarette inside of it. "Was it you?"

When he sees the case, he lights up. "Where did you get that? I've been looking everywhere for it."

He snaps it from my hand. The motion startles me, and I pull back, but not for long. I can't let him feel how scared I am of him.

"I know what you did, Chip," I say, trying to sound as matter of fact as possible, given the situation. "And don't give me any more of those lies. I saw you when you pushed her into the water."

He sends me a look of surprise, then glares at Ryan. "What's she talking about now?"

He's still grinning until I pull out the gun and point it at him.

"I know you killed Vera."

"WHOA."

Chip puts his hands up and steps back.

"Ryan, what is this?" he asks. "Please, tell your wife to calm down."

"Laurie," Ryan says. "Please put down the gun."

I shake my head. My hands are trembling.

"Laurie," Chip says. "I didn't kill anyone; please, calm down and explain. What are you talking about?"

"Vera," I say, struggling to get her name across my lips. "She was killed, and I saw you push her over the railing. I saw you put the gun against her head, then pull the trigger and drive away in your truck, the blue truck!"

Chip steps forward. "Laurie, please, stop this insanity. I haven't hurt anyone. I don't know why you'd think this. I don't even have the blue truck anymore."

"What?" I stare at him but don't lower the gun.

"It's true," Ryan says. "He sold it two weeks ago."

"And the case?" I ask. "The e-cigarette case I found on the ground where you and Vera stood. You have an excuse for that as well?"

Chip looks down at it, then turns it in the sparse light from the window. "Actually, I don't. I haven't seen it for several days. I thought I had left it somewhere, or maybe Lotty had thrown it out. You know how much she hates that I vape."

"Laurie," Ryan says. "I think... I don't think you're

well."

I can't think straight. I look into Chip's eyes, and I don't know what to believe. I have known him for years. Our kids played together. I trusted him with my husband's life when they deployed. I suddenly don't know what has gotten into me. Am I wrong? Could I be mistaken? I look at Ryan and feel confused. I don't know if I can trust either of them. I don't know if I am the one who's lost sight of reality or if they're playing games with me. I don't know if Ryan is right.

Am I the one who is insane here? Am I just being paranoid and seeing things?

"Laurie, hand me the gun," Ryan says. "Then, we can talk."

I look at him, and our eyes lock. My nostrils are flaring, my heart pounding so hard it almost hurts. I shake my head. I don't know what to do.

"I...I..."

"Laurie," Ryan says and gets that tone to his voice, the one that makes me feel like a child. My throat grows tight, and I touch it with the hand not holding the gun while I remember the look in his eyes when he tried to strangle me. I am reminded of seeing the same look in them when he shot our daughter and blamed me afterward.

"Laurie, hand me the gun before anyone gets hurt."

I shake my head again, this time violently. I lift the gun high and point it at them. "No. Stay back. Don't come anywhere near me, you hear?"

They both back off, and I turn around, then run for my minivan. As I race back toward the exit, I fear they might have called the security forces on me, to arrest me, but I slide through the gate with no problem. Tears spring from my eyes and spill onto the steering wheel as I hit the accelerator and floor it on my way home.

Chapter 48

FRANK IS A MESS. After Vera's funeral, he comes up to me and leans onto my shoulder, crying. I feel sick. Ryan and Chip are there too, as are the rest of their unit. They stick together like glue. I have paid my respects to Vera's parents, Sammy and Hattie, and told them how sorry I am. It's unbearable to look into their eyes, knowing they have been told it was a suicide. The police investigated for about a week before they came to that conclusion, apparently completely ignoring my statement. I have a feeling that Investigator Rick Thibodeau might have had a finger in that, disregarding the value of my testimony. Maybe he's a part of it all too, I wonder. Maybe they all are, and I'm just one person trying to fight them, up against a brutal and massive force, fighting a fight I know I can't possibly win. I know that I have messed it all up. If I hadn't taken the e-cigarette case, maybe the police would have found it and used it as evidence. Now, I have messed up any chance of taking down Chip.

Maybe it doesn't matter anymore.

"I can't… I can't…" Frank says, his eyes red-rimmed.

I hold him close. "You don't have to. Not now. How about we get out of here? You need to get away. Spring break is coming up. My sister has a cabin up in North Carolina. Let's go up there for a couple of days, just the two of us. My sister can take the kids. She'll like that. She misses them, and she recently moved, so Ryan doesn't know where she lives. They'll be safe there."

Frank sniffles and looks into my eyes. His face is strained in deep pain. I can't imagine how deeply it must hurt to have lost two sisters in such a short amount of time. I feel painfully guilty for Vera's death, and it is eating me up. I'm the one she was supposed to meet. I keep thinking it wouldn't have happened if we hadn't planned to meet. I keep thinking I should have kept her out of it from the beginning. I fear she was killed to shut me up—to scare me —which I have to admit was a success. I am so terrified that I barely sleep at night.

"I'd like that," he says, wiping his eyes with the sleeve of his black shirt. "I'd really like that."

* * *

I HAVE another reason for taking Frank to the cabin in Bryson City, besides getting him away and maybe helping him feel better. I have thought it through a lot and decided I want this to be Frank's child. I want to tell him I am pregnant, both because I think he'll be very happy and because it's time. I'm not getting any smaller, and since we're sleeping together, he'll start noticing soon. I'm ninety-percent sure it's his, or maybe seventy-five if I am honest. But I don't care about that. I want Frank to be the dad, whether he is so biologically or not. He'll be a great father, and he and I will make a good couple. If he asks for a DNA test, I will make sure to get one, but if he doesn't, then there's no need for us ever to know. In my eyes, he is the father.

We drive there in my minivan and drop off the kids at my sister's in Jacksonville on our way. Luckily, they both love Alicia, and no one is crying or even angry that they have to spend three days at her house. She lives right on the beach, so I'm sure she'll be able to keep them busy while we're gone. They're bringing Rosie and the bunnies with them too, so they won't be alone. It'll be good for them.

I'm nervous as we get back into the car and drive up and through Georgia, then into the Carolinas. Not because I'm worried about my children; I feel confident they're safe where they are. I'm not worried about my parents either since they have taken a trip to Colorado as they like to do at this time of year. They go for hikes, and my dad fishes while my mom reads. They have a place they like to visit up there with some friends every year, so I feel confident they're safe too. Plus, it'll be good for my dad's recovery to get closer to nature. What I am worried about is Frank. How will he take it once I tell him about the baby? How will he react to the news that he is suddenly going to be a father? Will he run away? Will he be happy? We never discussed this. Does he even want to be a father? And how will it all work out? Will he want to marry me? Do I want to get married again? How will the kids react? Will they welcome Frank into their lives?

So many uncertain things make my stomach churn as I drive the long stretch up the mountainside. There are cabins hidden between the trees, but there's a lot of distance between them. I see a car in one of the driveways, but most of them are empty. The sun is shining down on us as we drive upward and is reflected in the sparse snow on the sides of the road that is left from winter while we drive up the gravel road and finally reach the cabin. It is well hidden behind a row of pine trees, and as we drive into the driveway and get out, the view opens up to us of the valley below. It is breathtaking. We are surrounded by mountaintops hiding behind a light cloud cover—giving the place the name The Smokey Mountains—and we can see the creek that is running in the back behind the cabin. Birds are chirping in the tall trees covering us from the road, and the air is so cool and fresh, you can almost feel how healthy it is when breathing. I am suddenly feeling less worried as we carry our things and groceries inside. For the first time in days, Frank is smiling behind those sad eyes.

As we cook the chicken we bought on our way here, I almost manage to forget about Ryan and Chip, and even Vera isn't on my mind anymore. At least not constantly like she was back at home. Frank seems to lighten up as well. He kisses me and serves me a glass of red wine. I take it with a smile and pretend to be drinking, but don't drink any of it. I hope he doesn't notice since I'm not ready to tell him yet. I want to wait until the right moment, and that isn't now.

We spend the evening by the fireplace, me curled up against him on the couch, the fire crackling. He sips his wine, and my glass just rests on the table. I stare into the flames, feeling calm, listening to his heartbeat close to my ear. This is exactly what I need right now—being there, with him, alone. This place has such a calm to it; I feel like all my troubles have been left behind. I know I am just fooling myself; I know my problems are far from gone. Nothing has been solved yet, but I allow myself to enjoy this moment, to tell myself that maybe life can be good again.

Maybe.

Chapter 49

I WAKE WITH A GASP. I am frightened. I don't know why. Is it my dream? Is it that sense of dread that is constantly with me, eating me up from inside, making me feel this deep sense of being sick? Is it worry? Nervousness? Anxiety? My thoughts are a mess. The more I think, the worse it gets. I breathe and focus on calming myself. Frank is in bed next to me. My heart is hammering, and it won't stop.

Why am I so scared?

Frank snores lightly then turns in his sleep. The sun is peeking out behind the mountaintops, and its rays are hitting his face through the window. Frank has soft skin, and the sunlight bounces off him and makes him almost sparkle. I try to imagine myself being married to him, having a child, growing old. The thought is soothing to me. It makes me feel better. Frank makes me feel better. He makes me feel safe. And that is what I need right now.

Frank opens his eyes and looks at me, then smiles.

"Hi, there."

I lean over and kiss him. He is still smiling as our lips

part. "How are you so beautiful when you've just woken up?"

I chuckle and push his shoulder gently.

"It's true," he says. "You look stunning."

Instinctively, I touch my stomach as I am reminded of what it is carrying. I grow serious; my fingers caressing his skin.

"What?" he asks.

I stare at him, biting my lip. I know I have planned to wait for the right time, but I make the decision quickly. This might as well be the right time. I reach over and grab his hand, then lead it to my stomach. I place it on my skin and look up at him. Our eyes lock. His grow wide as the realization slowly sinks in.

"Are you trying to tell me something?"

I stare into his eyes. He barely blinks. I can't read his face; I don't know if he is happy, or just surprised. Is he mad? Scared? What is he thinking? Does he want to run away?

Then, I nod. I am still biting my lip and holding his hand on my skin.

"You mean to say you're…?"

I nod again.

"Yes, Frank. That is what I'm saying."

His hand is removed, pulled away forcefully. Startled at this, I look at him. His eyes are blank. I still can't tell what his reaction is.

"You're pregnant?" he says. I know he has realized this, but he wants to be sure. He wants me to confirm it, to say the actual words.

"Yes, I am pregnant."

"And it's mine?"

I hate that question. It assumes that I have slept with

others—makes me feel like a slut. But, of course, he has the right to ask. I am, after all, still married, and we've not been together for that long.

"Yes, it is yours."

He is barely breathing now. I can tell he is fighting his emotions.

"And you're sure about that?"

I sigh and close my eyes briefly. "Not one hundred percent, no." I lift my glance, hoping my honesty is the right approach. "Listen, we will do a test to be sure. But you're the guy I want to be the father of this child, no matter what."

He is staring at me. He can't find words. I can tell he is struggling. His lips are moving, but no sound is coming out. Not until after a few seconds when he finally manages to say, "So…I'm gonna be a dad? Like a real dad?"

His eyes are lighting up now, and I can see a smile as it lingers in the corners of his mouth. It is pulling his lips into a smile.

"Yes, Frank."

"I'm gonna be a father, a real father? We're having a baby? We're having a baby together?"

I chuckle. "Yes. That's what people usually do. Have babies together."

He places his hand on his face, then rubs his stubble. "Oh, my God. I can't believe it. I am having a child? I'm gonna be a daddy?"

He is smiling now and leaning forward to kiss me. He kisses me on the lips, on the forehead, on my cheeks, and then he leans forward and kisses my belly.

"Hello there, little one. I'm Frank. I'm gonna be your daddy. Do you hear me?" He looks up at me for reassurance. "Does he hear me?"

I shrug. "Probably. And just to be clear, it might just as well be a girl, you do know that, right?"

He laughs. "A girl? I'd love a girl. I love girls. And I think I'm doing a pretty decent job with Isabella, right? I mean, she likes me, doesn't she?"

I nod with another chuckle. "Actually, she does. She is quite fond of you."

"See? I can have a girl. I can't believe it. I'm gonna be a father. This is big. This is huge." He pauses. "You must be hungry. I bet you are; you're eating for two. How about I start by making you some pancakes, huh? And eggs, you should have eggs. No, don't get up. I'll bring breakfast to you in bed. From now on, you won't have to lift a finger."

He jumps out of bed with a happy sound, then gets dressed and rushes downstairs to prepare breakfast. I lean back in the bed, smiling. I realize that all my fear is gone. My heart is no longer pounding. I don't have that sense of deep dread inside me anymore. I am overwhelmed with joy at this moment. It is over. I told him, and now we can move on to the next chapter of our lives. Maybe I can even persuade him to move away with the kids and me. Get away from Ryan and his buddies to a safe place, where we can raise the children together. Maybe we can get a fresh start somewhere. Yes, that's what we need—just to get away.

Start all over.

WE EAT BREAKFAST IN BED. We go for a long walk, hiking a trail in the mountains. It's beautiful, and we're happy together. We're holding hands, and we're kissing, we're cooking dinner together when we get back and holding hands while staring into the fireplace after we're done eating. It's the perfect day. I can't remember a time in my life when I have been as happy as I am at this moment. Not since Ryan and I were younger, at least. But back then, it was different. We had so much going on that we barely had time to enjoy my pregnancies; we hardly ever looked each other in the eyes the way Frank and I are doing now. We were young and restless; we had no time just to stare into the fire, or even enjoy this precious moment.

Frank seems like he feels the exact same way too. We take pictures of us together on my phone, we goof around, and we even read to one another from a book we found in the cabin. It's a scary book, and I tuck myself under the covers as we sit on the couch, curled up together. That's when I feel the baby kick for the first time, and I jump.

"What was that?" Frank asks.

I stare up at him. "The baby...it..."

"It kicked?" he asks, smiling from ear to ear.

I nod, then grab his hand and put it on my stomach. Of course, nothing happens.

"Wait for it."

"I can't feel anything," he says.

We wait. I pray the baby will do it again for Frank's sake. I want him to feel it. It's awesome and amazing and nothing like anything else in this world.

It kicks again. I gasp slightly and look up at him.

"There. Did you feel that?"

He laughs. His entire face lights up. "Oh, my God. That was intense."

I smile while he leans over and kisses me again. It feels good...like we're one now. Like we have always been together and it is meant to be.

Frank bends down and kisses my stomach, then caresses it gently. I laugh because it's tickling me when my eyes fall on something outside the panoramic windows.

A shadow.

"What is that?"

Frank sits up straight. "What is what?"

As I look outside, the shadow suddenly moves, and soon it is gone. "Out there. There was someone there. Someone was standing over there by the row of trees."

Frank gives me a look. "All the way out here? It can't be. Who would come all the way up here? We're so far away from everyone. The next-door cabin is all the way up on the hill, and it's empty. We walked past it earlier on our hike, remember? There was no one there, not a single soul. Not even a car parked outside."

"That's why I don't like it," I say. "It's not a joke. I'm telling you. There was someone out there. I am certain, Frank. I saw someone move by the trees."

"Are you sure this pregnancy isn't making you paranoid?" he asks with a grin. I don't find it funny at all and ignore him.

"I don't like it, Frank."

Frank gets up and walks to the big windows, then looks outside, shielding his eyes from the light from the living room.

"I don't see anyone," he says, shaking his head. "I don't think there's anyone there."

"But I saw someone. This person was standing there, over there by the trees, and then when I saw him, he moved away, running away fast."

"Maybe it was a bear?" Frank says. I realize he's just trying to calm me down, but I know what I saw. "Yeah, that's probably it. They have a lot of bears up here, that's why they have those extra locks on the bins outside, so the bears can't get into the garbage."

"No," I say and get up from the couch. "That was no bear."

I look out the window myself, toward the trees. There's nothing there, at least no one I can see. But I know I saw someone, and it was no animal. It moved like a human. And I know deep within me that's what it was. It was a person. It was a person who was looking in at us.

Chapter 50

I RUN up to the bedroom and grab my suitcase and start packing. Frank comes up to me a few minutes later. He is standing in the doorway.

"Hey. What are you doing?"

"We're leaving."

Frank steps forward. He stops me and grabs me by the shoulders. "You gotta calm down, Laurie. I looked out, and there was no one there."

"I saw someone," I say, almost in tears. "I saw someone looking in at us."

Frank stares at me, then exhales. "Okay, say you did see someone. Maybe it was just a homeless guy or someone walking their dog late."

I shake my head. "What if it's Chip? What if he's coming for me? I saw him on the bridge. I saw him push Vera. I am dangerous to him. If he killed Vera and all the others as well, then he'll see no problem in killing me too, to make sure I don't talk."

"I thought you said you weren't certain it was him?"

Frank says. "You saw the truck, and you found the case, but…the truck was sold two weeks earlier, right?"

"I know. I know what I said," I moan and sit down on the bed with a heavy sigh. I feel so confused like I have all these pieces to a puzzle, but I have no idea how to make them fit together. My head is hurting. I hide my face between my hands. Frank sits down next to me, an arm wrapped around my shoulder.

"These past several months have been tough on you, Laurie. But you need to try and relax. You're beginning to sound a little paranoid lately. I went outside just a minute ago to check if there was anyone there, and I walked all around the cabin. I saw nothing. You're safe here, Laurie. Not Chip, nor Ryan can come anywhere near you."

I lift my head and look into his eyes. There's something about Frank that makes me feel so safe.

"I am seriously worried about you, Laurie. It's destroying you. You're not sleeping; you're barely eating. You're in a worse state than me. I'm the one who's lost two sisters."

"I know; I know," I say. "I'm sorry for making this about me. I'm just…"

He kisses my lips to shut me up. I let him. I don't want to say anymore. I am so tired, so exhausted from the lack of proper sleep for weeks, and the constant worrying and wondering. All it has done is to make me feel like they're right about me, that I am just crazy. Did I really actually see a guy with Vera on the bridge? The police have asked me this over and over again. What was he wearing? What did he look like? And I can't answer. All I remember is the blue baseball cap. It bothers me greatly that I can't remember anything else. They've told me they believe I might have imagined it—that maybe my mind played tricks on me because it was too hard for me to realize that my best friend might kill herself. I am beginning to fear they are right. The more days that pass, the more I feel like maybe have just been fooling myself all along, seeing what I wanted to see. But what about the bruises I got at Duke's house? They were very real. There was someone there, someone trying to stop me. I was attacked. Just like I did see someone on that bridge.

I shake my head and push Frank away. He looks at me intently.

"I am not crazy," I say.

"I never said you were," he says.

I smile, then pull him onto the bed with me.

WE SLEEP IN. I have a good night's rest for once, and I feel a lot better when we wake up. It's raining today, making everything gray and wet outside. It's warmer today than the day before, and the rain is making the small piles of snow disappear, washing them away. Soon, it's like there's water everywhere, running from the top of the mountain anywhere it is allowed to. It creates a small flood running past the house and into the creek below, turning the ground into mud. The wooden porch outside, facing the creek, is wet and nasty. The fog covers the mountain-tops in front of us. We stay inside, drinking our coffee and eating pancakes. Frank puts more wood in the fireplace and lights it. I cover myself with a blanket and read to him from the book we started reading. Hours go by until we finally grow tired of the story and put the book away. I call the kids and ask them what they've been doing. Damian has been on the beach all day, while Isabella preferred to stay in my sister's condo. She tells me she doesn't like the sun or the beach anymore. I tell her she used to love the beach and that I couldn't drag her out of the ocean when she was younger and that she might change her mind when she grows older, but she doesn't believe me.

"People change," she says, then adds that she'd much rather just watch her favorite YouTubers or play Skyrim on her computer.

I don't want to get into a fight with her, so I tell her I have to go, then say goodbye. Frank is in the shower as I hang up. I stare at my screen, then at the number that texted me after I was attacked at Duke's house and called me from my parent's place. I have tried to call it numerous times and texted all my frustrations to it, yelling at the bastard that I'll come for him. I have also given it to the police, but they can't trace it since it's a burner phone, they say. Probably thrown out in a trash bin somewhere. I put my phone in my pocket, then walk upstairs to find a sweater. I am freezing.

I walk into the bedroom, where I have put my suitcase and Frank his sports bag. The water is running in the bath-room as Frank is still in the shower. I grab my suitcase, then go through my things, looking for something warmer, but the only sweater I brought isn't comfortable. I look at Franks' bag. He has the best hoodie that I love to wear. It's so soft on the skin and so big on me that I can almost use it as a dress. I love that one and go to his bag to find it. I'm sure he won't mind. I dig in and rummage through the bag. I find his denim shirt, a couple of T-shirts, his jeans, and then there it is. The blue sweater I love so much. I grab it, and, as I do, my hand touches something else, something that makes my stomach flip as I pull it out and look at it.

A cell phone.

It's not the iPhone that he usually uses; this is a small cheap-looking phone that I have never seen before. I sit down on the bed, looking at the phone in my hand. My pulse is quickening, and I can hear my own breath. I debate within myself whether to turn it on or not, but it's useless. I know I'm going to since there is no way I'm going just to leave this alone. A phone like this can't be good news.

As I wait for it to turn on, I tell myself it might be nothing, that maybe it's for his work, or maybe it's an old phone he forgot to get rid of, but I know deep in my heart that's not it. I know I am about to step out in deep waters, and that there is no way back.

Heart hammering in my chest, I stare down at the display as it lights up. It needs a password to open, so I can't look into it. I am almost about to put it down; then a thought strikes me. Fumbling nervously, I grab my own phone, then find the number that texted me after the incident at Duke's house. My finger misses at first since it is shaking so terribly, but finally, I manage to press Call.

The display on Frank's other phone lights up, and it plays a song. My body starts to tremble violently, just as the shower turns off and Frank walks out, a towel wrapped around his waist.

Chapter 51

FRANK GRINS. He's drying his hair with a second towel, rubbing it in the back. "How about we go to town for dinner? I saw this Italian place on our way up here that looked really quaint."

I stare at him. My hands that are holding both phones are still shaking. His has stopped ringing, and Frank hasn't seen them yet.

"Why are you looking at me like that? Is something wrong?"

I hold out the phones. His grin is wiped away instantly. He freezes.

"W-what is this? Frank? What the hell is THIS?"

I press the call button again, and his burner phone lights up. I want to make sure he gets it.

"Laurie, I can…"

"It was you? It was y-you all along? I trusted you. I let you in my home? I let you hang out with my children? I…I made love to you? We were gonna…we were going to have a baby?"

Frank is watching me. A deep furrow is growing

between his eyebrows. He's looking for what to say, what to tell me to calm me down.

"Frank?" I say, bursting into tears. "Y-you attacked me at Duke's house? You…you attacked my parents? You… you killed…Sandra? Ted? Was that you, Frank? Was that all you? I mean, it makes sense, doesn't it? You're a forensic scientist; if anyone can make it look like a suicide, it's you, right?"

Frank is approaching me. I am suddenly aware that my gun is downstairs in my purse. "Laurie," he says, reaching out a hand. "Let's not get ahead of ourselves here, okay? Calm down."

"It all makes so much more sense now," I say. "Clarice, right? It was because of what happened to her. She was deployed and came home in a casket. You looked at her autopsy and realized she had been hurt. You fought for justice for her but didn't get any and were only met with closed doors from the Air Force. Then you decided to get rid of them on your own. Everyone who appeared in the report, all who you believed gave false testimony and tried to cover for what really happened. Sandra was the first to go. Suicides are common, and no one raises a brow over one; no one suspects foul play when a soldier who has been to war kills herself once she's back."

Frank looks at me, his nostrils flaring slightly. I can tell I'm right. He's not objecting. He's not trying to tell me I'm wrong. We're past that now. We're down to damage control. His muscles are flexing in his jaw, and he speaks through gritted teeth.

"Laurie, please…you don't know what it's like…when they all lie to your face. No one wanted to listen, and I… they all killed her, Laurie. Everyone in that unit killed her. I just know they did. They were covering for one another. She was raped and murdered, and we were getting no justice. Yes, I went to Sandra Mulcahey's house. I wanted to confront her and ask her about what really happened. We ended up fighting, and I sedated her using liquid Fentanyl—not in her coffee but with an injection. Then I dragged her upstairs and placed her in the tub and slit her wrists. Later, I went to Ted Kenopensky's house and broke in through the back door. I injected the Fentanyl into his system, then hung him up. Yes, I attacked you at Duke's house, but what else could I have done? You might have revealed me. I didn't want to hurt you, but you gave me no choice, Laurie. I didn't mean for it to get this far, Laurie. You must believe me."

I swallow the lump growing in my throat. It's so hard to wrap my mind around this. How had I not seen this earlier?

"How, Frank? How am I supposed to believe anything you tell me after this?"

He steps toward me. I wince, and he stops. He points his finger at me.

"One in three women who join the military will be sexually assaulted or raped by men in the military. Those are the facts, Laurie. Clarice was just a number in the statistics. And even more alarming is the rate of women coming home in caskets. Ninety-four U.S. military women have died in Iraq or during Operation Iraqi Freedom. Thirteen U.S. military women have been killed in Afghanistan during Operation Enduring Freedom. Of the ninety-four U.S. military women who died in Iraq, the military says thirty-six died from non-combat related injuries, which included vehicle accidents, illness, death by 'natural causes,' and self-inflicted gunshot wounds, or suicide. Thirty-six! From Fagrad Air Base alone right now, fifteen more deaths have occurred under extremely suspicious circumstances, where the relatives have received no acceptable explanation. This is not just about Clarice, Laurie. This is about the military and what they allow to happen to our sisters, to our girlfriends, and our wives."

I stare at him, not even blinking. I still have my phone in my hand, and I fumble with it, trying to call nine-one-one. Frank doesn't see it. He scoffs.

"Don't you understand how terrible it is what they do to these girls? To their relatives who'll never know the truth? Do you have any idea what kind of pain this has inflicted on my parents? How about all the other relatives who'll never know the truth? Clarice was badly bruised. She had teeth imprints on her skin; she had scratches all over her body. Her nose was broken, and her teeth knocked backward. One elbow was distended. The back of her clothes had debris on them, indicating she had been dragged from one location to another. Don't tell me they aren't lying. And she's not the only one this happened to. As I started digging, I found one story after another similar to hers. You wanna hear? I can name them for you. Also, at Fagrad Air Base, Private Gail Lavesque, twenty years old, was raped by a fellow soldier in February two years ago. The Air Force said she was found dead in her room by a self-inflicted M-16 shot, a suicide they called it, only ten days after she reported being raped. Her parents were told it was suicide, but they don't believe it. They talked to her several times after the rape, and even though she was upset, she was not suicidal, they say. Her family continued to challenge the eight-hundred-page-long investigative report that contained many suspicious elements, like how they believed she had used her toes to hold the weapon when shooting herself. Yet, the Air Force never investigated her death as a homicide, only as suicide. And on top of that, the rape charges against the soldier whose sperm was found on her body were dropped a few weeks later—no explanation to her family as to why. Also, at Fagrad, six months earlier, Private Mabel Jolander's death was ruled an accident as the Air Force claimed she fell or tripped out in front of a military vehicle as she crossed the road, walking from a guard tower to a latrine. The suspicious part is that the vehicle that ran her over was driven by a drunk sergeant from her unit who had first sexually assaulted her. The sergeant was convicted of drinking in a warzone and received a fine, while her death was ruled an accident. Do you want me to continue? Because I know all these cases by heart. There are so many of them; you won't believe it."

I am shaking my head in disbelief. I am trying to make the call in my hand without him noticing it, but it doesn't work. Frank continues, "And then when you started talking about Ryan and how you believed he might have killed Sandra, that was when I got the idea to make it look like it was him. I played along and helped you believe that. I started following him around and made my move as soon as he was out of sight."

"And in that way, you'd get him too. If his wife thought he was a killer and left him for you, that was great revenge. You wanted to see how far I would take it; maybe I could get the police to start investigating Ryan. You made me think my own husband was…a murderer?"

I hold up the phone, his burner phone, toward him, my hands shaking heavily in anger. "You destroyed my family."

"I didn't mean for it to go this far," he says, reaching out toward me. "You must understand this, Laurie. I tried to stop you. I tried to warn you, but you…you were relentless. You just kept pushing and pushing, and…I thought you'd stop after Duke's house and after I sent you those texts, but you didn't, and then…I was desperate, Laurie."

I narrow my eyes. "So, you attacked my parents in their own home just to scare me off."

He takes another step toward me. He drops the towel and starts getting dressed, his movements aggressive as he puts on his jeans.

"I was desperate. You wouldn't stop. You left me no choice. It's actually your own fault when you think about it. But it also means we're in this together, Laurie. You and me. No one needs to know what really happened. It'll be our secret."

The rain is pounding on the window outside, and my breathing is ragged and shallow. Frank looks up at me, his pupils are huge. There's panic in his eyes. We're standing in front of one another like two cowboys in a western movie. Sizing one another up, wondering what the next move will be. Who will go first? I'm thinking about the gun downstairs, wondering how to get to it. I also wonder if he knows I brought it. I'm calculating whether I can reach the stairs before he can get ahold of me. I just need to get down those stairs first, before he can stop me. We drove here in my car. I remember putting the keys on the counter when entering. I pray they're still there.

"What do you say, Laurie? Are we in this together? You and me, forever joined by this secret?"

I make the decision quickly since I figure it is now or never. I put the phone in my pocket and jolt for the stairs, pushing myself forward, sprinting for them. I get to the top of them, my hand on the railing, so I don't fall when I hear him spring for me, his bare feet accelerating on the wooden floors. I feel his leg as it hits me in the back and pushes me forward. The push is forceful, and I scream as I fly down the stairs in an explosion of pain.

Chapter 52

I HIT the steps below face-first. A white light flashes before my eyes as the pain shoots through me. I skid downward, hitting more steps until I slide onto the floor. I feel confused, unable to focus, or even lift my head. Frank is on the steps, hurrying down toward me. I can hear his bare feet tapping on the wood. I tell myself to act, to get up now, but nothing happens. I feel his hands on me, on my hair, and then him pulling me across the floor, dragging me into the living room. He drops me down on the floor and stands above me, hovering, his legs on each side of me. I try to focus, to lift my head, but everything is a blur, a haze. I am kicking my legs, hoping to hit him, but he doesn't move. He bends down, then grabs my shirt and pulls me up. Then, he slaps me. I feel the burning sensation across my cheek, but I can't open my eyes properly. He slaps me again, forcefully, and I feel like I am about to pass out.

Frank then tries to land a punch in my stomach. Realizing this, I know there is no time to waste. I clench my fist and swing it at him, hitting him directly on the nose. Startled at this, Frank stumbles back, holding his bloody nose.

It's a lucky punch, I guess, but just enough for me to get to my feet and swing at him again. Frank is pushed back toward the fireplace, stumbling and leaning on the wall of rocks behind him. While he is gathering himself, I land two quick punches on his jaw.

"You coward," I roar with satisfaction. I am panting in agitation. I anxiously feel my stomach with my hand. It doesn't feel wrong in any way and I am not bleeding. There is no pain to indicate something is off. But it's too early to tell. That fall from the stairs was hard. At this point, I can only pray the baby is all right.

"You sick coward!"

Panting, he glares up at me. Blood is running from his nose, spilling onto his white shirt he has put on so quickly that he hasn't even noticed it is turned inside out. I take another swing at him, but I have underestimated him. He grabs my arm mid-air and pushes me back. I fly backward and land on the floor, sliding across it. Then, he is on top of me fast. His weight holds me down, and with a hand on my throat, he has me pinned to the floor. I can't move.

"Squeal all you want to," he says, speaking close to my ear. "Scream if you can. It won't matter. No one is coming for you."

He is staring down at me, his eyes steady, unafraid. He knows he has won. He has me down, and there is no way I can escape. I look into his eyes and wonder if the baby has the same eyes—the eyes that have been the last that so many people have seen before they died. His hand tightens around my throat, and I can't breathe. I am gasping for air, trying to kick, but not hitting anything. I try to jab an elbow into his stomach, but with no success. I am panicking and can't think straight. The pain on my throat becomes deeper; the fear enveloping me completely. I stare into his eyes as he strangles me, his face strained in effort.

He is yelling and growling, his eyes popping out, and his teeth clenched. He is fighting so hard to kill me that he doesn't even hear the quick footsteps on the wooden porch outside.

I SEE him in the window first, and immediately, the panic is substituted with hope rising in my chest. Seeing the change in my eyes, Frank follows my gaze over his shoulder and takes in the sight of Ryan as he bursts through the door, breaking it open with his shoulder. He storms inside, a gun gripped between both hands.

"Time to end this, you bastard," he says.

Frank loosens his grip on my throat, and I gasp for air.

Ryan fires the gun and shoots Frank in the back. Frank collapses, falling on top of me. Frantically, I push him off, and he slides onto the floor. Frank is writhing in pain, trying to get up, making it to his knees. Ryan walks to him, places the gun on his head, and fires again. I scream and hold my hands over my head as Frank's body slumps to the floor, rag-doll limp.

Ryan runs to me. He kneels next to me.

"Are you okay? Are you hurt?"

There is panic in his voice as it is rising. I am still fighting to breathe, gasping and coughing, finally able to let the soothing air slide freely into my lungs. Ryan holds me by the shoulders, his eyes looking at me desperately.

"Laurie, are you okay?"

I manage to nod, and I sit up straight while I slowly get my focus back. I look at Ryan. He looks terrible. He is panting and agitated still, while the air of determination he had carried on his face when entering the cabin slowly subsides. His eyes become calm and affectionate when he looks at me, and he reaches up to caress my bruised cheek. Suddenly, he's exactly the man I remember, the one I cared for so deeply once.

Seeing this, I burst into tears, and he pulls me into a deep hug.

"It's okay, Laurie. It's gonna be okay. Don't you worry; it's all over now, it's over," he whispers.

And for some reason, I believe him.

Chapter 53

HE TELLS me to go lay down upstairs. He'll take care of everything. He'll call the police, but it'll be a while before they get here. At least an hour in this bad weather.

"You might as well rest, Laurie. You need it."

I am in complete shock and unable to think. I do as he tells me to and crawl under the covers, barely able to pull them up with my trembling hands. My heart is pounding so hard, and when I close my eyes, I can still see Frank's piercing eyes as he tries to kill me. I start to cry, sobbing heavily, crawling into a fetal position, hugging my knees. There is so much I still don't understand. I have never felt such anxiety deep within my chest, but I still try to close my eyes and rest. Right now, it's the only thing I can do. I think I manage to doze off because when I open my eyes again, it's dark outside. I gasp, feeling even more confused than earlier.

Why am I still asleep? Why didn't Ryan wake me?

I scramble to my feet, feeling dizzy as I get up. I lean on the dresser for a few seconds when I hear footsteps outside and turn to look out the window. I glance down and see Ryan come walking up in the rain and walk into the light from the porch outside. He is wearing a raincoat and boots that are covered in mud. He is whistling. I don't see any police cars, no ambulance, no blinking lights, or anyone in a uniform.

Just Ryan.

What is going on here?

I turn around and feel the room is spinning, then hurry to the stairs. I walk down just as Ryan comes inside. He takes the coat and boots off and leaves it all by the door. He smiles when he sees me.

"Hey, you're awake? Are you feeling better?"

I swallow; there's a growing sense of urgency in my throat. I try to remain calm. "Ryan? Where are the police?"

I turn to look at where Frank was shot.

"And where is the body?"

Ryan takes a deep breath. "Now, before you get mad…"

"What did you do, Ryan? What did you do?" I almost yell.

He steps toward me. He grabs my hands in his and smiles. "Calm down, okay? Let me explain."

"What did you do with Frank's body, Ryan?" I ask, almost out of breath.

This can't be happening; this can't be real.

"Ryan?"

"Let's sit down, okay?" he says and gestures toward the couch behind us. I do as he says and sit. He's still holding my hands in his like he's afraid I'll run away.

"I decided…and now, hear me out first before you go all crazy, okay? I decided to get rid of it."

I can feel how my eyes grow wide. I can't believe what

I'm hearing. I keep thinking it's a bad dream. It has to be. It's the only explanation.

"What do you mean you got rid of it? Ryan? What have you done?"

"I threw it in the creek. The water will carry it far down the stream to the big river. No one will ever know, Laurie."

"But…but why…*why* would you do that?"

"Don't you see? To protect you, of course," he says, smiling gently at me like I'm a young child who needs everything explained. He grabs a lock of my hair and puts it behind my ear.

I shake my head in disbelief. "Me? Why…"

"Sh, sh," he says and places a finger on my lips. "Don't worry. I told you it'll be just fine. I was scared you'd get in trouble."

"Why would I get in trouble?" I say. "He was trying to kill me. You shot him. It makes no sense, Ryan." I stand to my feet, pulling my hands out of his. "You're not making much sense here, do you know that? I mean…first of all, why are you even here? It was you I saw last night outside our window, wasn't it? What were you doing out there? What are you doing here?"

Ryan tilts his head and smiles again. "What am I doing here? I'm saving you, of course. Aren't you glad I was here?"

"Of course, I am, but why, Ryan? Why did you come? How did you know we were here at all?"

"I followed you, of course. I knew this guy was bad news. I needed to protect you."

I narrow my eyes, trying to think. What exactly is he telling me here? "You were following us? How long have you been following me?"

He wrinkles his forehead. "What do you mean? Are

you telling me you aren't happy I just saved your life? I did you a favor, getting rid of that body for you, so you wouldn't have to go through all that trouble with the police."

"He was the murderer," I said. "He killed Sandra, Ted, and Vera, and he tried to kill Duke too, making it look like suicide. Did you know this?"

Ryan's face grows serious. He nods with an exhale. "I did. I started suspecting him after Ted's death. I knew both he and Sandra had given testimonies in the report investigating Clarice's death. That gave him a motive. I tried to warn Duke, but he wouldn't believe me."

My shoulders come down. "You knew? And that's why you followed me? Why didn't you tell me?"

He shrugs. "Would you have believed me?"

I scoff. "Probably not."

"I figured as much. After Sandra died, you changed, and suddenly, I couldn't talk to you at all. You kept rambling on about all this crazy stuff, and you wouldn't listen to me. I know I'm not well; I know things have been difficult, but I'm still the same man. At least most of the time. I am no longer drinking and no longer doing drugs. But the thing is…you wouldn't believe me, no matter how much I tried to warn you."

I sit down. "Oh."

He puts his hands on top of mine. "Listen. I know you wanted to go to the police and everything, but I got scared. I'm sorry I did this, that I got rid of the body without telling you, but I just…I panicked. I feared one of us might have to go to jail, and I just hoped…well, I hoped we could find one another again. It might be too late, but I was hoping it wouldn't be. I hoped there still was a chance for us. I miss you, Laurie. I can't live without you. I hope you know this?"

He is squeezing my hands, and tears spring to my eyes. I am so tired, so confused. I look into his eyes and see them grow soft. I feel like such a fool for all I have put him and us through.

"We were a family, Laurie. We are a family."

"I know," I say and let the tears roll down my cheeks. "I know, and I'm not sure I can live without you either."

He chuckles and kisses my forehead. "And now, you don't have a choice. We've committed a murder together and covered it up. That binds us together forever. This will be the secret we take with us to the grave. Together."

He leans over and kisses me, and I let him while wondering if what he said was meant to be romantic or if it was a joke. To me, it sounded more like a threat. The thought brings shudders to my stomach as Ryan pushes me down on the couch and leans on top of me.

Chapter 54

THE RAIN HAS GROWN fiercer outside and is whipping against the windows. Ryan is lighting the fireplace while I sit on the couch, wrapped in a blanket and my thoughts. I am calmer now, yet my hands are still shaking terribly. But my mind is calmer, and I'm thinking clearer now. I watch Ryan as he puts firewood in and lights it. He uses an old newspaper we found between the books. I'm wondering what to do next and whether I really trust Ryan or not. He seems out of sorts like he's not completely there. I keep thinking I should get away from here as soon as possible— go to the police station in downtown Bryson City. Tell them everything.

Will they believe me? Even if I tell them we got rid of the body?

Probably not.

They'll think you're trying to cover up a murder.

I exhale and rub my forehead excessively. Ryan comes to me and sits next to me. "We should get something to eat," he says. "Maybe I should cook? You're in no state to; that's for sure."

I send him a weak smile. I'm starving now that he mentions food. But I fear my stomach is in too many knots to be able to eat.

"That sounds wonderful," I say.

"I know what you're thinking," he says and leans closer.

"Oh, really? And what's that?" I ask nervously. Does he know I'm thinking about running to the car right now and driving away? That I want to find my phone and call nine-one-one, that I am terrified of him and what he might do? That I have just seen him kill someone in cold blood and then dump the body like it was nothing, and that scares me to the core? Yes, he was saving my life, and I am grateful for that, but there's just something wrong; something tells me to run for my life.

He pokes my nose. "You're thinking we should get out of here before the police come and ask questions, am I right?"

I smile again, trying to seem like that is what I was thinking. "Well, yes. They'll find Frank's body soon enough."

He grins. "Well, that's why you need me, honey. You see, with all the rain that has been pouring down over the past day or so, no one will find him till he's far away. The extra water rushing through the creek and into the river will carry him very far before he's found. Besides, we can't really leave now. The rain outside has turned the area into a mud pile, and there's real danger of a mudslide. Flash flooding and mudslides are not something you want to meet out on a dirt road going down a mountainside, just sayin'. We'd do best by staying here and trying to enjoy ourselves. The rain will probably end tomorrow, and then we can get going, okay?"

He doesn't wait for my response. He kisses my nose,

then gets up. "All right. Let's see what we have that I can make for dinner. Did you buy any meat?"

He walks to the kitchen and opens the fridge, then pokes his head inside.

"Is that lamb?" he almost squeals. "You know how much I love lamb."

RYAN MAKES AN AMAZING MEAL. The entire cabin soon smells divine with rosemary and garlic. He pops open a red wine for me and takes a beer for himself. I give him a look, thinking I was so certain I just heard him say he wasn't drinking anymore. As we sit down, he sees me look at the beer when he sips it with a grin.

"It's just one beer, Laurie. Hardly gonna make me drunk. I'm kind of shaken up too, you know. It makes me calmer."

I smile and nod. I sip my wine, glancing toward my purse on the counter. The gun is still inside of it; the car keys are on the counter next to it. The rain is still pounding on the windows. I decide that Ryan is right. It's too dangerous to go anywhere tonight.

"It's really good, Ryan. The meat is so tender," I say as I taste the piece of lamb he has placed on my plate.

"Did you try the roasted potatoes, huh? Try the potatoes too," he says.

I do as he tells me. They taste great as well. I chew and smile at him, nodding, wondering if I can even manage to swallow it. The knot in my throat is growing out of proportion. I pretend to be fine, then smile and nod, still chewing, feeling like the potato is swelling inside my mouth. My stomach is a jumble; I am sweating heavily and struggling to keep my calm face on, so Ryan won't notice.

"Good, huh? What did I tell you?" he says, drinking more from his beer. The more he drinks, the more the look in his eyes changes. He sets the bottle down so hard the silverware clanks.

"Good thing you have me, right? To save you and now cook for you, huh?" he points at me with his fork. "I bet you're glad you're married to me now and not that Frank fellow."

He chews and mumbles something I can't hear, then finishes his beer and gets up to get a new one. He opens it and returns to the table. "I am telling you; I knew he was bad news. I tried to tell you…that family is…they sure are something." He points the beer at me, then drinks from it, gulping it down loudly, and looks at me once the bottle comes down again.

"Him and that…dyke of a sister."

He looks at me again, then puts the bottle back to his lips and gulps the rest of it down. I stare at him, eyes growing wide, then drop the fork onto my plate.

"It was you," I say.

Ryan gives me a look of surprise.

"What do you mean?"

"You raped her. You were the one who raped Clarice."

"Watch your mouth, Laurie. I'm warning you."

I stand to my feet. "Of course, you were. Why didn't I see this earlier? She was openly gay. You hate everything that has to do with homosexuals, ever since your mother…"

"Don't you dare talk about my mother!" he yells, but I'm not listening anymore. All the pieces fall into place. Frank killed those that had molested and murdered his sister. Of course, Ryan was the main victim. That was why he tried to take everything from him. Killing Ryan wasn't enough since he was the one in the center of it all; he was the one who had raped her. Sandra had to have told him who it was on that day they met when he ended up killing her. She had probably told him the truth…that it was Ryan. That was why Frank wanted to hurt him—make him feel deep pain like he had. First, he tried to make it look like he was the murderer, hoping he'd take the fall; that was why he was so eager for me to mention Ryan's name in the article and kept pushing me to go to the police. When that didn't work, he went for his wife—winning me over, taking me from Ryan. Finding out I was pregnant with his child had to have been the victory he was hoping for.

"You don't get to talk about my mother!" Ryan says, pointing his finger at me.

Seeing how upset he is only makes me want to continue.

"Ever since your mother fell in love with her psychiatrist and came out as a lesbian, you have hated everything that even has to do with homosexuals. Because it ruined your father; it ruined your childhood. You raped Clarice as revenge because of what your mother did to you."

Ryan's face grows white as a corpse. His nostrils are flaring, his hands opening and closing into fists.

"She was going to report us," he says, slamming his fist onto the table. "Said she didn't like the way we interrogated our prisoners. Well, she was nothing but a disgusting dyke; I'll tell you that much. Going behind our backs like that!"

"So, you showed her, didn't you?" I say. "You and your buddies, you decided to teach her a lesson?"

"Damn right, we did."

"Give her some manhood because that's probably why she was a lesbian, right? Am I right, Ryan?" I say, my voice rising as I get agitated. "Because she had never had a *real* man."

Ryan's eyes are glowing with hatred as he speaks. "She brought all…*that*…into our unit, and then she had the audacity to try and tell us how to do our work. Hell, yeah, we gave her something to think about. Chip held her down while I had my way with her. She knew what was coming, at least she should have."

I pause. My heart is pounding now. "Did you shoot her too? Did you? Did you kill her, Ryan?"

He reaches out his arms and leans forward, his eyes burning in anger. "Yes, I did. Are you happy? I shot her to shut her up, and then we all agreed to lie on that report."

"Even Sandra?" I ask.

He scoffs. "It's not like we gave her a choice. She knew what might happen to her, had she not done as we told her. She knew the game. She knew what she got herself into when joining the Air Force. She was smart."

"Unlike Clarice, who believed in justice and thought joining the military would mean doing something good, making a difference in the world. I get now why she was so disappointed."

Ryan doesn't say anything else. He is just standing there with his fists opening and closing. Silence grows between us, and only the pounding rain on the window and the roof is heard in the cabin with the vaulted ceilings. The mountains are covered by the darkness outside, and I can't stop thinking about Clarice. For some reason, I am reminded of the time she brought me flowers after I had given birth to Damian. Back then, I had already sensed resentment from Ryan toward her. I just hadn't been able to place it, to figure out where it came from. He never invited her over for barbecues when we invited the rest of the unit. She was never one of the guys and it had me wondering back then since I knew Sandra was accepted as one of them, so it wasn't a gender thing.

Now, I finally understand why.

Sandra played by the rules.

"You make me sick," I say.

Ryan suddenly moves. He stumbles across the room and grabs me by the shoulders. He is holding me steady, his beer breath hitting my face, making me want to throw up.

"Careful what you say," he hisses.

"Why? Or you'll kill me too? Is that it, Ryan?" I say. "Is that just your answer to everything? Get rid of the problem. The body, the girl…who knows what you've done?"

He lifts his hand in the air, fist clenched, and stops mid-air.

"Don't you dare talk to me like that; don't you DARE!"

I am waiting for the punch, closing my eyes. Ryan is shaking terribly, restraining himself, and struggling to do so. He wants to hit me; I can tell by the look in his eyes. I know that look a little too well.

"By the way, I'm pregnant," I say. I don't know why I say this now. I want him to be angry. I want this. "And I'm pretty sure it's Frank's."

Ryan's hand comes down, but the anger isn't gone; on the contrary. It's flaming more wildly than ever. Instead of hitting me with his fist, he pushes me forcefully. I fly back until I hit the wall behind me. He's coming at me, yelling at me, almost screaming.

"You whore! You goddamn whore!"

"R-Ryan," I say as he swings his fist at me and hits me in my stomach, knocking the wind out of me. I slide to the floor, coughing and spitting, thinking I'm bleeding, but I'm not. I cry, worrying about the baby, thinking it's all gone wrong as I try to get back on my feet, but they won't hold me. I land on my knees, and, gasping for air, I crawl forward toward my purse on the counter.

Ryan grabs the beer bottle, then smashes it against the table, shattering it, then comes for me, the beer bottle held out in front of him. He grabs my hair and yanks me backward so hard I am sure I hear something snap in my neck.

"Where do you think you're going, you bitch?" he yells and places the bottle against my throat. I can feel the sharp edge against my skin. He's spitting in my face as he speaks.

"I should just have given you a proper beating like Chip told me to when you started to get out of line. But better late than never, right? I told you it would end badly for you if you didn't stop sticking your nose where it doesn't belong."

"R-Ryan," I whimper. It sounds like I am talking through water. "S-stop."

"Oh, now you're begging me, huh? Say it out loud, Laurie. Tell me to stop; tell me to let you go, beg me. I wanna hear you say it."

He is pulling my hair still and scraping the bottle across my skin, not putting pressure on it yet, just letting me know he can cut my throat anytime he wants to if I don't do as he says. He pulls my hair again. It hurts so outrageously that I scream. It only makes him grin.

"Say it! Beg me!"

"P-please," I say. "Please, stop, Ryan."

"Say it again!"

"Please, Ryan. You're hurting me!"

He kicks me in the stomach twice, and I fall down, crying. He lets go of my hair while I cough, worrying about the baby. I glance up at the purse, and, unfortunately, he sees it. He then makes a quick move. He grabs my purse, then lets it hang from his hand.

"Was this what you were going for, huh? Let's see what's in here?"

He reaches inside my purse and pulls out the gun. It is dangling between his fingers. "Now, what is this? What do we have here, huh?"

Chapter 55

"THAT IS SO TYPICALLY YOU, LAURIE," Ryan sneers. "To have your gun in your friggin' purse!" He takes it in his hand and weighs it. I feel the hope glide from my body. I am in pain, and now I see my only possibility for surviving this being taken away. He walks to me and looks down at me. He then grabs his cell phone and dials a number, a grin growing on his face.

"What are you doing, Ryan? Who are you calling?" I ask.

He points the gun at me, then cocks it. He signals with it for me to be quiet, placing it on his lips, then points it at me again.

Someone picks up. I can hear most of what is being said.

"What's your emergency?" a female voice says.

Ryan grins again.

"She's dead," he says. He makes his voice sound like he's sad…like he's desperate.

"Excuse me? Who is?"

"The woman."

"What woman?"

I hear Ryan say the words. I hear him speak to the dispatch woman, and my heart starts to hammer in my chest, drowning out the sound of his voice. He is acting differently—like he's upset like he's someone who has just found a body and he wants the police to come. But it's not some body he's talking about.

It's my body.

I whimper as I hear him tell the woman the address, and then when she asks how I died, he tells her I was killed.

"Did you kill her, sir?"

"Yes," he answers, looking down at me.

"And you're sure she's dead?"

Ryan pauses. He closes one eye like he's aiming and pushes the gun closer to me. I stare up at him; I want to beg him to stop, to stop the games and talk to me, but I can't speak. He smiles as he says the last part, the thing that causes my blood to freeze.

"She will be."

RYAN HANGS UP. He is staring down at me, a grin growing across his face. "Guess there's no way back now, huh? The police will be here in approximately an hour. Maybe a little bit more. They won't be able to drive fast in the rain and have to be careful when coming up the slippery mountainside."

"Ryan, you don't have to do this," I say.

"Oh, no?" he says and places the gun on my forehead. He leans close to me as he speaks. "But the thing is, I want to. I have actually been looking forward to this part."

"Ryan, please, think of the children…"

I say the words while clenching my fist. Ryan is so close to me, I can reach out, and I grab his collar, then pull him down while stretching for the gun with the other hand, tearing it out of his grip. The gun slips out of his hand, then slides across the floor, while he pushes me back, hollering, "Oh, no, you don't!"

I hold onto his collar, using all my weight to pull him down toward me, so he can't get to the gun. With my foot, I manage to kick it, and it slides even farther away. He presses his hand into my face, pushing me downward, groaning in effort. It hurts like crazy, and I am forced to let go of his collar. He then springs for the gun, leaving my side. I scramble to my feet, then make a run for the sliding doors. I skid on the slippery floors but get back up fast, even though my hand slips on the floor. I grab the doors, then pull them open, Ryan bellowing behind me.

"Come back here! You're not going anywhere, you hear me?"

I feel his hand grab for my hair, but I am faster than him and jolt outside into the pouring rain.

IT'S NOT easy to run across the wet wooden porch in my bare feet. I am slipping and skating around, falling, getting up, and trying to gain some speed, but end up tumbling forward. I hear him behind me, panting, roaring, bawling my name, trampling after me.

"You get back here, Laurie. You get back here now!"

This time, I feel his hand on my shoulder, pulling me back. I yank myself free, so he reaches down and grabs my arm instead, then pulls me backward. I fall flat on my back, and he's caught my neck, wrapping his elbow around it, squeezing me, holding me in a tight grip. He has the gun in his other hand, and he places it on my cheek. What scares me senseless right this moment is the fact that his hand isn't even shaking. There isn't even a tremble to his voice as he speaks to me.

"I told ya. You're not going anywhere, Laurie. You hear me?"

He's holding me tight in his grip. I writhe and worm my body, but he isn't letting go. I manage to turn myself a little sideways, just enough to get my arm twisted loose. I clench my fist, then land a punch on his face, just hard enough for him to let me go. He screams and curses my name when I jolt out of his grip and spring forward. I jump up over the railing, then let myself fall to the lawn one story below. Only the lawn is turned into a pile of mud, and, as I land, I am covered in mud from top to toe. I can taste it in my mouth and feel it in my nostrils. I look up and see Ryan above me, hollering my name.

Then, I run.

I run, and the mud is splashing up against my legs and my back, while the rain is still pouring down on top of me. I hear Ryan as he runs for the slope next to the house and comes down toward me, avoiding having to jump. He is faster than me, and soon he is running toward me down the sloping backyard, sliding in the mud toward me, his legs first, trying to trip me. He misses, and I continue toward the road I know is there somewhere because I just walked it with Frank a few days earlier. But it's no longer visible. It's covered in mud, and big parts of the edge have been dragged into the valley by the water.

Still, I continue carefully so I won't make a wrong move and get dragged down with the water. It is gushing down the sides of the mountain, making big muddy rivers that I have to jump over and land in the mud on the other side, face-first. I am fast on my feet, though, as I hear him yell behind me. He sounds like a drowned mouse, and the rain soon clears my face and hair, washing away the mud.

I make one more jump across a river gushing down, and slide onto my back on the other side, then get back up and run, panting, gasping for air, when I suddenly reach an edge and stop. I almost don't see it in the darkness, but as I come close enough, I realize there is no more road. It has been washed down the valley. I turn around and see Ryan coming toward me. He stops running when he realizes I have stopped. He is walking closer, pointing the gun at me.

"This is it, Laurie. End of the road for you. You hear me? This is it, Laurie. You're done running! Ha! You thought you could just slip away, didn't you? But that ain't happening. No, not tonight. Not ever, Laurie. You'll never get away from me."

He laughs, walking closer, then fires the gun. It's probably because it's so dark that he only hits me in the shoulder. There's only a little light from a lamppost on the street above us, shining down through the trees. Or maybe he does it on purpose so he'll get to torture me a little longer because he's usually a very good shot. It still hurts like crazy, and I fall back into the mud. Ryan is walking closer, grinning, while I am screaming in pain and holding a hand to my shoulder.

He is getting close, hovering above me, pointing the barrel of the gun at me.

"Say goodbye, Laurie. Say goodbye now."

He has his finger on the trigger, and this is where I think this is the end; this is it for me. I don't know if it is God holding his hand over me, or what it is, but at this very moment, a wall of water breaks loose from above us, then hits him and washes him away and takes the part of the road he's standing on with it. He drops the gun, and I hurry to pick it up as it is about to be washed down as well.

I can't see him; I can't even hear him scream until I finally spot his head sticking out. He is dangling from a tiny branch sticking out of the mountainside, holding onto it for dear life. Water is gushing down the sides and is about to grab me too, but I put the gun in my waistband, then manage to grab onto a bigger branch with my one good arm and swing myself onto a place higher up, where there is still solid ground to stand on. The water is moving fast and fiercely below me now, roaring into the valley below.

"Help! Help me!" Ryan screams.

He is close enough for me to be able to. I can help him if I want to. I can reach out my hand and let him drag himself up to me and save him.

But I don't.

Instead, I just stare at him, look him straight in his eyes as water and mud gush down on him, and the branch he's holding onto threatens to break free. I look him straight in the eye, and I don't do a darn thing.

He is still screaming for my help as I climb upward toward drier ground. I stop for a few seconds once up there, but I don't look down at him. I don't dare.

But I do hear as the branch gives way, and I hear his scream as he is pulled down with the mud.

Chapter 56

LAURIE REACHES for the box of tissues and grabs one. She is trembling as she wipes the tears from her eyes and catches the ones that have rolled down her cheeks, dabbing the skin gently. Jonathan watches her. He realizes he has been holding his breath while she told the last part.

Laurie closes her eyes for a second to compose herself, then looks at them again. Detective Grande is shifting in her seat. Jonathan noticed she, too, was spellbound by the story while Laurie told it.

Laurie exhales and places her hands on top of the covers. "Somehow...I'm not sure how, but somehow, I manage to get back to the cabin. It's all a haze right now, as I was probably in deep shock. But I remember walking in the rain, crawling through rows of trees, areas of mud piles, and finding the remainder of the road. I remember spotting the cabin in the distance, and I remember getting back up on the porch and coming inside, getting to shelter, then the feeling of great relief when closing the doors. I remember I then slid to the floor and cried. The last thing I did was to crawl up in the chair in the living room and put the gun on the table so the police could see it once they entered. I remember leaning my head back in the chair, pain throbbing in my shoulder, then hearing the soothing sound of sirens approaching in the distance."

"And that's where our officers found you," Grande says. "When they got to the cabin."

Laurie nods her head. "And that's the story. Every little part of it. As you can hear, it was all self-defense, and that is the truth. Now, you do what you need to do, but I know I didn't kill anyone."

Grande sniffles and wipes away a tear before she glances at Jonathan like she hopes he doesn't see it. Jonathan turns off the Dictaphone app and looks at his notes. Grande sends him a look and nods. She gets up.

"I think we're done here. I want to thank you for taking your time," she says as she reaches out her hand and shakes Laurie's.

Laurie smiles. "Is that it? You don't have any more questions for me?"

Grande looks at Jonathan, then shakes her head. "I don't think so. It was obviously self-defense. I am sure whatever evidence is found up there will support your story. We won't bother you anymore. I am sure you're eager to get home to your children."

Laurie swallows, then nods. "I sure am, thank you, Detectives."

Jonathan reaches out his hand and squeezes Laurie's, then smiles gently. "Thank you, Mrs. Davis."

She sniffles and nods. "Thank you both."

Jonathan shares one last glance with Laurie then walks to the door and holds it for Grande. As he is about to leave, he hesitates, then looks back at Laurie.

"Oh, there was one more thing."

"Yes?"

"There was the matter of Vera."

"Yes? What about her?"

"We never really got the story of why she died. She was Frank's sister. Why did he kill her?"

"Oh, really? I never said that? That's odd. Well, he killed her because she threatened to reveal him, at least that's what he told me. And also to get back at me, you know. Because I wouldn't back off."

"Uh-huh, and what about the truck and the case?"

"He placed them there so the police might come looking for Chip. He bought the truck from Chip two weeks earlier and stole the case from the glove compartment. He used it to get back at him since he played a part in the rape as well. He was the one holding her down."

Jonathan nods, biting his cheek.

"Listen, I don't pretend like I know all of Frank's motives. I just know what I told you."

Jonathan nods again, then smiles. "Of course."

He pauses and is almost about to leave when he turns to look at her again. "And what was her last name again? Vera's? I don't think you mentioned that."

Laurie's eyes narrow.

"I didn't say that? Huh."

Jonathan shakes his head. "I would have remembered that. I have a thing with names."

Laurie pauses. For a second, the two of them stare at one another, sizing each other up. Then her shoulders come down, and she smiles.

"It was Donovan. Her full name was Vera Donovan."

Jonathan smiles again. "Of course, it was. Thank you so much."

"Thank you, Detectives."

Jonathan walks out to Grande, who is waiting in the hallway, shaking her head. "I know I shouldn't let her go till we have it all verified and have made the calls back home, but that can take days, and I just thought she needed to get back to her children. I, for one, have lost all my suspicion toward her. A story like this, I mean come on, you can't make that stuff up."

Jonathan nods and looks down at the small detective. He holds the door for her as they walk out to the elevators. "You're probably right. You're probably right."

He presses the button to the elevator, and as soon as it has arrived and they walk inside, he turns toward her and says, "But I want you to do one thing for me."

"Yes?"

"The book. The one she said they were reading from while staying at the cabin."

Grande wrinkles her forehead.

"What about it?"

"I need you to get it for me."

Grande lifts both eyebrows, and a frown grows between them. "You want the book? Why?"

The elevator dings, and they walk through the lobby and out to their cars. He pulls out the keys to his car.

"Just indulge me with this one, will you?"

She shrugs, then walks to her own police cruiser. "As you wish. I don't see what you want with an old book, but if that's what you want, you got it."

Chapter 57

"ANYTHING else I can get for you, hon?"

Jonathan looks up at Joanne. Her nametag is crooked today, and he wonders if she was in a rush this morning. Maybe she overslept. Her hair looks perfect as always, though, and so does her make up. He tries to imagine her with morning hair and no makeup—just the way God created her. He would like to see her in the morning, would enjoy waking up with her. Jonathan shakes the thought. He had the Mountain for lunch, which is a special Everett Street burger with BBQ pulled pork, onion rings, and creamy coleslaw, and he is kind of full. But the glint in Joanne's eyes makes him want to buy more. How can he say no to her? He wants to make up excuses to stay longer than just for lunch.

"Any pie today?" he asks.

"I got a key lime and coconut cream pie."

"Key lime, please."

"You want some whipped cream on that? I know you have a sweet tooth."

He smiles gently, feeling his cheeks blush. "Yes, along

with coffee, please. And keep it coming. I'm waiting for something, so I have some time to kill."

Joanne winks. "You got it, sugar."

He watches her intently as she gets the pie and coffee for him. He puts in some sugar and a little milk, then sips it and eats the pie. A couple enters the diner, and Joanne is busy taking care of them next. He watches her every move while finishing his pie, and then his phone rings.

"Yes?"

"It's Grande. I have the book you wanted."

Jonathan smiles. "That was fast. I barely got to finish my pie."

"Do you want me to bring it to you?" she asks. "I can come down to the diner if you like."

He takes a deep breath, then finishes his coffee. He leaves a bill, including a huge tip for Joanne as usual. He waves at her and rushes out the door with the phone still clutched to his ear.

"No. I have a better idea. Meet me at the hospital."

GRANDE'S CHEEKS are flushed as she enters the hallway. Jonathan is already standing outside the door to the hospital room when she walks in, holding the book in her hands. She lifts it up.

"It was the only book up there," she says. "So, I figured this had to be it."

"Let me guess. *Dolores Claiborne*?" Jonathan asks.

Grande stops, holding the book mid-air. She wrinkles her forehead. "How did you know?"

She hands it to Jonathan, and he flips through a couple of pages. "An old Stephen King classic. Have you ever read it?"

She shakes her head. "Can't say I have."

"I figured as much," Jonathan says.

"I'm not sure I understand. Are you going to tell me what this is all about? The book? Us being here? I have a lot of work to do."

"I think you'll be glad you came here instead," he says. "Gonna save you a lot of time and effort."

"Are you all right?" she asks. "You're kind of talking in riddles here. I'm not sure I completely follow where you're going."

"You will," he says, holding up the book. "In a few minutes, it'll all be very clear to you. Just follow my lead."

LAURIE IS DRESSED when they enter. She's standing next to the bed. The technicians have brought her the suitcase with the clothes from the cabin, and she has gotten her phone back. The jeans she is wearing are too big, and it looks like she's lost a lot of weight. They're also slightly too long, so she has folded them at the bottom. Her face lights up, even though her voice breaks a little as she sees them.

"Detectives? I thought we were done? I'm just about to leave."

"Oh, but we are. Almost," Jonathan says. "There was just a small matter that I was hoping you could clear up for us."

"Well, of course, Detective. Anything." Laurie sits down on the bed and crosses her legs. Her smile is insecure, and she clears her throat nervously. "What's going on?"

Jonathan holds the book in the air. "We found the book. The one you told us you were reading with Frank while staying at the cabin."

He places the book on the bed in front of her. Laurie picks it up and looks at both of them, puzzled.

"And?"

Jonathan exhales. He grabs a chair and pulls it close, then sits down, making sure she understands he is in no hurry.

"Well…now, Grande here has never read it, but I have, several times. I even saw the movie, the one with Kathy Bates. I watch almost any movie with her, but that's not the point. Now, Grande here doesn't know what it is about, so I thought I'd clarify it briefly. To make it brief, it's basically a book about a woman telling the story of how she got away with murdering her husband."

"Oh, really?" Grande asks.

"That is very simplified," Laurie says. "There's a lot more to it than just that."

"But that is the essence of the storyline, isn't it?" Jonathan asks.

Laurie exhales. She's biting her lip anxiously. Her shoulders slump, and her face flusters.

"When did you know?"

"I figured it out pretty quickly. At first, it was the thing about you not being used to the heat, when you grew up in Florida. That struck me as odd. You mentioned the weather a lot like it was a surprise to you. Also, the way you described a roach like you had never killed one before. I am a Florida man myself, and when growing up down there, you're used to roaches, snakes, and even gators roaming the neighborhood. That was the first time I started wondering. But what had me most interested were the names. It wasn't until you were about halfway through your little story that it occurred to me. I had heard those names before. They are all in this book. All the names in your little story were taken from it. Like…let's take Vera

Donovan, for instance. In your story, she's your friend and sister to the woman who was murdered in Afghanistan. In the book, she is the woman Dolores Claiborne works for. Her sister Clarice is also the name of Vera's sister in the book. Lisa McCandless, also called Lotty in the book, was a friend of Dolores, while Chip was her doctor. Frank was a police officer, Sandra someone who used to work for Vera, and Ted Kenopensky was a friend. Do you want me to go on? Because there's a lot of them. All the way down to the names of the people in your childhood, Mike Stargill and Shawna Wyndham. All are names you can find in this book. The only names that weren't made up were Laurie, Ryan, Isabella, and Damien. Because you had to keep those real to make them match the driver's license and the ID of the man we found drowned in the mud. But you made the mistake of thinking that none of us were Stephen King fans and would remember the names from one of his books. But I guess you were out of luck. As I said, I have a thing for names. I tend to remember them."

Detective Grande stares at Jonathan, mouth gaping. "So…wait a minute…you're telling me, it was all a…lie?"

Jonathan sends her a compassionate smile. "Not all of it."

He looks at the woman sitting on the bed. She is looking down at her fingers, rubbing them excessively.

"Come to think of it, I think a lot of it was true, actually," he continues. "The names were changed to make it harder to verify. Clarice was the story of a real woman who was raped and probably murdered during deployment. Laurie was a woman who thought her husband had killed their neighbor and other people from his unit. Frank was also the brother who tried to revenge his sister by killing those involved. But I don't think he was alone, was he? He had his sister to help him. I think they worked together on this, on revenging the death of their beloved sister."

Jonathan is looking at the woman on the bed, waiting for her to start talking. She doesn't say anything. She doesn't even look at him.

"His sister?" Grande says. "You mean Vera?"

"Yes. Except that isn't her real name."

"But…she died," Grande says.

"That's the part of the story I don't believe is true," Jonathan says. "That is why it was left out when Frank confessed to having killed so many people. See, the thing is, you forgot that he needed a motive. You wanted us to believe Vera was dead, so we wouldn't go looking for her, so we wouldn't suspect that she is really…you."

Grande points at the woman. "But…this is Laurie…right?"

Jonathan sends her another smile and waits for the dime to drop.

"Oh. So, she's not Laurie?"

"No," Jonathan says. "She looks like her; they both have red hair, and she could pass for her when looking at her old driver's license in her purse. But the pants are too big and too long. This is Laurie's best friend, passing for her, trying to get away with murder by calling it self-defense. See, Vera here, or whatever your real name is, was close to Laurie. Laurie told her everything, down to the smallest detail. It was easy for her to tell us Laurie's story instead of her own, especially when it's your secret dream to become an author and coming up with stories is what you are darn good at. See, that was another mistake you made. For someone who never read books, Laurie knew a little too much about famous mystery characters."

"So…you're telling me this is Vera, and she has been

telling us the story seen from Laurie's perspective?" Grande asks.

"Yes, by pretending to be Laurie, she hoped she could get away with murder. She knew everything there was to know about her best friend—all she had gone through when thinking her husband was a murderer because she shared every detail. This way, she hoped to buy herself enough time to get away, maybe start a new life in Canada or somewhere else. She knew we'd eventually check her story but hoped she could make it away before we did."

"Why do you keep mentioning Laurie in the past tense?" Grande says, narrowing her eyes.

Jonathan nods and bites his lip. "Because I think she's dead. Isn't it true?"

He looks at the woman in front of them. She's still not talking. He's trying not to get himself worked up or raise his voice at her, even though that's what he wants to do. He needs her to start talking soon.

"I think if we take an extra look up at that cabin, we'll find her body, am I not right? But it must be well-hidden for the technicians to have missed it. What did you do with her body? Bury it?"

He can tell he's getting to her now. Her nostrils are flaring, and she's shifting on the bed like she can't sit still properly.

"What did you do with Laurie's body!" he says, finally raising his voice and giving in to his temper.

She's looking at her feet now when a tear escapes her eye. Then, she nods. "There's...an old swing in the backyard by the big magnolia tree. I buried her behind that. I covered it up by placing a couple of rocks on top of it. She's not buried very deep. I didn't have much time."

Jonathan exchanges a look with Grande, who rises to her feet with her phone in her hand. She calls someone, and Jonathan listens to her to give them instructions before she hangs up.

"They're on their way," she says, then returns.

Finally, the woman looks up, and her eyes meet Jonathan's. He sees honesty and vulnerability in them that he hasn't seen any other day when hearing her tell the story. This is the real deal; this is her: no façade, no more acting, no more lying.

"I didn't kill her, though," she says in almost a whisper.

"So, who did?" Jonathan asks. "Tell us who killed Laurie."

She exhales, her hands shaking. "Laurie went to the cabin with Frank, whose real name is Stephen Wilkerson. And he is…was my brother."

"And he's the one whose body we found in the river, right?" Grande says.

"Yes," she says. "He was shot twice."

"By Ryan Davis, right?" Jonathan says.

"Yes. That part was true. Laurie figured out what Stephen, or Frank, had been up to, and he tried to get rid of her, but Ryan came to her rescue. He shot my brother twice and then threw the body in the river."

"And you know this because…where were you at this time?" Grande asks.

"I was watching Ryan. I followed him as he drove up there to face Stephen."

"You were supposed to have killed him while Laurie and Stephen were at the cabin, am I right? You and your brother planned it that way, but then he suddenly drove off toward the mountains, and you couldn't get to him till he was up there."

"It wasn't supposed to happen," she says. "Stephen was supposed to take Laurie away, so she wouldn't suspect anything. It was supposed to look like suicide. I couldn't have foreseen what would happen. I tried to call Stephen once I realized where Ryan was going, but he didn't pick up his phone. Ryan watched them from outside at night, and then the next day, he burst inside and shot Stephen. I should just have killed him when he walked back to his car, but I hesitated. I didn't want it to happen here. I didn't want Laurie to find out."

"And then what happened once your brother was killed?" Jonathan asks.

"I watched Ryan as he got rid of the body and threw it in the river. And then he attacked Laurie. I saw it happen while standing outside on the porch, looking in. I was determined to kill Ryan after what he did to Stephen. I was so destroyed with grief; I just wanted him to hurt. I walked in there as he was fighting Laurie. When he saw me, he laughed. Just flat out laughed at me, even though I was holding a gun to his face. He attacked me out of the blue and got the gun twisted out of my hand while we were wrestling on the floor. Laurie was screaming, trying to help me, but he slapped her, so she slid across the floor. As soon as he had the gun, he picked up the phone and made the call to dispatch. As soon as he hung up, I saw him look at Laurie, and I knew it was too late. Before I could run to her, he had shot her. I screamed and ran to her lifeless body, but it was too late. She was gone. And that was when he came for me. I stormed outside through the sliding doors and onto the porch. The rest, you know. He chased me out to the edge and was washed down by a mudslide. And that's how you found him. I then walked back to the cabin. I took Laurie's phone and ID from her purse, then buried her in the backyard. I then walked back into the living room, grabbed the gun, and shot myself in the shoulder to make sure you wouldn't doubt my story of self-defense. Then, I waited. It took hours from when the call was placed until the police arrived, probably because of the muddy and dangerous roads."

The woman claps her hands together with an air of finality. "That's it. That's my story. The real one."

"And I believe this is the real one. There is only one thing you haven't revealed to us yet," Jonathan says.

"What's that?"

He smiles. "Your real name."

She scoffs and looks down at her feet. "Oh, yeah. I almost forgot about that one. It's Dolores. Dolores Claiborne Wilkinson. My mother had a thing for Stephen King's books. My brother, she named after the author himself. We had a dog named Cujo, and my sister, the one who died in Afghanistan, is named Carrie. As a child, I read *Dolores Claiborne* over and over again. I always wanted to write a story like it."

"And in a way, you did," Jonathan says with a scoff. He looks at Grande, who nods. She grabs a set of handcuffs from her belt, then walks up to the woman. She turns her around, then cuffs her while reading her rights.

Chapter 58

JONATHAN DRIVES up in front of the diner and gets out. Just as he steps onto the pavement, a voice comes up behind him, calling out his name. He turns to look at Detective Grande. She walks up to him. It's spring now in Bryson City and warming up pretty fast. It's gorgeous now with all the wildflowers and trees blooming and the snow completely gone, along with the mudslides and long days of rain. Jonathan can hear a bird chirping in the distance, and the air is so fresh, he takes a deep breath just to feel it in his lungs. When you grow up in Florida, you never feel air like this. That's why he moved away when he grew older and went to Virginia, where he later joined the FBI. Well, that's part of it.

Now, that time is almost over, and a new life is about to begin. He thinks about this while glancing down briefly at the listing in his hand.

"I'm glad I caught you," Grande says.

"Well, I'm glad you did too," he says. "Looking delightful, as always. Is that a glow I detect? Are you…are you expecting?"

She blushes. "How did you know?"

"I've seen it before."

She chuckles and touches her stomach gently. "We're not telling people yet."

"Oh, no. Too early for that," he says.

"I can't stop thinking about Dolores, though. Having a baby while in jail can't be easy."

"She'll have to give it up," he says. "She has confessed to helping her brother murder three people. She's going away for a long time. Did she ever say who the father is?"

"She did. And it's not pretty. She was raped on base. She never saw their faces because they were wearing ski masks. Once it happened, she went to her brother, and that's when they decided to start taking matters into their own hands. They went to Sandra first, to get her to give them all the names of the people who had been involved in Clarice's murder."

"Maybe she doesn't even want to keep the baby then. But it makes more sense when thinking about what she and her brother did afterward."

"The ME examined Laurie's body after we dug it out of the dirt behind the cabin. She wasn't pregnant at the time of death," Grande says.

"No, Dolores just made that a part of the story because she knew we'd find out somehow, either because we were told by the doctors or could see it in the papers. She left no stone unturned. Clever."

"Almost got away with it too. I have to say; I could never have figured all this out alone. I sure am glad I had you here to help me. She had me completely fooled at the end. I was so certain of her innocence. But I feel terrible for those children back in Florida. Lost both of their parents, just like that. They're staying with their grandparents, but who knows what this will do to them once they learn the truth."

Jonathan exhales. "Makes me kind of happy this is my last case."

"Really? You're retiring?"

He shrugs. "I have to—turning fifty-seven in a month. It's time to go. But to be honest, I'm beginning to look forward to what's next."

"That is wonderful. So, what is next? Now that we're done here, I expect you're heading home?"

That brings a huge smile to Jonathan's lips. "As a matter of fact, I'm thinking about sticking around for a little while."

He lifts the hand holding the papers with active listings of cabins for sale in and around Bryson City, just as Joanne comes out of the diner, putting on her jacket on top of her uniform. She leans over and kisses him on the cheek.

"I thought they'd never let me go. You ready?"

He smiles even wider and kisses her cheek as well. "Never been more ready in my life."

They walk to his car, and he holds the door for Joanne, then turns around and winks at his new favorite detective.

"See you around, Grande. You be careful out there."

She salutes him as he gets into the driver's seat, turns the engine over, and waves as they take off.

THE END

Dear Reader,

Thank you for purchasing *Sorry Can't Save You*. This book is fiction, and many of the places are fictional as well. The Air Force bases both in Florida and Afghanistan don't exist. Neither does Dundee Beach. It bears some resemblance to my hometown, Cocoa Beach, but since the topic in this book is so controversial, I wanted to keep it in the world of fiction.

What isn't fiction is actually the theme. I got the idea for this book when I came across several stories of women being raped in the Air Force and parents who doubted the explanation of what happened to them that they got from the military. There are quite a lot actually, and the numbers in my book are taken from the real world. One in three women who enlists is actually sexually assaulted or raped by men in the military. There are numerous stories of women coming home in caskets and their death being under suspicious circumstances. You can read more about them by following these links. The first one is the inspiration for Clarice's story.

https://www.independent.co.uk/news/world/middle-east/us-interpreter-who-witnessed-torture-in-iraq-shot-herself-with-service-rifle-1674399.html

https://thesource.com/2014/01/21/justice-for-lavena-johnson-raped-murdered-or-suicide-the-evidence-says-one-thing-u-s-military-says-another/

https://www.commondreams.org/views/2008/04/28/there-army-cover-rape-and-murder-women-soldiers

The rate of suicides in the military isn't fictional, either. Since 2008, more than 60,000 U.S. veterans have taken their own lives. In ten years, more died by committing suicide than during the entire Vietnam War.

https://www.mentalhealth.va.gov/suicide_prevention/data.asp

https://allthatsinteresting.com/veteran-suicide

Finally, I want to thank the women living on base who helped me bring this book to life, providing me with details into the life on base that I have no way of knowing. You know who you are.

Thanks again for reading, and don't forget to leave a review if you can. It means so much to me.

Take care,

Willow Rose

About the Author

Willow Rose is a multi-million-copy best-selling Author and an Amazon ALL-star Author of more than 80 novels. Her books are sold all over the world.

She writes Mystery, Thriller, Paranormal, Romance, Suspense, Horror, Supernatural thrillers, and Fantasy.

Willow's books are fast-paced, nail-biting page-turners with twists you won't see coming. That's why her fans call her The Queen of Plot Twists.

Several of her books have reached the Kindle top 10 of ALL books in the US, UK, and Canada. She has sold more than three million books all over the world.

Willow lives on Florida's Space Coast with her husband and two daughters. When she is not writing or reading, you will find her surfing and watch the dolphins play in the waves of the Atlantic Ocean.

Tired of too many emails? Text the word: "willowrose" to 31996 to sign up to Willow's VIP Text List to get a text alert with news about New Releases, Giveaways, Bargains and Free books from Willow.

Cover design by Juan Villar Padron,
https://juanjjpadron.wixsite.com/juanpadron

Special thanks to my editor Janell Parque
http://janellparque.blogspot.com/

To be the first to hear about new releases and bargains from Willow Rose, sign up below to be on the VIP List. (I promise not to share your email with anyone else, and I won't clutter your inbox.)

http://bit.ly/VIP-subscribe

Tired of too many emails? Text the word: "willowrose" to 31996 to sign up to Willow's VIP text List to get a text alert with news about New Releases, Giveaways, Bargains and Free books from Willow.

Contents